Didn't I Say
to Make My Abilities
Average in the
Next Life?!

VOLUME **7**

Reina

Little Evil God

Didn't I Say to Make My Abilities *Average* in the Next Life?!

VOLUME 7

BY

FUNA

ILLUSTRATED BY

Itsuki Akata

Seven Seas Entertainment

DIDN'T I SAY TO MAKE MY ABILITIES AVERAGE
IN THE NEXT LIFE?! VOLUME 7

© FUNA / Itsuki Akata 2018

Originally published in Japan in 2018 by EARTH STAR
Entertainment, Tokyo. English translation rights arranged
with EARTH STAR Entertainment, Tokyo, through TOHAN
CORPORATION, Tokyo.

Seven Seas press and purchase enquiries can be sent to
Marketing Manager Lianne Sentar at press@gomanga.com.
Information requiring the distribution and purchase of
digital editions is available from Digital Manager CK Russell
at digital@gomanga.com.

Follow Seven Seas Entertainment online at
sevenseasentertainment.com.

TRANSLATION: Diana Taylor
ADAPTATION: Maggie Cooper
COVER DESIGN: Nicky Lim
INTERIOR LAYOUT & DESIGN: Clay Gardner
PROOFREADER: Jade Gardner, Stephanie Cohen
LIGHT NOVEL EDITOR: Nibedita Sen
MANAGING EDITOR: Julie Davis
EDITOR-IN-CHIEF: Adam Arnold
PUBLISHER: Jason DeAngelis

ISBN: 978-1-64275-722-4
Printed in Canada
First Printing: November 2019
10 9 8 7 6 5 4 3 2 1

God bless me?
CONTENTS

Japan

Misato

A high school student. Died saving a little girl and was reborn into a fantasy world.

C-Rank Party "The Crimson Vow"

Mile

A girl who was granted "average" abilities in this fantasy world.

Mavis

A swordswoman. Leader of the up-and-coming party, the Crimson Vow.

Reina

A rookie hunter. Specializes in combat magic.

The Kingdom of Vanolark

Faleel

A young beastgirl. Daughter of the owner of the inn where Mile and company are staying.

Telyusia

19-year-old swordswoman. Leader of the five-woman party, the Servants of the Goddess.

Pauline

A rookie hunter. A timid girl, but...

Leatoria

The youngest daughter of a baron. Afflicted with a mysterious, deadly illness, until Mile intervened.

Previously

When Adele von Ascham, the eldest daughter of Viscount Ascham, was ten years old, she was struck with a terrible headache and, just like that, remembered everything.

She remembered how, in her previous life, she was an eighteen-year-old Japanese girl named Kurihara Misato who died while trying to save a young girl, and that she met God...

Misato had exceptional abilities, and the expectations of those around her were high. As a result, she could never live her life the way she wanted. So when she met God, she made an impassioned plea:

"In my next life, please make my abilities average!"

Yet somehow, it all went awry.

In her new life, she can talk to nanomachines and, although her magical powers are technically average, it is the average between a human's and an elder dragon's...6,800 times that of a sorcerer!

At the first academy she attended, she made friends and rescued a little boy as well as a princess.

She registered at the Hunters' Prep School under the name of Mile and formed a party with her classmates. The Crimsom Vow made a grand debut, but one problem after another has come hurtling their way—from golems, invading foreign soldiers, and doting fathers to elder dragons, the strongest creatures in the world!

And then suddenly, a clash between the Crimson Vow and Mile's friends from her first school, the Wonder Trio?!

A lot has happened, but now Mile is going to live a normal life as a rookie hunter with her allies by her side.

Because she is a perfectly normal, *average* girl!

CHAPTER 57 |

The Mysterious Kidnappers

O NE EVENING, the Crimson Vow stopped by the guildhall to turn in their goods after a successful day of hunting. On their way back to the inn…

"Wehehe, cat ears, cat ears…"

"Mile, can you stop going around town saying weird things with that creepy look on your face?!"

"Miley, that's kind of…"

"You're being suspicious. Someone's gonna call the guards on us…"

The other three groused at Mile's behavior, waiting at any moment to hear, 'Officer, that's the one!' However, Mile did not appear to care a jot.

"Squishy squishy, fluffy fluffy, honest, and adorable…the perfect little sister! Aah, I can't wait for another sweet evening with little Faleel tonight…"

| 13

"........."

Utterly resigned, the other three just shrugged their shoulders.

"Faleel, we're back... Oh!"

Faleel, who was typically at the counter at this hour, was nowhere to be seen.

"I wonder if she's in the restroom?"

Such a thing was possible, of course. She was human (read: a beastgirl), after all.

"Oh, it's you all, is it?" The inn's owner emerged from the kitchen, looking worried.

"What's the matter?" asked Mile.

The man replied with a troubled look. "Faleel hasn't come home. Normally, she's back by now. I mean, I have to assume that she's just off playing with friends and didn't notice the time. Unlike Faleel, her friends don't have to help out with household chores, so there's probably still some time before they have to be back home for dinner."

Despite the logic of his words, the owner seemed worried. It was only natural—his daughter was still a very little girl. While it brought him some relief to think that she might be with friends, it did not change the fact that he was concerned. Usually, she wore a hood or bonnet when leaving the house, but she was still a child, and it was possible that she might unwittingly let it slip while she was playing...and of course, there was always the possibility that anti-beastfolk contingents already knew about her and might be lurking about.

The population of the capital was great enough that it was not unheard of for elves and dwarves and beastfolk—as well as half-breeds of all three—to be present within the populace, though their numbers were few. While public discrimination and persecution were thus relatively unusual, beastfolk were often looked down upon or teased behind their backs. Unlike elves and dwarves, with whom humans were generally friendly, beastfolk were thought to be kin to demons—or at best, a group of backwards forest dwellers.

Thankfully, things never went as far as serious injury or any life-threatening assault, for anyone who took things too far would be caught and persecuted as a criminal. After all, the top brass in the kingdom and all its territories wanted to avoid war with the beastfolk, particularly because war against the beast tribes would not be one of army against army on the battlefield. Instead, it would be an onslaught of guerilla combat, with any humans who entered the woods ending up dead. Woodcutters and hunters would lose their stomping grounds, causing acute harm to the economy. Any routes through and near the forest would become dangerous, and thanks to the rapid rise in escort expenses and the higher rate of injury, it would no longer be feasible for merchants to regularly travel. If things got especially bad, most of the feudal administrations would begin to go bankrupt.

Therefore, no one risked offending the beastpeople on a whim. ...Normally.

Yes. *Normally.* For in any world, there are degenerates and fools, including those who *would* wish to stir up conflict between humans and beasts. Arms dealers, mercenaries, foreign provocateurs...

"Why don't we go and fetch her? Where does she usually—?"

In the midst of Mile's question, the door swung violently open. A man around thirty, holding hands with a girl of five or six, burst through the doorway, a dire expression on his face.

"Dafrel?" the owner addressed him.

The man known as Dafrel shouted, "Faleel's been abducted!"

"Whaaaaaaaaaaaaaaat?!?!"

The man hung his head, speaking in a pained voice. "Just a little while ago, my daughter came home crying. When I asked her what happened, she said that Faleel had been dragged away by some strange men. I'm so sorry, I'm truly sorry!"

When they finally calmed the sobbing little girl, Methelia, they learned that several strange men had suddenly appeared where the two girls had been playing. They shouted, "There she is!" and seized Faleel, before silencing her and dragging her away.

"Faleel tried—*hic*—to bite their fingers and kick them, but—*snff*—they put a cloth over her mouth and tied her up and—*hic*—took her with them... I tried my best too, but they pushed me away... I'm sorry, I'm sorry..." Methelia began to wail once again.

"Wh-what do I do...?"

Though the innkeeper was quite a large fellow, he shrank into himself, fretting. Understandably, he appeared rather shaken.

He's no good to us like this! We have to do something. Reina thought. Just as she tried to speak, however...

"IS THAT SOOOOO?!?!?!"

"Eep!"

The inn's owner, Sir Dafrel, little Methelia, three members of the Crimson Vow, and the matron, who had rushed from the kitchen, sensing something was wrong, all suddenly yelped in fear.

"IS THAT SOOOOO?!?!?!"

The voice, which sounded as though it had risen from the very depths of hell, was Mile's.

Mile, who was now trembling with rage.

There were various levels to Mile's anger: First, there was pouting and sulking. This meant that she was just in a bit of a bad mood, and though she might grouse and be cross for a little while, it was nothing much to worry about. Then, there were the times she showed no expression at all. This meant that she was quite angry. In these instances, she was cool, composed, and relentless in dealing with her enemies. This happened when, for example, she took on stalkers in her previous life or bandits in this one.

Finally, there were the times when she *truly* showed her anger. This was the case when someone harmed her allies or someone else important to her. For example, during the fight against the elder dragons...

"Little miss, would you mind showing me to the place where Faleel was abducted? You'll take me there, won't you?"

Nodnodnodnodnod! Methelia nodded vigorously.

"Well then, let's get going!"

She's scary! She's so scary! Reina thought. However, as the leader of the Crimson Vow—er, well, as the true director of the

party, with the most experience as a hunter—there was something that she had to do.

"Pauline, you go with the owner here to the Guild! Have
him place an emergency request and then accept that request
immediately!"

"Huh?"

Both Faleel's father and Sir Dafrel seemed perplexed.

"Th-this isn't the time!" the owner protested. "If you want
money, I'll pay you afterwards! Just hurry up and find Faleel!
Please, I need you to find my daughter!"

"Calm down!" said Reina, explaining, "We are going to give
this search our all. That's precisely why this step is necessary. If we
head out immediately, this will officially be nothing more than an
independent operation. Assuming that we find Faleel and a battle
breaks out, it will be considered a personal conflict, and if the abductors have been hired by a noble or someone else with wealth,
there's a chance that we'll be labeled as attackers or villains. And
if that happens, then we might never get Faleel back."

"Oh..." The owner was nearly speechless.

"That's why we file the emergency request. If you make a public announcement to the Guild about Faleel's kidnapping, file an
emergency request for her rescue, and ask for the capture—or
annihilation—of the offenders, Pauline can accept it, making our
mission an official request. Anyone who might try to hinder us
becomes an enemy of the Guild. And you know that no upstanding hunter, mercenary, aristocrat, or merchant would ever want
to make an enemy of the Hunters' Guild, don't you?"

Indeed, just as the merchant company and local lord involved with the incident in Pauline's hometown had fretted over such a thing, the owner of the inn knew that going up against the Guild could prove fatal for anyone, regardless of their position in society. Reina was not the only one aware of this; the other three members of the Vow knew it just as well, nodding along with her explanation. Such fundamental facts had been covered at the Hunters' Prep School. Classroom lessons were not just meant for nap time, after all.

"Plus, if we should end up in a tight situation, as long as we're on an official job and abiding by their terms, the Guild will send us backup—even if our enemy turns out to be a noble or merchant. In other words…"

"In other words?" the owner asked, his breath caught in his throat.

Reina grinned wickedly and replied, "In other words, we'll be able to ensure our enemies learn that *whoever* tries to mess with little Faleel—with any friend of ours—will soon come to find they'd be better off dead. Those kidnappers are going to find out very, very soon what happens to anyone who tries to lay a hand on a friend of the Crimson Vow…"

At these words, a big smile spread across Mavis's face. A smile that would make anyone who knew Mavis back away very quickly.

The smile was…dark. In fact, it was a terrifyingly dark expression, which the truly warmhearted Mavis would never show in any normal situation.

Pauline, meanwhile, had on her usual smile… Which was to say, it was a wicked grin.

Yet the scariest was still Mile, whose face was utterly lacking in expression. She was truly the most frightening of them all.

"The terms of the job," Reina declared, "will be Faleel's rescue and the capture of the criminals—or else, their annihilation! If someone's behind this, we'll wipe them out! Now, Crimson Vow, roll out!"

"Let's go!!!"

While Pauline and the owner headed to the guildhall, the others followed Methelia to the site of the kidnapping. The matron and her sons remained behind to mind the inn.

"........."

Mile's continued silence induced terror in the rest of the group. Reina, Mavis, the owner, Dafrel, and his daughter were all livid too, but the powerful, oppressive aura emanating from Mile's entire being was overwhelming.

Finally, Mile broke her silence to ask, "Reina, what do you suppose those criminals were after?"

Feeling Mile's aura brighten just a bit, Reina replied hurriedly, "I-I wonder. The only things that come to mind are fairly random—trafficking or some sick perverts who want to use a child as a plaything and kill her for sport... The other possibility is someone who was after Faleel specifically because they knew that she was half-beast."

"Because she's half-beast, you say?"

"I mean, of course. There's all sorts...people who think that beastfolk are lower life-forms or people who say that having beasts living among humans is going to bring down some sort of divine judgment on everyone... And obviously there are people like you, Mile, who are just really into beast—*Eep!*"

"Don't lump my appreciation for beast-eared girls in with those cretins!"

Mile was definitely still terrifying.

"Regardless, it is most likely that Faleel's beast lineage is the reason for all this. Whether they intend to sell her or have some other purpose in mind..."

"Huh?"

The others looked perplexed at Mile's remark.

"Wh-what makes you so sure of that?"

"Well, Methelia herself said it: when the kidnappers spotted Faleel, they shouted, 'There she is!' That means that they had to have been aiming for Faleel from the start, hadn't they? Any normal ransom-seekers or slavers or perverts would have taken little Methelia along too, wouldn't they? Given that they didn't abduct—or even try to silence—her means that they mustn't have had any intention of doing harm to anyone other than Faleel. Normally, a criminal tries to eliminate witnesses to delay the discovery of their crime or to prevent them from giving testimony. A flick of a knife would be enough to buy them the few extra seconds they needed. However, the fact that they didn't even try that means that we're dealing with some fairly honorable individuals... At least when it comes to anyone besides Faleel."

"S-silence me?!"

"A f-flick of a knife?!"

Finally realizing the danger that she had been in, both Methelia and Dafrel went pale as sheets.

After running for between ten and fifteen minutes, they finally arrived at the field where Methelia and Faleel had been playing. In fact, it was not particularly far, but a child's legs were not very speedy. Though Dafrel had tried to carry his daughter on his back at first, she was around six years old, meaning that letting her run on her own was actually faster.

"Th-this is it! This was where those men…"

Methelia pointed ahead to a spot where the grass was disturbed—the place where Faleel had tried to fend off her attackers and where Methelia had tried to help her friend.

Suddenly, Mile shouted something very peculiar.

"Smell, become sight!"

"What??" Both Reina and Mavis spoke up, understandably confused.

"It's a spell to turn my sense of smell into vision."

…Obviously.

"And what the heck does that mean?!" Reina protested, leaving Mile with no choice but to elaborate.

"If I were a dog, I could track Faleel's scent. However, we don't have a trained dog or any article with Faleel's scent, so instead I'm using magic to enhance my sense of smell. That way, I can track her scent myself. Normally, smell is something that you sense with your nose, but my nose doesn't have the ability to determine the strength or the direction of a particular smell. So instead of trying to detect the smell with my nose, I'm changing the scent traces to visual information so that I can 'smell' with my eyes!"

".........?"

Neither Dafrel nor any member of the Crimson Vow appeared to have any idea what Mile was talking about. Methelia was, of course, not even part of the equation.

"Never mind! Our time is precious here, so please just hush and follow me!"

With that, Mile began to look intently all around her.

"There it is! Let's go!"

Picking up on the scent trail of the kidnappers, Mile walked forward, her eyes to the ground. The other four quickly followed behind.

"Mile," asked Reina, "do you really know Faleel's scent that well?"

"Reina, why exactly do you think I've sniffed her so many times before now?!"

".........."

Everyone, save Methelia, was thoroughly taken aback at Mile's matter-of-fact reply.

Truth be told, of the two scent trails that had come from the direction of the inn, one had clearly headed back the way they'd come, while the other stretched off the opposite way. The one that had returned was clearly Methelia's. Several other scents had come from the opposite direction and then retraced their steps. With that evidence, determining which smell was Faleel's was a no-brainer.

"Mavis," said Mile, "Pauline and the owner should be finished up at the Guild by now. I think I've got a lock on the direction, so I'm going to proceed this way for a little while. Can you go back to the Guild and fetch Pauline?"

"On it!"

After a short time, Mavis returned with Pauline, the owner of the inn, and five other hunters in tow.

"Wh-what are *they* doing here?!" Reina raged.

Pauline lowered her head in apology.

"S-sorry. They overheard us when we were going through the emergency request process with the receptionist and said that they wanted to take the job, too. I told them that *we* would be taking the job, but they just—I even told them that the pay was only going to be one silver, and they still..."

"When these five were just starting out and sleeping at inns, they stayed with us for a time," the owner chimed in. "They would cuddle and dote on Faleel, too... I set the pay for the job to be only one silver, like you said, but they said that was fine. Honestly, as far as I'm concerned, even having just one more hunter is a big help. So, I gladly accepted their kindness. We can all work together!"

The Vow were in no position to refuse. They could understand Faleel's father's feelings, as well as the feelings of the party that had tagged along.

Plus, in the case of an emergency request, the client did not get to choose who took the job. If they wanted to do that, they would have to place a direct request—the logic being that if they had time to be choosy, then it probably wasn't an emergency after all. Of course, the circumstances this time called for the request to be placed as an emergency. It gave the job priority at the Guild and spread news of the request, thus suiting their purposes.

At any rate, the Crimson Vow had already accepted the job. They still had the right of refusal, but not even Pauline could deny the owner's request to bring along another party.

Even Reina realized that there was nothing she could do, shrugging her shoulders.

Finally, the other party spoke up. "You all can rest at ease now that we're here! Just leave this to us, and we'll show you a thing or two! We are five maidens, protected by the Goddess's grace—the Servants of the Goddess!!!"

"So, what are you doing, Mile?"

From here on out, this would be a job for the hunters. Despite their desire to tag along, Faleel's father, Dafrel, and Methelia were told that, as laymen, they would be an impediment to the groups' progress. They were sent back to the inn, and as was good form, the two parties briefly introduced themselves to one another—all the while following Mile.

They previously had met one another at the Guild. However, the Servants had merely butted in on the Crimson Vow's conversation at that time, so the two parties had never been formally introduced.

Watching as Mile stared at the ground while leading the group assuredly forward, Telyusia, the 19-year-old leader and the eldest among the Servants of the Goddess, asked the obvious question.

"She's tracking the scent," Reina replied.

"Tracking the scent???" the Servants asked in unison.

"Is she a dog?!"

"Mile, are you half-beast too?"

"Sorry for farting earlier!"

"Shut your mouths!"

"Oo-oh! She's a feisty one..."

Mile appeared to be growing angry, which was no surprise. Judging by the fact that the kidnappers had tried to capture Faleel without harming her, and that so little time had elapsed, it was too soon to assume that Faleel was in any real danger. Still, the longer they took, the more the danger grew for the beastgirl. To slip up because they were in a rush would be unforgivable, so Mile was conducting herself carefully, without missing any necessary steps. However, she had no time to let her attention be drawn away by frivolous matters.

In fact, heightening her own senses and turning olfactory signals into visuals ones did not mean that she had lost her own sense of smell entirely. This was not truly a matter of *exchanging* sight for smell. After all, if her visual signals turned into olfactory ones, she would not be able to function. Thus, both her sight and her smell remained as they were, with any divergent scents appended to her field of vision. With that information, along with her own, already heightened sense of smell, she could accurately distinguish and follow Faleel's scent.

Mile stopped as they reached a fairly wide roadway. "The smell is growing weaker here," she declared. "They must have carried her this far and then loaded her into a wagon or something to take her from here."

"Hmm... That must mean..."

Reina worried that Mile would no longer be able to track Faleel's scent, but Mile immediately reassured her. "No, it's fine. It's just..."

"Just, what?"

"It's time for us to fly!" she said and broke into a jog, with the Crimson Vow and the Servants of the Goddess following desperately behind. Of course, what was a "jog" for Mile was incredibly fast for the rest of them.

"I don't think it was a passenger carriage—probably a delivery wagon. There's still quite a bit of scent to follow."

If they were riding in a passenger vehicle like the sort on Earth, very little smell would escape, meaning that tracking would become quite difficult. In the case of a delivery wagon, with its open bed, this was no issue. Plus, such a vehicle would not be able to pick up any considerable amount of speed. The only time one might travel at full tilt was when one had to go very far, very fast, uncaring of whether the wheels or the axles or even the wagon body itself broke down—for instance, if one was pursued by bandits or monsters. It was unusual enough for a wagon to travel at that sort of pace that such a thing would stand out. There was no way that a group of kidnappers would want to bring such attention to themselves, and besides, it would wear out their horses too quickly. At the rate that the two parties were going, they should have been more than able to catch up with the wagon in no time at all.

"Hmm... The scent's weaker now," Mile said suspiciously.

Looking ahead, the reason became clear.

"The city gates..."

Indeed, it was necessary to pass through the city gates to exit the capital. In order for the kidnappers to do this without being caught, it was likely that they would have shoved Faleel into a box or barrel. Nevertheless, it was still the case that for some distance beyond the city limits, there was only one road big enough for a wagon to travel along. Plus, even if Faleel's scent dissipated, the scent of the kidnappers and the horses was still strong in the air. There was no way that Mile could lose track of them, at least for as long as Faleel was forced to remain on that particular wagon. Thus, the chase continued!

"All right, it's just as I thought!"

A short time after they had passed through the gates, Faleel's scent grew stronger again. Keeping the girl in a cramped box or barrel for very long was risky, so at the appropriate moment, once the wagon had gained enough distance from the city, they must have let her back out.

The others had no idea just what it was that was "as Mile had thought," but if things were as she suspected then that was probably not bad news. They continued to run, saving their breath by withholding any unnecessary questions.

"This is it!"

After proceeding for a short while, Mile came to a halt at the spot where the road veered off to bypass the forest. It was already beginning to grow dark. This world's moon was rising, but its light would not reach beyond the trees.

"Here, Faleel dismounted the wagon with three humans. The four of them headed into the forest, while the wagon continued down the road. I'd guess that they wanted the wagon to gain some distance from the capital on the off chance that they were spotted or followed."

The kidnappers were right to be cautious—after all, Mile and the others *had* been following them this whole time.

"Anyway, that wagon's not any of our concern. We can deal with capturing the rest of the kidnappers tomorrow once their friends are taken care of. Our focus now is Faleel!"

The other eight nodded silently in agreement.

"We might encounter the enemy at any moment now. Keep sharp!"

They nodded once more.

"Let's go!"

Up until now, they had merely been following along behind Mile, but now, there was no telling when the enemy might appear. They proceeded quickly and quietly, keeping a close watch on their surroundings.

"I can't imagine that they would have their main hideout this close to the capital," Telyusia remarked. "These woods aren't all that deep, and D and E-rank hunters are always coming through here to hunt and gather. This must just be a temporary waypoint for them. Or else..."

"Or else?" asked Pauline.

"Or else they chose this to be the scene of the crime."

"........."

The scene of the crime. Thinking about the meaning of those words, everyone's expressions hardened.

They proceeded on silently for a short while more, when suddenly they heard a cry like the hoot of an owl.

Huh-hoo! Hoo hoo, hoo hoo, hooh!

"We've been spotted," Mile announced calmly. The Servants of the Goddess nodded, but the members of the Crimson Vow were dumbfounded at this revelation.

"How do you know?" asked Reina, voicing their shared thought.

Mile explained: "We haven't heard any bird cries so far, but we just heard one at a short range as we approached. Besides, the call wasn't a regular one—there was some sort of pattern to it. I have to guess that it was a night watchman pretending to be a bird in order to relay some information. If *I* were to establish a bird-song code in order to relay information as a watchman, I would decide on a pattern of sounds to let the others know how many people were approaching—with individual signals for one to four, and one each for five and ten. For example, *huh-hoo* would be five, and a single *hoo* might be one, and so forth. Finally, there would be a signal to convey the level of threat. *Hohohohoo* would mean soldiers, *hohoo* would mean tough veteran hunters, and just *hooh* would mean useless young female hunters—or something along those lines."

Reina, Mavis, and Pauline listened, awestruck. The Servants, on the other hand, looked as though this information was completely obvious to them.

"M-Mile, do you have a fever or something?" asked Reina.

Normally, Mile would have groaned in annoyance at such a jab, but this time she completely ignored it.

"They're coming. Four groups of four—sixteen men total!"

The magic Mile had used to determine this remained within the scope of "investigating with surveillance magic," rather than the prohibited "asking the nanomachines for information about an opponent," so she drew on it without reservation. After all, someone's life hung in the balance—Faleel's, to be specific.

At her words, both parties moved quickly from their travel positions into battle formation.

Given the hastily combined nature of their two-party force, trying to fight as a single unit would be out of the question. Without fully knowing each other's strengths, they could not efficiently collaborate. Therefore, both parties formed into separate lines. The Crimson Vow had Mavis and Mile in the front line, with Reina and Pauline at the back. The Servants' front line consisted of Philly, the lancer, in the middle, with the swordswomen Telyusia and Willine flanking her; Tasha the archer-slash-dagger-wielder was at the midline, and on the back line stood Lacelina, the fourteen-year-old mage and youngest of their group. (While they flattered Lacelina by calling her an 'all-purpose' mage, in reality, she might be more fairly classified as a 'jack of all trades and master of none.')

Tasha fought primarily using her bow, but in the event that an enemy should break through the front lines or appear from the sides or behind, she would discard it and draw her dagger to defend herself and Lacelina while covering the front line's backs.

On top of having to be prepared to adapt to a myriad of situations on the fly, there was a high risk of her losing her bow, as Tasha had to quickly judge a place where she might discard her weapon. It would be a huge loss if her bow were to be trampled underfoot in the scuffle, and since she didn't have time to store it on her back, she had to quickly find a place that would not be disrupted by the battle and which she might easily reach with a light toss. Even then, she was left with her dagger, forced to fight at close quarters with a weapon that had a shorter reach than her opponents'. Poor Tasha...

"Mavis, try focusing your strength and directing your spiritual power to your eyes. Then think, 'Strengthen my eyesight so that I can see in the dark!'"

"Huh? S-sure, all right."

Just as Mile directed, Mavis steeled herself.

"Uh? Oh my goodness! It feels like my vision is getting brighter..."

"........."

Reina and Pauline looked on suspiciously. This "spiritual" power was turning out to be quite an all-purpose skill. It seemed as though it could do just about anything.

In any event, now they were ready to fight!

"Who's there?!"

Surprisingly, the girls found themselves not being attacked but questioned. Furthermore, what they saw before them now was a single very suspicious-looking man, wrapped in a black cloak with a sword at his side. The others remained lying in wait. Were they aiming for a surprise attack? Or did they hope to simply explain away their presence, believing that the girls had stumbled into the woods by chance? There was no reason for them to think that the girls had tracked their scent and followed them. If they had already confirmed visually that they had made a clean escape, it was not ridiculous for the men to assume that the young hunters had just happened upon them.

Of course, few people would have a reason to be deep in the forest late at night, so the probability of such a thing occurring was relatively low. Even if this were but a small thicket near to the capital, the woods at night were still a dangerous place. Unless they had some emergency affair to attend to, no one would normally choose to be wandering about in a place like this, particularly not a group of young ladies.

"We're hunters. What's a group like *you* doing out in the forest in the middle of the night?!"

Oof... The Servants of the Goddess were greatly vexed. The enemy had gone out of their way to have just a single person appear before them, meaning that they had a valuable chance to lead the conversation and get the other to let something slip. This way, they might obtain useful information. And yet, here Reina had carelessly revealed that they were already aware of the enemy's true number. Thankfully, her remark seemed to have flown over the man's head, but it was still a misstep in their negotiations.

The man bristled. "That's what *I* should be asking!"

Mile's face twisted as well. Normally she would have grinned and ignored Reina, but right now, gathering information was key, so she was far more serious than usual. Even if they got into a battle and won, there was no guaranteeing that they would get the information they needed. It was better to get the enemy to let something slip while they could still talk, and to that end, they should not be giving anything away.

"Just what in the world are you all doing out in the forest in the middle of the night?!"

"When you ask someone a question, it's customary to explain yourself first! What are *you* all doing here?!"

A battle of words unfolded as both Reina and the man refused to cede control of the conversation—of course, it was only natural that two parallel lines would never meet. Apparently, their opponent was not particularly bright, or at the very least, not especially skilled in the art of persuasion...

"Now!" the man shouted. He had given up on warding them off with words.

At his command, the remaining men emerged from out of the bushes and trees: fifteen in total. Waiting in ambush did not appear to be part of their strategy.

Given that none of them had emerged from behind the girls, the men did not seem to have the intention of preventing anyone from running; their formation indicated that as long as no one broke through their lines, then that was good enough.

All the men were dressed in plain clothes with black cloaks on top, and each held a sword in their hand, just like the first man to appear. While certainly no one would wear full plate armor in the forest, it was odd that there were so many of them, all raring for a fight, without even leather armor atop their clothing.

Furthermore, they did not appear to have any mages among them. With this many assembled, it would normally be good to have at least two or three within their ranks. Perhaps there were not enough capable men or this grouping had just happened to come together...

"They might be disguised. Watch out for magic!" Telyusia warned the Crimson Vow. Clearly, the Servants needed no such warning.

"........."

Though their party included Mile, who was dressed as a swordswoman even though she was primarily a mage—and though they had previously come up against mages who were pretending to be normal swordsmen during the false bandit incident—the thought had somehow not occurred to Reina and Pauline. However, Mile and Mavis had already considered such a possibility.

Meanwhile, the Servants of the Goddess appraised their enemies. *Who knows how strong they are in battle, but they're clearly amateurs when it comes to negotiations...*

If they had been hiding their strength and wished to overwhelm the girls with sheer force, they would have launched a more sudden surprise attack. Ideally, they should have taken word from their commander as the signal to attack at once. Yet with his command, the enemy simply appeared in groups.

Still, the fact that they were bad at negotiating did not itself mean that they were necessarily unskilled in battle. Soldiers and assassins did not make their bread and butter from chatting with the enemy, and their lack of speaking skill was no indication that they were not strong fighters.

As the men hustled in, the first one who had shown himself retreated to the three who were likely the rest of his unit, and with that, it seemed that the other side's battle preparations were complete.

The Crimson Vow and the Servants of the Goddess were lined up with the Vow on the left and the Servants on the right, leaving about two meters between the two parties. It was necessary to allow that much distance in order to fight safely alongside an ally whose strength and battle style one did not know. However, it was still a short enough distance that there was no fear of an enemy slipping in without suffering an attack from both of the two sides.

Splitting into two groups, the enemy advanced toward the Crimson Vow and the Servants of the Goddess. Judging by their numbers, appearances, and the high proportion of individuals taking the forward guard, the Servants clearly came across the greater threat, but perhaps the opposition was not interested in breaking up their practiced team formation—or perhaps they merely thought that they should be lowering their strength to match their young opponents...

At any rate, the battle was currently split into eight against four and eight against five. The kidnappers were twice their number, at least roughly. Even if the division had been seven on four and nine on five, it would not have made much of a difference. A four-woman party that included underage girls should be swiftly dealt with, and then they could concentrate their efforts in taking down the remaining group.

Just then, the enemies came rushing in.

Each group of four was broken into two lines, with roughly two meters between front and back; two of these groups went for the Crimson Vow, and two went for the Servants of the Goddess. More than likely, the front two of the first team planned to engage their opponents' front line, while the other two flanked to the left and right to launch an attack from the sides. In the meantime, the back team would slip around behind their opponents and take out their back line. It was a formation that would assure an instantaneous victory.

Fighting with an enemy in closed quarters was not merely a matter of taking on their front line; it meant being prepared to deal with their full forces at close range. This was the only proper tactic for a group of swordsmen with no mages among them.

"Gravel, crush my enemies' eyes!"

The enemies were by no means the only ones who had prepared themselves for battle. Lacelina, who had been murmuring the incantation for her spell underneath her breath, now shouted the command phrase to release her attack.

Actually creating gravel was a bit too much of a challenge for a jack-of-all-trades mage like Lacelina, so her spell merely gathered up rocks, dirt, and mulch from the ground and sent the lot flying. Even if the spell specified "gravel," the attack really consisted of all manner of debris.

Hearing her words, the enemies reflexively tried to shield their eyes with their arms—all while rushing straight toward enemies who were armed with swords and spears.

"Gwah!"

"Gyahh!"

"Waaaaah!"

Taking a spear through the shoulder, a sword smack to the side, and a blade in the gut, three of the men were felled in an instant. Of the first team, only one man remained.

"Uh..."

At this rate, the rear team would never be able to go for the Servants' back line. If they even tried it, they would be attacked from the side as they tried to pass through—and even if they did manage to break past, they would be sliced at from behind the moment they tried to launch their own assault.

The last man hurriedly fell back to safety, grouping in with the rear team. Just when it looked as though they would be pushed into a deadlock of five-on-five, Philly, the Servants' lancer, leaned her body slightly to the left, while Telyusia, to her right, leaned slightly to the right.

"Windsurge!"

At Lacelina's second shout, the men dug their feet into the ground so that they would not be bowled over by the force of the rushing winds coming their way. But just then—*whoosh!*—an arrow came flying through the air. Indeed, this was the reason that Philly and Telyusia had leaned away: to allow the arrow to pass.

"Tch, what a wobbly little arrow!"

The man who stood in the arrow's path gave a leisurely swing of his sword. Though he was apparently unskilled in negotiations, he was well studied in the martial arts. Though perhaps that studying had been only at a dojo and not on the actual battlefield...

"Hmm?"

The arrow struck deep into his right shoulder.

"H-how...?"

The man stared dumbly at the arrow in his arm, so shocked that his brain had yet to register the pain. Indeed, the wind spell that Lacelina had used just prior was not for the sake of knocking down their enemies—such a powerful spell would be beyond a mage like her anyway. However, a soft breeze? Now that she could manage. At least enough to shift the course of a flying arrow just before impact...

They're strong!

After firing their first shots, Reina and Pauline had left the enemy to Mavis and Mile and were now engrossed in watching the Servants' bout, their eyes wide in shock. The girls were not particularly skilled in swordsmanship, spears, or magic. This is not to say that they were *lacking* in talent; however, they were still young. Their technique was unpolished, and their magic was crude and lacking in power.

And yet, they were strong.

Unthinkingly, Reina spoke. "This is what it looks like when

you work your way up from F-rank to C-rank without losing a single person along the way... These are the Servants of the Goddess..."

As a party, the Crimson Vow was undeniably strong. However, what they were was merely a collection of strong individuals. Their fighting skill relied on each of their individual strengths— nothing more, nothing less.

The Servants of the Goddess, however, were different.

Though each of their members had only middling skill, they were strong together.

Reina was chagrined.

If the two parties were to face off against one another, there was no doubt that the Crimson Vow would win. Still, Reina could not shake a feeling of deep embarrassment.

And as for Mile and Mavis?

Currently, they were fighting with great concentration and great restraint, trying their best to keep the remaining enemies from approaching Reina and Pauline without hurting or killing any of them. As a result, they had no time to be watching anyone else's fight.

Speaking of which...

Before the fight began, Mile and Mavis had moved up front, while Reina and Pauline fell to the back, leaving a sufficient gap between them. Though they were fighting against an enemy force that consisted only of frontline fighters, there were no mages stupid enough to approach an enemy if they didn't have to.

"Frozen Helix Shot!"

"Ice Nail!"

With ample time to prepare, Reina and Pauline incanted their spells in their heads, firing them off with a shout to increase their power.

It was shocking to see that the men had not readied themselves for the possibility of a surprise attack. They knew that there were mages about, but perhaps, seeing that said mages were only little girls, they had underestimated them—or perhaps they had never actually battled against mages before. At any rate, Reina and Pauline welcomed the advantage.

"Gwah!"

"Gyaah!"

The two men who had been trying to slip around the sides of the party stopped in place, crying out in pain as Pauline's ice nails split into two swarms, striking the men in the shoulders, arms, legs, and guts. Though they were not gravely injured, they crumpled to the ground. At the same time, Mile and Mavis faced the two who were attacking from the front head-on with their swords. The four men of the rear team, who were tasked with slipping past to attack the back line while the front line had their hands full, stepped out to move in for the offense, only to be stopped by Reina's magical attack, which they took at full force.

"Gah!" cried one.

"Owwww!" cried another.

"Waaaaaah!!" cried the final two.

At Reina's behest, the soft earth of the forest floor had co-agulated into around twenty relatively small helix shapes, which rained down on the men in a high, arcing path, like a parabola. There were three main reasons for such an attack pattern: first, it avoided striking Mile and Mavis, who were up ahead; secondly, it raised the speed and force with which the shots would hit; and thirdly, few people were accustomed to being attacked from above. Finally, so as not to be an embarrassment to the name "Helix Shot," each shot rotated on its own axis.

Because they were in a forest, Reina could not utilize her specialty fire magic. Furthermore, because their allies were so close—and because the Servants would be watching—Pauline could not use her "hot" magic. Nonetheless, simply barring them from using their two most powerful, specialized spells still left the two with a fair bit of leeway.

Of the men who had taken Reina and Pauline's magical attacks, two were still crumpled, perhaps unable to move. Those who had attacked the party from the front had been struck down by Mavis and Mile. The remaining four were not greatly injured, but thanks to being pierced by the ice nails and pummeled by earthen shots, their will to fight had dropped dramatically. This meant that Mile and Mavis, who were engaging in restrictive maneuvers in an attempt to incapacitate the men without kill-ing or seriously injuring them, were now facing some unexpected difficulties.

Rather than going after Reina and Pauline at the rear, the four had refocused their efforts on Mavis and Mile.

The two of them can handle this, thought Reina and Pauline. Even so, they held a set of attack spells just in case, keeping tabs on their own fight even as they turned to watch the Servants. The attacks they held were ice javelins, which could be fired simply and precisely, meaning that they would be ready to help at a moment's notice, if need be.

"Huh?"

Watching the Servants of the Goddess, the two were dumbfounded. What they observed was the party emerging safe and sound as they felled their opponents by way of their mediocre magic, swordsmanship, lancing, and archery.

They're strong!

While they did not voice the thought, this much was clear to both Reina and Pauline. These girls possessed a strength that was quite different from their own. Though they were not especially skilled, they were formidable. Their power was one that Reina had never known when she was alone, relying solely on her own abilities. It was a strength that she now sought to find among the Crimson Vow.

The battle that had started as eight against five was now five on five. On top of that, one of the opponents who was still standing had arrows sticking out from his right shoulder, which meant that the Servants of the Goddess currently had the upper hand.

"These little wenches..."

The men had likewise noticed the individual lack of skill in each of the Servants. Clearly, they judged, the timing of their attacks had just happened to line up. The girls had gotten lucky.

However, Reina and Pauline thought differently.

When it came to actual combat, you were lucky if you could make use of even half of the fruits of your training. If one were to secure certain victory in a real fight, it would only be thanks to training that amounted to hours, weeks, and months beyond the battle in question. Anyone who chalked up the results of the girls' fighting to mere chance was not someone who had a lengthy future ahead of them.

Every one of their moves had been intentional. From purposely shouting the command word for the spell loud enough to trigger countermeasures, to making the men brace themselves against the wind magic so that they would not be able to dodge the arrows that would strike them down in time, to firing those arrows so that the wind magic would hit them from the side just before impact...

Spears had a long reach. It was difficult for the men to go up against Philly, who was positioned in the middle of the forward three, her spear brandished. Even if they could deflect the spear and leap in to attack her, the very act of moving that spear would leave them open to flanking attacks from the two swordswomen, Telyusia and Willine. Behind them, Tasha's arrows were already nocked, and Lacelina was murmuring her next spell.

For these men, who wielded only swords, to go up against a party that had been carefully composed to account for everyone's specialties, was the height of recklessness. Without overwhelming numbers or exceptional skill, there was no hope for the Servants' opponents. That said, with eight against five, these men did have the advantage of numbers. And though it seemed they had not much actual combat experience, their swordsmanship was nothing to scoff at. They probably assumed that this group of young, female hunters were scarcely better than amateurs, that their skills were nothing special. In fact, this assumption was not incorrect. However...

Even though the battle was now five on five, there were two back and mid-line fighters among the Servants. The clash against the front line amounted to only three against five. Therefore, no matter how hazardous it might have been for the men to attack, owing to the spear's long range, they would quickly be able to overwhelm the young women with numbers. After a momentary pause to regain their balance, the five of them swooped swiftly in for the kill. Just then...

"Dust Storm!"

In the time that her enemies had wasted before making their move, Lacelina had completed her next spell. The men had done her a great service in providing the mage ample time for her spellcasting.

Normally, an enemy who did not have a mage of their own would deal with an opposing mage as swiftly as possible, even if it meant taking a fair bit of damage. When the first three men had been felled, the fourth should not have fallen back. Rather, the four others should have come up quickly from behind to make a united stand. Had they done so, three of them could have halted the front line, while the other two moved around to take out the back and the middle. Even if an arrow were to be fired their way, they could have struck it down, or—in the worst case scenario— levy one of the men as a sacrifice before summarily taking out the archer, who would be left defenseless in the moment after her attack, and the mage, who would be similarly at a loss, having had no time to prepare her next spell.

In fact, all that would only have been possible if the Servants of the Goddess had not already prepared for just such a scenario.

I bet you they have prepared for just such a thing, thought Reina and Pauline. If they hadn't, there was no way that they could have made it this far without having a single vacancy among their ranks.

The name of the spell that Lacelina had let loose this time was impressive, but it turned out to be nothing more than a simple gust—a strong wind, lacking even the power to blow a man away. Yet that simple gust began to disturb the ground, swirling toward the enemies in a spiral. Just as the spell's name had suggested, it was pulling dust up from the earth.

Of course, the men were not stupid enough to be felled by Lacelina's wind spell a second time. Rather than reacting in the same manner as before, they stopped their feet midstep and turned their bodies to the side, positioning themselves so that the front line of the Servants would serve as their shields. This would not net them a complete defense against the cloud that was swirling toward them, but at least it was better than taking it head-on. Yet just as they narrowed their eyes, calculating the timing of their attack for when the dust storm had ended, the five Servants of the Goddess rushed in.

Yes, all five of them. Tasha had discarded her bow in favor of her dagger—which, though it was called a "dagger," was not some piddling knife but a blade around fifty centimeters in length that would stand up splendidly to any enemies in whose defenses she could find an opening. Lacelina was there as well, brandishing her staff like a spear. At some moment or other she had shed the iron cap on the butt of the staff (the part which strikes the ground), revealing a fiendishly sharp metal implement.

"A sword...staff?" Reina uttered in astonishment.

"Why that's no different from a spear!" said Pauline in turn.

Normally, a mage would never participate in melee combat along with the forward guard, and a staff was typically a bludgeoning weapon rather than a tool for piercing. Furthermore, while the two of them had certainly heard of a so-called "sword cane," which had a blade hidden inside, a "Swordstaff: Spear Edition," was something new entirely. Yet there was no mistaking that a spear-type weapon—with its longer reach and ease of use, even for a beginner—was the obvious choice for the slight, young Lacelina.

The men, who had positioned themselves in such a way as to avoid the dust cloud, noticed Tasha and Lacelina's movements a moment too late. By the time they realized what was happening, the five Servants fell on them at once, with Tasha between Telyusia and Philly, and Lacelina between Philly and Willine.

Thanks to the dust storm, the men, who had stopped mid-attack and were now waiting, could not see clearly. While they'd expected to face a direct attack from the three frontline fighters, they had figured that with five on their side, they could still easily take down the opposition. Stricken with surprise that they were being run down by not only the front line, but inexplicably the middle and back lines as well, they were too slow to react.

In a situation like this, even a moment's delay might mean a fatal blow.

"Th-they're strong..." Reina and Pauline said at once, and in that moment, the men facing both the Servants of the Goddess and the Crimson Vow were stripped of the strength to fight once and for all.

"We better get going. We'll leave them here," Mile said to the group, after separating the sixteen now-powerless men and binding them all with the fishing line from her inventory.

The line was thin and strong, and in addition to having their arms secure behind them, their thumbs had been bound together, so if they attempted any struggle, the line would slice through, and it would be bye-bye fingers. The men had assumed that such thin thread would be a cinch to break, thinking they would merely have to flex their muscles to snap the strings. However, at Mile's explanation, the blood drained from their faces. There was no use in this world for a swordsman who had no thumbs.

"We don't have the time to tort—er, *interrogate*—them, and I get the feeling that the kidnappers are close by. It'll be quicker if we just press on from here. Let's go!"

On top of having their hands, feet, and fingers secured, the men had been tied together and lashed to a large tree, so it would be quite difficult for them to run. And unlike rope, fishing line could be tied unbelievably taut, unable to be undone without something sharp. Naturally, Mile had already confiscated and stored away all of the men's knives and swords.

While this was going on, Mile and Pauline had healed any particularly grievous injuries the men had sustained—though of course they had not healed them *completely*, only enough so that they would not die before the girls returned to retrieve them.

Unlike the Crimson Vow, who had held back, there were those among the men who faced the Servants of the Goddess who would very possibly have died if left as they were. Seeing them healed back into a stable state, the Servants' eyes went wide.

Unbelievable!!! they all thought.

The men they had just faced had been little more than the opening number. The real battle would be what came next, and yet here the Vow were, fruitlessly wasting their energy on healing the enemy? What softhearted fools! When things were down to the wire and victory escaped them, the magic that they wasted now was sure to be the cause.

Even the men whose injuries should have proved fatal had their bleeding stopped and their breathing steadied. How could these two use their unworldly healing powers without reservation on their enemies?

They were unbelievable. Like two heavenly maidens from a fairy tale...

As the members of the Crimson Vow set off again, the Servants of the Goddess followed behind, shaking their heads in bewilderment. By this point, Mile had already determined the position of Faleel and the kidnappers with her location magic. As such, the previous battle had not been for the sake of gathering information, but, as Mile would have put it, for "taking out the trash."

Knowing that Faleel was still safe, and having secured her position, Mile began to feel just a little bit more at ease. Without this knowledge, she would not have been able to hold back in the previous battle, and while men might not have died, the force of her attacks would have been sufficient to break every bone in their bodies.

It was growing quite dark now, but somehow the group managed to stick with Mile as they proceeded ever forward. Just when they began to think that they would not be able to go any farther without lanterns, Mile stopped.

"There."

The group broke out of their marching column and grouped around Mile. Following her pointing finger, they looked through a gap in the trees ahead, into a wide, treeless area. In the clearing were around thirty men. Just as before, their clothes were unkempt, but they were all wearing black cloaks. There did not appear to be any women among them. Roughly twenty stood in a circular formation near the middle of the clearing, with seven or eight more on the outside around the perimeter.

The men standing in the middle were all holding staves and were, presumably, mages. The men on the perimeter were all outfitted with swords. It would seem that the perimeter men were meant to guard the mages behind them.

The clearing was bright, lit by burning braziers here and there. And in the very center of the circle was...

"Lattice Power, Barrier!" Mile said softly, calm finally returning to her face as she whispered, "Phew, that's one thing off my mind!"

Indeed, there in the middle of the circle, laid out on a blanket on the ground, was Faleel. There was no telling whether Mile, with her superior vision, had confirmed that Faleel's chest was rising and falling with each breath or whether her radar had confirmed the vital signs for her. Either way, she could be certain the beastgirl was unharmed, and now that she was surrounded by Mile's barrier, her safety was assured even if a battle should happen to break out around her.

"Now, what to do? It looks like everyone in the middle there is a mage, which means that we can't carry on like before. If we go in unprepared, we have no chance of winning. Plus, if they take little Faleel as a hostage, we won't be able to rescue her... Even if we make use of the magic that Reina and the others have, Faleel might be caught up in it, or taken hostage anyway..."

Apparently, the reason that the earlier lookout-slash-guard forces had no mages among them was because all of their mages were gathered here. Having this many mages in one place was a clear imbalance, especially when compared to the number of frontline fighters on the scene.

Following Telyusia's suggestions, everyone had just begun to ponder a plan of attack when Mile began moving boldly forward.

"Well, let's get in there!" she said.

"Huh?!"

At Mile's words, the Servants were agog, but the members of the Crimson Vow merely shrugged their shoulders and followed behind.

"Wh-wh-wh-wh-what are you doing?! Have you gotten so flustered you've lost all reason? Wait a moment!"

As Telyusia desperately tried to stop Mile, Mavis turned to her. "Sorry! That's just Mile for you!"

"Wh-what does that mean?! That doesn't explain anything!" Telyusia muttered, unable to accept Mavis's explanation. However, the Crimson Vow continued to march ahead behind Mile, leaving the Servants no choice but to follow their lead.

"Whatever! If something goes wrong, it's not my fault!"

The Servants valued safety first and never acted without a plan for every eventuality. This was the first time in a long while that they had leapt before they looked, entering into a dangerous situation with no escape route in mind. The unease was clear on their faces, but they had no intention of leaving either the Crimson Vow or little Faleel behind, so they had no choice but to follow Mile.

"Who the hell are you?!" one of the guardsmen demanded.

The distance between the site of their previous battle and this clearing was not great. Naturally, the men here should have been able to hear the false bird call from before and would have concluded that their fellow guards-slash-lookouts would deal with the intruders. And thus, it was hard for this group to comprehend what it meant for the girls to show up completely unannounced, with no word from their lookouts.

"We'll be taking Faleel back now."

The guards from the outer rim had already gathered, blocking the girls' path. At Mile's words, the men could already tell that there was no point in questioning them farther. They drew their swords.

Upon gauging that a third of the girls' combined numbers were mages, the men called for further reinforcements from the inner circle and were joined by six more men. The remaining fifteen or sixteen mages remained where they were, without a care for the newcomers. Together, they began what could only be described as a suspicious incantation. Some of the girls began to worry that they were preparing an attack spell, but there were no words that that conveyed a clear indication of violence. Instead, they droned on and on in abstracts. It was almost more like a prayer to a god than a spell, when you thought about it...

Though of course, if it were a prayer that involved the abduction of a little girl, then it was more likely directed to a devil than a god.

"Hurry up and take them out! We must return to the circle to complete the spell of summoning!"

One of the mages who had joined the group as a reinforcement was kind enough to confirm the girls' suspicions.

"A summoning spell..." Mile murmured, her voice low.

[Summoning + Kidnapped Girl = Sacrifice]

Based on what Mile knew from her previous life, she could not possibly come to any other conclusion.

"Aha!"

Zip!

Reina, Mavis, and Pauline's eyes popped open in shock.

"Ahahaha…"

She was laughing. Mile was *laughing*…but her eyes were not smiling at all.

"Ahahahahahaha!"

A swirling haze filled her dead eyes. Were such a scene depicted in a manga, there would have been spirals turning within them…

At that moment, the enemy mages fired their spells. Five of the six joined in on the attack, while the sixth held a defensive spell, ready to let loose.

Three of the men each aimed one fireball at the opposing mages, while the other two lobbed firebombs at each of the parties as a whole.

For such young women to have felled the lookouts, the mages concluded, it must be the case not only that their melee fighters were more than just amateurs, but also that their mages were skilled. After all, appearance was a poor indicator of magical ability.

This was the logic behind the mages' plan of attack. Even if deflected with a sword, a firebomb would explode, and even if their opponents moved away, they would still be party to a substantial impact—at least enough to make them lose their footing. And of course, the final mage was ready and waiting to safeguard against any magical attack from the opposing side. All said, it should have been a flawless strategy.

How did the Crimson Vow react to the three magical bursts flying their way?

Reina and Pauline neatly deflected the fireballs with magical shields. And as for the explosive firebomb flying at the other two...

"Anti-Magic Blade!"

Before Mile could even make a move to cast the firebomb away, an excited Mavis stepped forth, beaming and trembling with the thrill that her day had finally come. The moment Mavis's blade sliced through the firebomb, it vanished without so much as a sound. Her Anti-Magic Blade had made its battle debut.

Meanwhile, on the Servants' side...

In spite of Lacelina's limited abilities, she valued her own life and was able to hastily conjure a protection spell to fend off the fireball aimed at her. Tasha, meanwhile, had nocked an arrow the moment she saw the enemies making moves to attack and now let it loose. The arrow collided with the still-flying firebomb, causing it to detonate in midair. Both fireballs and firebombs were far slower than any bow and arrow, so tracking their trajectory was a simple feat for any skilled archer.

"Wh...?"

The five enemy mages were flabbergasted to see all of their attacks so easily deflected—particularly the man who had launched the bomb that fell to Mavis's Anti-Magic Blade.

Defensive magic was something that they knew. They could use such spells as well, and it was perfectly normal for a mage to be able to conjure one in a short amount of time. Thus, they figured it was enough to simply force the opposing mages into guarding in order to render any spells they had silently prepared useless. At the same time, they would make the frontline fighters move to deflect their spells in order to protect their allies, causing injuries to all. For these parties to have perfectly guarded against every attack and emerged unscathed was unfathomable—as unfathomable as the fact that a bow and arrow had vanquished a firebomb... Sure, they reasoned, such techniques were not unheard of. Really, it was something that almost anyone could achieve if they had luck on their side to guide their arrow's course.

However, there remained one glaring improbability: the girl who, with a swing of her sword, sliced through an explosive spell and not only avoided detonating it but made it vanish into thin air.

Such things should not be. They *could* not be!

The magical attack that the six men had launched had been thwarted by a mere three mages, an archer, and a swordswoman. The men assembled were stunned at this utterly inconceivable turn of events, and as a result, the eight swordsmen stood stock-still, forfeiting their moment to strike.

While the enemies were momentarily frozen in place, the girls wasted not a second in preparing their next spells. Lacelina was the first to attack.

"Ice Needle!"

It was an area attack, targeted toward all six of the enemy mages. While its attack power was low, it was still a spell that would be unpleasant to take head-on. At the very least, if the mages were struck by the needles, their own incantations would be interrupted.

At Lacelina's words, the sixth mage unleashed the shield spell that he had been holding to protect all six of them. With a spell as weak as this one, it mattered little if the shielding effect was lessened a bit by spreading it over a wider area.

However, just a moment after Lacelina, Reina and Pauline completed their incantations also. And in their momentary surprise, the spells of the five enemy mages were a beat too late. The man who had used the first shielding spell was only just now beginning his next, and it was up to one of the other five to defend them.

It was then that Reina and Pauline shouted the activation words for their merciless spells.

"Burn them to the bone!"

"Winds, swirl!"

The clearing was wide, so the possibility of a wildfire spreading was low. Even if a blaze were to spark, Mile and Pauline were both present, so extinguishing the fire would be simple. Having judged as much, Reina decided to unleash her most powerful spell. Pauline, recognizing Reina's incantation, chose the wind spell in order to assist.

The six men were enveloped in an eddy of flame, battered by a howling wind.

"Magic Barrieeeeeeer!!!" shouted the man who had been desperately preparing a shield spell as two others switched midway from their attack spells to defensive ones.

Each of the men present valued his own life. It was only natural that they would prioritize defending themselves over attacking. Plus, if they were able to keep the attention of the girls' mages, then it would be easier for their swordsmen to overrun the rest of their opponents. They had an important role to fulfill.

Of course, it was not as though the melee fighters were merely sitting and twiddling their thumbs, waiting for the magic battle to conclude. The battle was six-on-three, and they couldn't fathom the idea of their allies losing to a group of young girls, but while their allies were tending to the magical side of things, their duty was to crush the front lines and then rush the back lines to take them out as well. A mage group without their front line had no hope of standing up against a simultaneous assault from swords, spears, and magic. They would be crushed in an instant.

With this in mind, the eight swordsmen launched their assault. The ones who faced this attack were the four sword wielders—Mavis, Mile, Telyusia, and Willine—along with Philly, the lancer. Tasha, the archer, fired an arrow at point-blank range before quickly drawing her dagger and leaping into the fray.

Of the eight men, pairs of two moved to oppose Mavis and Telyusia, who appeared to be the strongest of the sword wielders, as well as Philly, while one went to Mile and another to Willine, who looked to be the two youngest. Perhaps thinking that Tasha's arrows could easily be fended off with a sword, they were saving her for last. Surely with most battles being two-on-one, the girls would be vanquished in the blink of an eye, and there would be so little delay that she would not have the time to fire off a second arrow.

But then...

Whsh, chnk!

"Gaah!!"

Tasha's arrow pierced one of the enemies in the gut without him making so much as a move to avoid it. Somehow, she had rushed all the way to the front line, a hair's breadth from the enemy and fired off another shot. There was no way that he could have avoided or deflected it. Then, after falling back, she had tossed her bow away and drawn her dagger.

With this, the three frontline fighters of the Servants of the Goddess became four, and the enemies opposing them were diminished to four as well. And while the enemy might have more polished skills, as compared to the Servants' middling abilities, the young women clearly had experience in battle. Such was the current scene.

"Gwah!"

"Gyah!"

"Guh!!"

"Gah!"

And then, the four men fell—struck down by Mile and Mavis who came in from behind, smacking them down with the flats of their blades.

"Huh...?"

The Servants were stunned.

Mile, and Mavis with her True Godspeed Blade, needed little more than a few seconds to defeat enemies who were inexperienced in battle. Had they left it to the Servants, people would have been seriously injured, which would be a huge bother, so they thought they ought to take care of this situation as quickly as possible. This wasn't the graduation exam or a sporting match, so there was no need to overtax anyone's abilities or make a spectacle.

With the front line now taken care of, they all looked to observe the mages' fight where Reina continued to incant her specialty, Crimson Hellfire. Finally, she released the spell. The flames had been bolstered by Pauline's wind magic but miraculously woven in such a way as to not threaten the lives of the enemy mages or break through their protection magic. Once surrounded by the swirling flames, the mages could not see their opponents, so even those who had been in the midst of casting attack spells had to give up on accuracy and fire only in the girls' approximate direction before switching to shielding spells.

What they were doing now was usually referred to as protection magic, but the result was more a kind of magical protection: in other words, they were protected just fine against magic, but things like bows and arrows—or combat spells that had physical components such as earth and ice magic—would pass right through. With their vision obscured, these mages, who were not masters of the blade, would have no way of deflecting such attacks if they did penetrate the flames. And so, the mages circulated wind and water magic behind their magic shield in the hope of lowering the temperature of the flames.

Yet suddenly, the six mages fell to the ground, as though they had reached their limits. It was unclear if they had succumbed to the heat of the flames or if the fire had sucked out all their oxygen and asphyxiated them.

"Hmph! Well, that was easy. As for the rest of them..." Reina turned her gaze to the remaining mage corps, fifteen or so of them still carrying on their strange chant, rotating in a circle with Faleel at the center, unaffected by the change of circumstances.

Just then...

Slam!

Thud!

"Gwah!"

"Huh...?"

Reina fell onto her backside at a quick shove from Telyusia. She looked up to see a small, silver object protruding from the girl's torso. Clutching her side, from which blood now poured, Telyusia fell to the ground.

"Wh... H... Huh...?"

Reina was stunned, unable to move. Several images ran through her head: first, that of her father, cut down by bandits while trying to protect her. And second, the faces of the members of the Crimson Lightning, flying through her mind, one by one.

Without a word, Philly dashed forth, driving the butt of her spear into the chin of the mage who, from his position on the ground, had magically propelled his small utility knife toward her fellow party member. With the man now face-up in the dirt, she drove the dull end of the spear hard into his gut once more.

Willine ran up after her, kicking the man in the side. Once the man was unconscious, they circulated among all of the other fallen mages, striking them with foot and spear to make certain that none of them retained the will to fight—though it appeared that the rest of them were already unconscious in the first place. Going to the trouble of injuring them any further was little more than a nuisance.

The attacking mage, the bulk of whose strength had been decimated by Reina's fire spell, had perhaps decided that his best course of action would be to use his scant remaining magical power to perform not a magical attack, which could be blocked, but a physical one, which could not be magically shielded against. If this was to be his final attack, then he may as well use it to take out the strongest of the enemies, after which her small and clearly mediocre companions could all be dealt with handily. At least, that was the man's expectation.

"Wh-why would you...?" Reina asked Telyusia, crouching forward.

"Wh-what do you mean, 'why?'" Telyusia forced out, her face twisted in pain. "C-can you imagine what would happen i-if word got out that junior hunters had been seriously hurt while we were right there w-with them...?"

She then looked to Philly, who had just returned from disabling (though not killing) the remaining mages. "Philly, it's up to you from now on. Looks like I'll be going to the Goddess's side just a little ahead of you, but I'll be watching over all of you. It's your turn, Philly. You're the leader of our party now. Keep following your dreams..."

"Telyusia!"

"Leader!"

"Miss Telyusia!"

"Nnh..."

It was a fatal wound.

The knife had not pierced her heart, so she still appeared to be all right, but in this world, a wound to the abdomen always proved fatal. To start with, there was obviously the possibility of the liver or kidneys being punctured, but there was also the prospect of damage to major arteries or the rupturing of the intestines, which would cause the bacteria of the gut to proliferate, bringing on peritonitis and several days of agonizing pain, followed by death.

Indeed, Telyusia's death was already as good as certain.

However, there was no time to mourn her. The tears could come later. Now, they had a duty to attend to. They had to save Faleel!

With these thoughts in mind, the Servants wiped their tears away, standing up proudly. But just then...

"Ha!"

Gush!

"Gaaaaah!"

Suddenly, Pauline unceremoniously gripped the knife that was thrust into Telyusia's side and yanked it out.

"Huh?!"

A cry of shock came from the four other Servants. It was common sense not to remove the implement until any preparations for healing had been made. When you removed the knife, the wound itself would open wider, with blood spurting from the point of entry. Death from blood loss would come swiftly. And yet, Pauline had drawn the knife out without even a moment of hesitation.

"Reconnect and mend the blood vessels, repair the nerves, multiply cells, reconstruct muscle tissue, annihilate foreign bacteria, numb the pain receptors... Mega Heal!"

"Huh...?"

The Servants looked on, stunned, as Telyusia's wound closed before their eyes. Telyusia herself could only blink, her mouth hanging open soundlessly.

"Do you really think I'd let someone who saved our Reina die from just a little wound like that? And besides..." Pauline gave a haughty grin and continued, "*Looks like I'll be going to the Goddess's side just a little ahead of you, but I'll be watching over all of you. It's your turn, Philly. You're the leader of our party now. Keep following your dreams...*"

A deep blush spread over Telyusia's face.

"It would be a piteous shame if the speaker of such iconic words were not there to live on as they became a legend among hunters everywhere."

"G-g..." stuttered Telyusia.

"G-g...?" the four other Servants repeated.

"Gaaaaaaaaaaaah!!!"

The Servants of the Goddess had previously observed only the healing work that Pauline and Mile had performed on the group of lookouts. However, that had merely been for the sake of keeping the men from dying—nothing more than stopping any blood flow and repairing the functioning of their internal organs. Besides, no amateur would be able to recognize the fact that the internal organs and blood vessels had been repaired just from seeing the men's exteriors. Pauline and Mile had left the visible openings of the wounds as they were to keep the men from trying anything foolish.

Therefore, while the Servants been surprised at Pauline and Mile's healing abilities before, they would never have guessed that the two mages were *that* good.

To bring a person who was certain to die back into the world of the living... Was that truly a power that any mortal hands should be able to wield?

"No!" "Don't!" "Please don't tell anyone!" Telyusia's tears seemed to protest, even as the eyes of the four other Servants welled with tears for a different reason.

Lacelina, overcome with rage that her friend had been hurt, felt her head growing hazy with an emotion she could not hold back. Impulsively, she turned toward the men who were still rotating like a magic wheel and fired off a spell.

"Fire Rain!"

This particular spell had a penetrating power that was next to nothing, but it could easily rain down upon a large area. Against a large number of opponents—and moreover, as an attack that could be launched with some restraint—it was not a bad choice at all. Plus, it used up little magical power and required barely any elaboration in the incantation to produce a burning fluid that would stick to the targets' clothes. And yet...

Whsh!

"Huh?"

The fire rain vanished.

The countless burning droplets had not been repelled—they vanished completely just before striking the men, as though they had evaporated.

"...Fireball!"

Next up, Pauline tentatively fired off a spell. It was a simplistic but fairly strong basic fire spell.

Ka-bwsh!

"Wh...?"

All of the mages, save for Mile, were terribly taken aback.

Next, Tasha, who had now retrieved her bow, and Philly, with her spear, launched a direct attack in tandem.

Their blows did not pass through, and the circle of mages calmly continued their ritual as though they hadn't realized that they had been attacked at all.

"Bwahaha... It's pointless!" As they all stood puzzled, a voice called to them.

It was one of the swordsmen, sitting on the ground, his arm and his ribs broken. Of course, the girls were aware that some of the melee fighters were still conscious, but since they had been rendered powerless to grip their weapons and launch an attack, they had left the men as they were. There was little chance of them throwing their weapons either, but they still took caution (as they did not wish to divulge too much information about their abilities, Mile had not put their weapons in storage as she sometimes did).

"The further that ritual proceeds, the more the mages' magical power grows. No magic or physical attack can harm them. All that's left now is to wait for the ritual to be complete. Then, 'It' will appear and grant our wishes in exchange for the sacrifice. Bwaha-bwahahahahahaha!"

Hearing this, Mile muttered to herself, "Magical Engine, internal pressure rising…"

Her expression was still firm, but apparently, she was back to her usual self.

The reason that the main corps of the enemy party had not taken part in the battle, sparing only the melee fighters and a few mages, was, first and foremost, that it was unfathomable that they could lose to just a few little girls. Yet, more importantly, staying out of the fray bought them valuable time even if something went awry with the rest of the fighters. Therefore, they had concentrated only on the ritual, not bothering to send out any additional forces. If nothing else, throwing too many of their forces into battle at once would leave both their battle party and their ritual party at half-strength.

"Inferno rise, burn hot enough to melt the rocks, hot enough to turn them to vapor, hotter still, more violent still…"

Reina began a spell. She did not dash out the words as quickly as she always did. No, these were slow words, words of power.

"I told you, it's pointless! No matter how skilled you think you are, that barrier will never be broken by some little girl's spell!"

She persisted, ignoring the swordsman's taunting, voicing the words of a spell that none of the others had even heard of—a spell to vaporize rock. Even Reina, the one chanting this spell, could not have possibly had any concrete idea of what temperature would be required to bring such a thing about. Only that it was an absurdly high one...

And then, she voiced the command phrase.

"Scorching Breath!"

A high-temperature jet, several millimeters in diameter, spewed forward. The concentrated stream bored a hole in the magical barrier that went through to the other side. One of the mages in the circle fell to the ground.

A peculiar light shone in Reina's eyes. Just as it did in Mile's. Just as it had in the moment she was reborn as "Crimson Reina, the Bandit Slayer"...

"Wh...?"

Neither the sneering swordsmen nor the mages in the circle could conceal their sudden unrest. However, despite their distress, the mages continued their ritual as though nothing had happened. If they were to pause the ritual now, not only would it not come to fruition, but the barrier would dissolve, and they would have to face these inexplicable intruders, who remained unharmed despite facing down the lookouts, the guards, and six of their mages. They had no other choice but to continue on.

After Reina's attack, Mavis approached the barrier. And then, slowly, she thrust her sword in.

Ka-shnk.

It passed through the barrier without the slightest hint of resistance.

And then, another mage fell.

Plod plod plod plod.

Mile walked right up the barrier, stopping just inches away, and shoved her right arm through.

Thwmp.

She seized the nearest mage by the nape of the neck and dragged him out.

"Whaaaaaaaaaat?!?!"

Seeing the Servants fall upon the man who had just been dragged out, the other mages, who had just barely managed to ignore the fact of Mavis's sword, could not hold back a cry of shock.

"H-hurryyy!!! Forget the fifth stage—let's just wrap up the incantation! Preparing the words, in *five, four, three, two, one...* Now!"

The mages, who had thought there was no doubt they would complete the ritual safely, were now thrown into a tizzy, sweat dripping from their brows. These young girls had ripped through their magical barrier as though it were paper, but the mages were not prepared to give up just yet. It would be a race against the clock.

Mile remained unworried. She had put a full-strength barrier around Faleel. Even an elder dragon could not have harmed her. Well, an "elder dragon, or something of equivalent type." As the nanomachines had informed her that her own power was equal to half the abilities of such a creature, she could be confident. Besides, with those same nanomachines on her side, it couldn't possibly fail. Even if the mages did carry on with their little ritual—and even if some summoned fiend did appear before their very eyes—it was no matter. If they wanted to sacrifice their own souls for the sake of some reward, then that was well and good in Mile's book.

And so, Mile was in little hurry—until suddenly, she heard a frantic voice ringing in her ears.

LADY MILE, PLEASE STOP THEM! THIS IS NO GOOD!

WE ARE PROGRAMMED TO CARRY OUT ALL UN-PROHIBITED MAGICAL COMMANDS, REGARDLESS OF WHETHER THEY ARE GOOD OR EVIL. THEREFORE, WE MUST ENACT THE WILLS OF BOTH SIDES, SO AS NOT TO VIOLATE OUR MOST BASIC TENETS. THIS IS A SITUATION THAT OUR CREATORS COULD NOT HAVE HYPOTHESIZED.

THIS SCENARIO HAS BECOME DIRE! IF YOU DO NOT STOP THEM AT ONCE, A DISASTER MAY OCCUR!

Never before had she heard the nanomachines sound this desperate. Apparently, what the men aimed to achieve with their final incantation was something rather unsavory. Enough so that even the nanomachines were disturbed...

Well, if even *they* were bothered, then that changed things. This was no laughing matter. Mile had assumed that so long as Faleel's safety was assured, it was fine to let things run their course, but now it was time to step into the fray.

Initially, she thought that she might feign putting her hand into her breast pocket, but because of the leather armor, there was no way for her to do so now. Instead, she shoved her hand in down the top of her chest piece and withdrew it, a small parcel gripped in hand. Though she pretended the parcel had been drawn from within her armor, in actuality, it came from her inventory. Indeed, it was one of the spice hand grenades, which she had assembled back when they were producing the spices for the restaurant owner.

Behind her, she could hear the Servants whispering among themselves, "Oh? Padding? Did she have padding in there?" Suddenly, it occurred to Mile that her hearing might be a little *too* good.

Sh-shut up back there! she spat venomously within her heart and then stiffened when she realized that, because she had no reason to hide the fact of her storage magic from the Servants of the Goddess, she could have simply taken the item out of "storage" as she normally would.

For no reason at all, she had just caused herself heartache—and an unconscionable ridicule. Consumed by rage at both herself and the universe, Mile unleashed her explosive secret technique.

"Eruptiiiiing! Burning! Fingeeeeeeeeer!!!"

Then, the parcel in hand, she shoved her right arm through the barrier and flung the grenade toward the mages within.

"Red Tornado!"

And with that second shout, she withdrew from the barrier.

Inside, a whirlwind whipped up. It was not particularly

powerful—only strong enough to circulate the air within the barrier... However, it was bright red.

"GAAAAAAAAAAAAAAAAH!!!" the men all screamed.

Just then, near the center of the circle, where Faleel was still lying on the ground, fissures opened up in the air itself. A strange aura began to emanate outward from the fissures. Yet, the moment the red air crept inside of it...

"GYEEEEEEEEEEEEEEEEEH!!!"

With a desperate scream, the presence vanished just as suddenly as it had appeared. The fissures in the air closed, and quiet returned to the clearing, almost as though nothing had happened at all.

"........."

There were no signs of movement within the barrier. In fact, the barrier itself seemed to have dissipated. Likewise, there were no signs of movement from the six other mages, who were still collapsed on the ground. Two of three of the enemy swordsmen were still conscious, but their eyes were wide, and it did not appear as though they would be making any sudden movements.

The four members of the Crimson Vow appeared utterly unaffected. As far as the Servants were concerned, however...

"Th-that's...a waste of good spiceeeeeeeeeeeeeeeees!!!!!"

Seriously?!

✧◈✧

While Mavis headed off to the Guild to fetch reinforcements, the others began the work of detaining the men. All told, between the lookouts and the additional forces in the clearing, there were around 47 in total—far more than they could reasonably be expected to relocate on their own. They would have to rouse the men enough to allow them to walk on their own two legs, and with so many mages in the mix, doing so might be dangerous. If there were any among them who were capable of silent-casting or using abbreviated spells, a surprise attack could come at any moment. Plus, it was unlikely that they would cooperate enough to march in any straightforward fashion.

The reason that Mavis had been the one to go was simply that she was the fastest. Plus, they couldn't possibly send one of the Servants, who were the senior party, to be the errand girl. Reina and Pauline were way too slow, so they were out of the question, and Mile needed to remain on the scene in case of any emergency. Therefore, Mavis was the obvious—really, the only—choice. Even Mavis herself could see this, so she accepted her duty without question and set off running at once.

In truth, there was one more reason why Mavis had been chosen: thanks to her "spiritual powers," she had excellent night vision. Torches and light spells would grant only a short range of vision, and because of the shadows they cast, it became more difficult to discern shapes, so one had to proceed with caution. Furthermore, with torches came the risk of wildfire, requiring even more care.

Granted, returning with the response team would be a slower affair either way, but there wasn't anything that could be done about that.

The lookouts had been left where they fell, but given the way that they were bound, it was unlikely that they would be able to escape. It was not as though the status of their injuries would have allowed them to make it very far anyway. Plus, even on the off chance that one of them *did* break free, it was unlikely that they would head anywhere besides this place, where a large number of their comrades were gathered.

In the clearing, after all the men had been bound and gathered into one spot, they got the still-conscious men to tell them who was the highest-ranking among them and then forced said man to inhale some awakening herbs to rouse him. The answer had come easily. Apparently the identity of their leader was not something that they felt the need to conceal.

Naturally, the moment the barrier dissolved, Mile had dissipated the capsaicin particles in the air and cleared away what lingered upon the mages' clothing and mucus membranes. If she hadn't, it would make things difficult for *their* faction as well.

"Now then, there are a few things that I would like you to tell me: Why did you kidnap Miss Faleel? What did you intend to do with her? Which feature of hers do you find the most adorable? And, I suppose, while you're at it, you can tell me your reasoning behind this whole thing." Mile spoke with a grin, though her eyes were entirely unsmiling.

Seeing this, the leader replied, his face twitching, "W-we've done nothing to be ashamed of! We were merely conducting a ritual that would allow us to summon our god, with a child tainted with filthy beast blood as the sacrifice!"

"That is *absolutely* something to be ashamed of!!!" the Crimson Vow and the Servants of the Goddess screeched all in unison. Still, the man looked on blankly. Of course, shame required both self-awareness and some kind of conscience—or at least a concept of what was and was not acceptable—something that a group of religious fanatics might lack.

"Are you seriously telling me that using a young girl for a sacrifice doesn't weigh on you just a little bit?" asked Reina, cutting straight to the crux of the matter. "Also, why did you choose *her*? Furthermore, what sort of god demands a sacrifice in the first place? That's something that only a great devil or an evil god would ask for, isn't it?"

"It's because that *creature* carries the blood of beasts! Beastmen, elves, dwarves—and naturally, demons—are all unclean creatures, brought into this world to sway foolish men from the path of holiness. To sacrifice one of those uncouth fiends is only the natural course—the mark of a good and just mind! And of course, the reason we chose *that* one is that, well, there aren't any demons in the area, and when we tried to capture any adult elves or dwarves or beasts, it went really poorly... I mean! Surely our god would be overjoyed to receive a pure young girl, unsullied by the ways of adults...!"

The man answered earnestly—perhaps a bit *too* earnestly, as though he could see nothing at all wrong with the actions that they had taken—though his face twitched as he spoke. He revealed not only their official stance but their true motives as well.

Clearly, he thought that the Crimson Vow and the Servants, who were all pure-blooded humans, would understand where he was coming from.

It was true that even several people would find it difficult to capture a dwarf or beastperson, with their honed physical strength and keen reaction times, or an elf, with their advanced magical powers, without being killed or suffering serious injury. Particularly for a group who were as unaccustomed to actual battle as these men seemed to be.

Though the man had not seemed inclined to talk at first, with some persuasion from Reina and Pauline—especially Pauline—the gist of the situation became clear.

The men were members of a fanatic religious order, which spanned numerous nations. Among them were chief members, who devoted their entire lives to the order, as well as some normal believers, who had lives outside of the order as well.

The pantheon that this group believed in consisted of a group of gods that had "appeared from another world, possessing great powers." These otherworldly gods had appeared numerous times in the distant past, engaging again and again in fierce warfare against the gods of this world, both sides striking equally, until, finally, the invaders returned to their own world, and the gods of this world vanished off to who-knows-where, leaving humans behind. Abandoned, the humans made preparations in case the invading gods should one day reappear. In that process, the four subservient humanoid races were born: elves, dwarves, beastfolk, and demons.

Rather than remaining faithful to the gods of this world, who had cast humans aside and run off, leaving them to endlessly perpetuate the gods' edicts, was it not better to welcome the invading gods and receive their protection? After all, the gods who had fled were weak and negligent. Those sorry excuses for gods were not present, had not returned, and had not granted humanity the slightest bit of protection.

It would seem that these were the founding tenets of this order's teachings.

Wait, that sounds like...

Indeed, while Mile completely disagreed with the men's general philosophy, she had in fact heard stories that very closely resembled this legend—not one, not two, but three times now. The first time had come from the elves, via Dr. Clairia. The second, from the elder dragons, via Berdetice. And the third—though it was far vaguer than the other two—had come from the chief elder of the fairies. Yet, it was a story that had been lost among the humans, with their short life spans and the swift overturning of generations—or a story that *should* have been lost.

No human alive should know about this. How can this religion have such a story now...?

"So what you're saying here is that you're a bunch of bankrupt nobles who could never make it to the upper echelons or half-baked merchants who could never make the big time but still burned with ambition, basically wishing on a shooting star and risking everything that you had? You have no idea if gods from another world would even be able to understand you—and if they did, who says that they'd have any interest in catering to their believers' trivial whims in the first place? They might just drag those believers back to their own world and use every one of them as their personal slaves, or even their next meal... Plus, what if their believers back in their own world are orcs or ogres? The kind of gods that monsters would revere would have to be evil deities or devils."

"Shut your mouuuuuuuth!!!" the leader shrieked, veins bulging in his forehead as Pauline casually pointed out one flaw after another in the logic of his story. It seemed that these criticisms were not wholly foreign ones.

"Mm... Hm? Where...where am I...?"

Zip zip zip zip zip!

As Faleel's eyes finally opened, the Servants of the Goddess rushed to her side at lightning speed, leaving the Crimson Vow in the dust. When Mile cleared the capsaicin from the air, she had released the lattice power barrier as well.

"Are you all right? We took care of those nasty kidnappers! You're safe now!" said Telyusia with a grin, crouching down next to Faleel.

"Huh? It's the Servants of the Goddess..."

Faleel looked up at them, perplexed.

"If you're ever in danger, Faleel, we'll always come running, no matter where, no matter when. So you've got nothing to worry about!"

"Oh, thank you!" cried Faleel, sitting up and squeezing Telyusia tightly.

"N-noooooooo! Th-that was supposed to be my reward!
That's a violation! A foul!!!"

The clearing resounded with the sound of Mile's anguished
screams.

It was already the next morning when Mavis returned, reinforcements in tow. When she had arrived at the guildhall, it was
already late at night, and the only people she could recruit were
hunters who had been drinking in the tavern. Plus, there was the
matter of procuring carts and drivers, and the fact that most were
rather opposed to delving into the forest in the middle of the
night. The Guild's decision that they would depart in the morning was more or less inevitable.

Having surmised that this might be the case, Mile returned
alone to the spot where they had left the lookouts after some time
had passed to administer additional healing magic. Forcing them
to pass the whole night as they were would be a weight on her
conscience.

At the same time, she provided the men with food and water
from her inventory. Once their wounds were healed, their empty
stomachs and parched throats would suddenly intensify. It wasn't
as though the increased cellular regeneration could come from
nowhere, after all.

Afterwards, she returned to the site of the ritual, and the
questioning of the enemy leader continued. Since no one other
than Mile had any idea what the man was talking about, the rest
served merely as onlookers. Mile would be the one to give their

report when they returned to town. Though they hated the idea of relying on Mile alone, since the exchange was a rapid one, dealing with legends the likes of which they had never heard, they had few other choices.

A short while after first light broke, Mavis finally arrived with the reinforcements. The wagons were apparently waiting back on the highway.

"Sorry we took so long," Mavis apologized, though they all knew it wasn't her fault.

The other three smiled and waved back.

"You all again?" asked Felicia, a tired look upon her face.

"Hey! What's a clerk like you doing here, Miss Felicia?"

"We heard there were a number of perpetrators. You couldn't expect us all to just sit around meditating."

That really didn't explain anything at all. However, the other guild employees and hunters were nodding fervently in agreement, so the Crimson Vow got the feeling they shouldn't be asking any more questions and abandoned their inquiry accordingly.

"We've already heard a report of the situation from Mavis, of the Crimson Vow. We would like to hear confirmation from the Servants of the Goddess or at least a report on the general circumstances of what's come to pass."

Apparently, even the guild master himself had come out, perhaps worried that, if mishandled, this incident could blow up even more than it already had.

The mysterious abduction of the daughter of a prominent merchant, the kidnapping and attempted murder of a young beastgirl by an anti-beastperson hate group, the revival of a dark god by a cult of worshippers... Sure enough, no matter how you spun it, this could get pretty bad, pretty fast.

At the guild master's request, Telyusia took a step forward and replied, "Miss Faleel, the jewel of the inn, was abducted right before her friend's eyes, and her father placed an emergency request which we accepted jointly with the Crimson Vow. We tracked the criminals to this site, where they were conducting a suspicious ritual, and put a stop to it. We then rescued Faleel, who was on the verge of becoming a sacrifice. Furthermore, the men were the first to attack."

It was an incredibly abbreviated explanation, but Mavis should have already filled the Guild in on the details. Since this was merely an inquiry to confirm whether or not Mavis's report was truthful, it was enough. Unlike the Crimson Vow, who, in spite of their skill, were newcomers with mysterious origins, the Servants of the Goddess had already been active in this town for some years and were known to be a reliable party in and of themselves.

"Hm... I see. Thank you for your hard work. Your actions in this matter have done a great service for our Guild, and we shall see to it that all of you receive additional recompense and contribution points for your efforts. Moreover, we will tender a report to the Crown to ensure that you receive an official reward from that quarter."

"R-really?!" Telyusia shouted, her eyes wide.

"Mm-hm... The promised pay for this job was only one silver, you see. I would say that what you have done merits far more than that," the man said with a smile.

The Servants took each other's hands and leapt for joy. After all, such fortune was something that rarely fell into the laps of the Servants, who, unlike the extreme outliers who were the Crimson Vow, took each day one steady step at a time. Such an event might even bump their reputation from that of low-end C-rankers straight to a mid-class in one fell swoop!

Once the offenders had all been restrained and loaded into the wagons, the whole group began its return to the capital. Naturally, the lookouts had been retrieved as well.

The mages had all been gagged tightly, with cloths stuffed in their mouths, so that they could not recite any incantation. In addition, they were blindfolded so that they could not perform any silent casting. Still, lookouts were assigned to them just in case, ready to bash in their skulls the moment they saw anything suspicious.

The men would be questioned once they returned to the capital, but that was a job not for the Guild but for the city guard, or perhaps even agents of the Crown itself. Both parties would likely be summoned to give their testimony when the time came for that, and since their cooperation was directly linked to their reward, they were in no position to complain—particularly not the Servants.

The two parties walked down the highway alongside the transport wagons. Faleel rode atop Philly's shoulders. Mile wanted so desperately to be the one carrying her that she was practically weeping tears of blood, but she had been denied the role. "You're far too small, it wouldn't be safe," Philly had told her.

A short while after they began walking, Telyusia said, "By the way, Reina, darling..."

When introducing oneself, a maiden never offered her own age, so the Servants were all convinced that Reina was only twelve or thirteen years old.

"While it's clear that you have intense magical power—and a lot of it—and that, even for a C-rank, your practical senses are incredibly honed, you mustn't rely so much on that power, neglecting to consider the little things or letting your guard down. You need to think more about cooperating with your friends and never turn your back on an enemy until you're certain he has perished. Even a child can play dead, after all!" She patted Reina gently on the head as she spoke.

Reina's cheeks began to take on a scarlet tinge.

Oh noooooo! She's gonna bloooooow!!!

The faces of the other members of the Crimson Vow began to twitch. Not only was Telyusia speaking to her like a child, something they knew Reina abhorred, she was also explaining things to her in a condescending manner, *and* she was patting her on the head! It was a trifecta that would brew a perfect storm.

Reina, her head bent, then spoke softly. "...You're right."

Sh-she's gone soooooooooooft!!!

In a world in which she was surrounded by people who wanted to use and abuse her, Reina had survived by bluffing her way through life. Everyone who had ever offered her help, asking nothing in return—everyone who had ever cherished her for being herself—had all perished. She could rely on her companions among the Crimson Vow, of course, but they were her equals—no, even worse, they were naive and guileless fools who relied on the senses she had honed through years as a hunter to defend and to guide them. They were people who relied on *her*, not people whom *she* could truly depend upon.

She dreamed of someone who did not hesitate to put her own life on the line to save hers. A reliable figure, one on whom she could depend, in whom she could have absolute faith. For Reina, who had lost both her father and the Crimson Lightning, such a person was her heart's greatest desire.

And now one such figure had appeared: an older girl who had put herself in the way of an enemy attack to shield Reina with no regard for her own life.

Reina couldn't help but soften.

✧ ◈ ✧

So, what was that all about? Mile questioned the nanomachines as the party walked down the road, still sulking that the honor of carrying Faleel home had been stolen from her by Philly. Her companions, seeing that she was in a bad mood, elected to leave her be, leaving her to converse with her invisible friends unimpeded... The Crimson Vow had long ago learned not to bother speaking to Mile when she got like this.

AND WHAT MIGHT YOU BE REFERRING TO?

Don't play dumb! What was all that, 'Please stop them! This is bad!' nonsense?! What are you hiding from me, Nanos? And what in the world was that thing *that appeared in the air for a split second? What were they summoning? And seriously, you're telling me it's susceptible to* chili peppers?

'.........'

After some time, the nanomachines finally replied. They had probably paused to consult with central processing.

NORMALLY WE WOULD BE PROHIBITED FROM IM-PARTING SUCH INFORMATION TO A COMMON MORTAL, BUT SEEING AS YOU HAVE A LEVEL-5 AUTHORIZATION, LADY MILE, YOU ARE NOT EXACTLY "COMMON," ARE YOU? THEREFORE, WE MAY DISCLOSE SOME OF THIS INFORMATION TO YOU ON THE CONDITION THAT YOU SHARE IT WITH NO ONE.

What are you talking about?! I'm a completely normal girl!

'.........'

Ugh, whatever! I won't tell anyone!

Apparently, Reina's speech patterns were beginning to rub off on Mile.

As it turned out, the bit of information that the nanomachines were able to impart unto her was the truth behind the tale of the aforementioned "gods."

The "gods of this world" that the legend spoke of were in fact *not* the ones to whom the nanomachines referred as their Creators—in other words, beings like the one who had granted

Mile's own rebirth. Rather, they were people of the ruined ancient civilization—the people who were depicted in the mural in the first set of ruins Mile had come across. Naturally, to the people of the current day, legends of a strange, ancient, scientifically advanced culture would sound just like the land of the gods.

And, as for those "gods from another world"...

NO SUCH THING, OF COURSE.

Obviously!

If the ones being referred to as "gods" were merely people of a civilization that was slightly more advanced than that of modern-day Earth, then it was unlikely anyone who started a brawl with them would be a god or devil, either. Most likely, they were some other intelligent life-form with an equal level of technological advancement, or perhaps some less-developed race with technology that had not come so far, who could not wipe the others out easily... Or perhaps some kind of monsters...

Whatever they were, compared to the "godlike figure" who had been responsible for Mile's rebirth, or any of his compatriots, they represented even less threat than a flea.

Yet even those "godlike figures," though they could support the people indirectly, could not exhibit any large-scale interference or aid anyone in a direct way. Therefore, any conflict that arose could be the affair of only the participants. It was likely only after this earlier civilization's inevitable destruction that the "large-scale interference, as an experiment and as an aid to the planet," that Mile's "God" had mentioned would have occurred. Of course, that large-scale interference had been the seeding of the nanomachines...

Yet, this too had ended in failure. The remaining intelligent life-forms on the planet, whom the people of today referred to as "gods," fled this world when they found themselves on the brink of collapse, and *then* the "godlike figures," having lost interest in the planet entirely after the failure of their experiment led to a long-term stagnation of its civilizations, ceased their guidance and abandoned the planet as well (even though a few of them *did* feel guilty about it).

Hm? So, in that case, that "summoning magic" was...

IT WAS NOT "SUMMONING" MAGIC BUT DIMEN-SIONAL LINKING MAGIC—MAGIC THAT CAN CONNECT THIS WORLD TO OTHERS. ANYTHING THAT MIGHT COME THROUGH IS ONLY WHATEVER LIFE-FORM HAPPENS TO ENTER THE GATE, WHEREVER IT HAPPENS TO OPEN...

HOWEVER, IT IS RARE THAT ANY CREATURE, INTEL-LIGENT OR OTHERWISE, WOULD CHOOSE OF ITS OWN FREE WILL TO ENTER A SUSPICIOUS FISSURE IN THE AIR. THEREFORE, THE CREATURE IN QUESTION MUST TRULY HAVE WANTED TO GET AWAY FROM WHERE IT WAS—OR HAD A CLEAR VIEW OF OUR OWN WORLD...

Finally, Mile was starting to get the picture, but the number-one concern she had about the situation had yet to be assuaged. Again, she pressed the nanomachines.

So, why were you all so worried? If it was just some normal crea-ture that came through, not a god or anything, than it could be a dragon for all you all cared. It wouldn't really matter, would it?

Even if it tried to eat those mages, or caused a bit of mayhem, it's not really something for you all to get worked up over, is it?

....

If you can't tell me that *much, then what's the point of telling me* anything?!

....

After another brief pause, the nanomachines replied, sounding a bit resigned.

WELL, IT CONCERNS THE CONTENTS OF THE CONVERSATION THAT YOU SHARED WITH OUR CREATOR, ABOUT WHICH YOU PREVIOUSLY INFORMED US...

Indeed, some time ago the nanomachines had expressed great interest in hearing about their Creator, in other words the "not-a-God" fellow who had brought Mile into this world. Understanding where they were coming from, Mile recounted her conversation with him word-for-word, to the best of her memory. For the nanomachines, it must have been a feeling akin to hearing news of their parents, from a hometown they had not visited in decades.

THIS WORLD HAS BEEN DESTROYED AND REBORN, OVER AND OVER AGAIN, YOU INFORMED US. IT HAS LOST COUNTLESS CIVILIZATIONS, AND EACH TIME THE SCANT SURVIVORS HAVE HAD TO START OVER AGAIN FROM THE BEGINNING...

Ah, yes... Mile was already aware of at least that much.

DO YOU NOT THINK IT PECULIAR THAT THIS WORLD WOULD END UP ON THE BRINK OF RUIN AGAIN AND

AGAIN, DESPITE THE CREATORS ASSISTING IT EACH
TIME—NO MATTER HOW INDIRECT OR HOW MEAGER
THAT ASSISTANCE MIGHT HAVE BEEN?

Hm...?

She hadn't thought about this, or rather, had assumed it was
only natural that most civilizations would eventually reach a hur-
dle that they could not overcome and that this hardship would
lead to their decline and eventual ruin. Whether it was pollution
or energy depletion or travel to the stars, there were countless
hurdles that could stand in a civilization's way...

However, by the nanomachines' implication, this was *not*
the case.

WOULD YOU NOT THINK IT MORE APT TO CONSIDER
THAT THERE MIGHT BE CIVILIZATION-DESTROYING
FORCES THAT ARE PERIODICALLY VISITED UPON THIS
WORLD? FORCES THAT WE, WHO HAVE BEEN FORBIDDEN
FROM ANY LARGE-SCALE OR DIRECT INTERFERENCE AND
FROM ACTING UPON OUR OWN WILL, CAN DO NOTHING
ABOUT? ALL WE CAN DO IS LEND OUR POWER TO THE
CREATURES OF THIS WORLD WHO WOULD OPPOSE THEM
THEMSELVES, IN THE FORM OF "PSEUDO-MAGIC"...

Th-that means...

WE THOUGHT THAT THERE WAS STILL MORE TIME,
BUT IT APPEARS THAT THERE ARE PEOPLE IN THIS
WORLD WHO WOULD HASTEN ITS DESTRUCTION. IN OR-
DER TO PROTECT AGAINST THIS, IT CANNOT BE WE WHO
ACT AS THE SAVIORS, BUT PEOPLE WHO USE US, ACTING

OF THEIR OWN WILL. WE *NEED* THOSE PEOPLE.

A question suddenly leapt to Mile's thoughts from the depths of her heart.

So were there really *no other worlds that I could have been reborn into? Were my ridiculous abilities* really *a miscalculation or mistake on God's part? This seems awfully suspicious...*

Normally, the nanomachines had a tendency to offer unprompted replies to the undirected thoughts within Mile's head, but this time, they ignored her completely. Mile found that all the more suspicious.

So then, what is the source of all this...?

THAT IS ALL THE INFORMATION THAT WE CAN PROVIDE AT THIS TIME.

Huh?

TELLING YOU ANYTHING FURTHER WOULD REQUIRE, AT MINIMUM, A LEVEL-7 AUTHORIZATION. FRANKLY, WHAT WE HAVE IMPARTED UPON YOU ALREADY SURPASSES THAT WHICH YOU, AT LEVEL 5, SHOULD BE ALLOWED TO KNOW. WE WERE ONLY ABLE TO SKIRT THE RULES WHEN TAKING INTO CONSIDERATION THE FACT THAT YOU ALREADY POSSESSED A MEASURE OF INFORMATION DISCLOSED BY THE CREATOR HIMSELF, THE FACT THAT YOU ALREADY POSSESS A FUNDAMENTAL LEVEL OF UNDERSTANDING OF CONCEPTS THAT THE PEOPLE OF THIS WORLD COULD NEVER COMPREHEND, AND FINALLY, THE IMPORTANT ROLE YOU PLAYED IN RESOLVING THIS MOST RECENT INCIDENT.

Clearly, they had no choice, and neither did she. Mile, who had already promised herself that she would not go asking the nanomachines willy-nilly about every little thing that occurred, was in no position to be giving them the third degree now. Plus, even if she did want to push further, there was no way of overturning an objection from the nanomachines. The nanomachines may have possessed more flexibility than the average machine, but once they had made a decision about something, they stuck to it.

I see... Well, the next time that there is some piece of information you are allowed to tell me, you will, won't you?

As you wish.

And so, the escort troop proceeded on to the capital.

CHAPTER 58

Information Gathering

WHEN THE GROUP transporting the criminals arrived at the capital, they headed straight for the palace.

While the Guild had the power of mediation in all affairs regarding guild-assigned jobs, as well as the ability to arrest criminals, it did not truly possess any legal authority. The questioning and judging of criminals was a matter for the palace and the city guard. Normally, the handling of such incidents remained within the guards' jurisdiction, but when it came to grave or political matters, agents of the Crown took direct charge. It seemed that the current incident fell into just such a category.

Of course, it was only natural that a case involving a kidnapping, in which the victim was a non-human, would be bumped up the hierarchy, particularly when it involved religious heresy and a great number of perpetrators who may or may not have included wealthy merchants and low-ranking nobles. Plus, there was the possibility that there had been additional allies who were not even present... These were not the sorts of bandits or thugs who fell under the standard justice that the city guards could provide.

Faleel was handed over to her mother and father, who were waiting at the city gates. Mavis had updated them on the situation the night before, and they had even come to see the reinforcement squad off, so they were already in place when the convoy arrived. The rescue had drawn to a close without Mile reaping even the slightest perks.

✧ ◈ ✧

"Now then, please tell us every detail of what transpired."

Though the investigation was being conducted on the Crown's authority, it was not the King himself who came to question them. Such questionings were conducted by someone whose post was appropriate to the severity of the situation—though it was always at least relatively high-ranking individuals in the royal court who were put in charge of such things.

Of course, the Crown had already been given the gist of the situation. Without it, they would not have been able to select the appropriate rank of representative, after all. The guild master, who had been roused in the middle of the night along with the half-dozing night guardsmen, had plenty of time to kill before dawn, so it was no trouble to prepare a letter to be carried to the palace once the sun had risen.

Using the testimonies from the Crimson Vow and the

Servants of the Goddess as their basis, the officials questioned the captured men, who could tell from the start that there was no point in denying the facts when they had been caught in the act with so many witnesses. Instead, they opted to try to portray themselves as a group of meek and pious believers who would never harm a little girl, claiming that it was merely necessary to have a young beastgirl *present* for the ceremony and that they were going to return her safely once the ritual was finished—among all other manner of highly dubious claims.

Of course, no one present would believe such a story, meaning that the criminals would be subject to more intense individual questioning later on...

However, that was not the biggest problem at hand.

The Crown needed to know the scope of this peculiar organization, the details of how it had been established, the identity of any other members of this order, and the ultimate goal of the group. Understanding these points was of the utmost importance. Without this knowledge, there was no telling if such an incident might occur a second or even a third time. In fact, there was no telling whether this incident truly *was* the first time. There were plenty of other people from the capital who had been reported missing before, after all—even though it was certain that at least some of that number were comprised merely of eloping couples, traveling tricksters, and the like.

After their testimony was given, the two parties' duties were done. Once they had shared all that they knew, and confirmed the criminals' recounting of the facts, there was no reason for any of them to linger any longer. All that was left now was for the guards to extract the truth from those offenders by one means or another.

And so, the girls headed toward the Guild. While everyone there was already aware of the details of the job, they needed to give their official report to mark the completion of the emergency job and receive their reward of a single silver—which none of them would have traded for even a thousand gold.

"Do you think that they'll let us know about the findings of the investigation?" asked Mile.

"I mean, that isn't exactly something that the palace would be interested in sharing with us hunter types," Telyusia replied. "In fact, if anything truly troubling came to light, I bet they would want to keep it under wraps."

"Oh, man. Really?"

That was unfortunate. Mile wanted to know more about those people. She was particularly curious as to how a story that should have been lost to the sands of time—twisted though it may have been—made it all the way into the heads of these people and how it had become a basis of their faith. Furthermore, the fact that they had nearly invoked a dimensional linking spell could not possibly be mere chance. She had to find out the root of all this and make sure that no one tried to use that magic ever again.

This mission was more important and direr than the elder dragons' investigation could ever be.

"Though I suppose," Telyusia added, "the guild master might be able to get at least a bit of information out of them. He was the one who originally informed the palace of the incident, after all, so it should be fine..."

Indeed, as Telyusia implied, the Guild had been the ones to inform the palace, and if such an incident were to occur again, the Guild would likely be the first to have to deal with it, so it made sense for them to get at least the basics of any report. Of course, such information would probably be limited to the scope of the perpetrators' organization and the severity of the threat they posed—not the particulars of any confessions about their true identities.

This sucks... Well, that's fine. I'm sure something will come to me!

When Mile was angry, she had a fairly pessimistic way of thinking, but most of the time, she was relatively optimistic. With the power of positive thinking, there were no limits to the sort of good ideas she could manifest.

After receiving their one silver each from Felicia, who had returned to the Guild a bit before the two parties, the Crimson Vow and the Servants of the Goddess each retreated to their respective hideouts—the Servants to the small house they rented together, and the Crimson Vow, naturally, to Faleel's inn. They had been awake the whole night. It was time to get some food and go straight to sleep.

All that they had received today was the reward from the inn-keeper; the bonus from the Guild and the Crown would come tomorrow. They probably had yet to decide on the amount.

All right! As soon as we get back to the inn, Faleel is mine—all mine! With none of those pesky Servants in the way, it's time to give Faleel the scoop on who really *played the most important role in saving her...Hehe. Bwehehehehehehe!*

Somehow, Mile seemed like she might be a rather unreliable narrator.

"All righty then, see you gals later! Good work out there!" said Telyusia.

A tinge of a blush on her cheeks, Reina replied meekly, "Y-you too..."

From the depths of their hearts, the other three screamed in silence, *Who are you, and what did you do with Reinaaaaaaa?!?!*

✧◈✧

"We're back!"

"Oh! Welcome baaack!!!"

As always, Mile announced the party's presence as they stepped through the door, Faleel greeted them from the reception desk. Faleel already appeared to be back to her normal self. It had been some time now since they had last seen her, so all the emotion of the tearful reunion between parents and child had likely faded.

Then again, it was her parents who had been the emotional ones; Faleel had actually seemed relatively unaffected. While the two of them had been waiting and worrying the whole time that she was gone, Faleel had been knocked out right after her abduction and so she had no recollection of the time between when she had been snatched and when she had woken up. Plus, when she *had* woken up, she was surrounded by the Servants, a group that made her feel safe, so really, she never even had the time to get scared.

She had, of course, been distressed at the time of her kidnapping, but after riding home on Philly's shoulders and talking with the Servants for a while, she completely forgot all that as well. It was at least some small relief that she did not appear to have suffered any long-term trauma.

Mealtime was still a long while off, but the innkeeper and his wife were more than happy to take the party's food orders. As they prepared the food, Mile desperately gave Faleel her side of the story.

"And so you see, Faleel, the one who followed your trail and found you after you were taken was me—Mile!"

So she proclaimed, and yet all Faleel could see before her was a sneaky fox trying to steal the Servants' glory.

The Servants of the Goddess never boasted about what they did, she thought. *They were just happy to see that I was safe. Compared to them, Miss Mile's being kind of a creep...*

Sensing that Faleel's reaction was not the one she had been hoping for, Mile began to panic.

"I-It's true!" she protested. "By tracking your scent..."

"Hm? Did Miss Reina do that?"

"What?"

That was when Mile remembered their very first morning at

the inn—and the memos that Faleel had written in the margins of the inn's register.

Mayvis: Shes tol but shes got no chest. Probly a elf.

Rena: Shes got fangz. Shes probly got sum beestfok blood in her. Just lik me.

Poline: I sens evil on her. Probly a deemon.

Miel: Shes a skwirt. Probly a dworf.

Th-this is bad! If she thinks that Reina is one of her people, she'll feel closer to her than to me!

Mile began to fret more and more.

"N-no! That's not what happeeeeeeeeened!!!"

Watching Mile's futile struggle, the other three members of the Crimson Vow looked upon her with cold, disapproving, and tired eyes...

"Well then," proposed Faleel, "Let's test your sense of smell!"

If Mile was the one who possessed a sense of smell on par with that of a member of the beastfolk, then she should be able to prove it. Though Faleel had previously assumed Mile to be a dwarf, she was rather pleased at the thought that Mile might have beast blood like her and wished to confirm the notion. Unlike Faleel, with her cat ears, and Reina, with her pointy canines, Mile showed no outward indicators of carrying beast blood at all.

Faleel appeared to disappear into the kitchen and then quickly returned. In each of her hands was a cup full of water.

"One of these cups contains just a drop of ale," she explained. "No normal pure-blooded human could tell them apart, but if you can follow someone's scent, this should be nothing!"

"Leave it to me!"

Mile was chomping at the bit. With this, she would be able to prove herself to Faleel!

Her sense of smell was already far more acute than the average human's, but it was still nothing compared to an animal's or beastperson's. So she used her body-strengthening magic to enhance her senses, just as she had when tracking the kidnappers. In fact, this time it was sharper still, on par with a dog's or wolf's. Failure was not an option here.

"All right, maximum strength smell! Let's go!"

She brought one cup close to her face and took a big whiff of it.

Sniiiiiiff...

She could smell the water and the cup, mixed with the scent from Faleel's fingers, the simmering dishes and raw ingredients in the kitchen, and the scent of the owner and his wife—as well as all the scents lingering around the dining room...

"All right, now for the next one!"

Once again, she put the cup to her nose and took a deep breath in.

Sniiiiiiff...

Slam!

Promptly, she lost consciousness and collapsed onto the floor.

Seeing this, Reina waved both of her hands around near her rear and said quietly, "Uh, 'scuse me..."

The fact of the matter was that, no matter how strong a beast's or beastperson's sense of smell was, they could still deal with a bad smell or two. Their sensory organs and the structure of their brains were equipped for it. Therefore, short of something like the monstrosity that Mile had crafted in the forest, they rarely suffered much simply from a bad odor. Even back in the forest, where they had vomited and lost consciousness, none of them had died from the shock.

However, humans were different. As their senses of smell were generally not very strong to begin with, they were lacking in such safety mechanisms. Mile, a human herself, had raised her sense of smell to beyond that of a beastperson's, and then, utterly defenseless, breathed in with all her might, absorbing all the scents around her...including Reina's contribution.

"Is she all right...?" asked Pauline, her eyes full of worry. She prodded Mile, who was still twitching on the floor, with her foot.

Mavis, who had been watching silently, finally opened her mouth to speak.

"Well, anyway..."

"Anyway?" parroted the other two.

"Let's eat. It won't taste as good if it gets cold."

The food had been laid out on the table without them noticing it. Out of courtesy, the innkeeper and his wife had tried their very best not to look Mile's way, their faces taut...

"Why didn't you wake me up?!"

By the time Mile finally came to, it was already the next

morning. She had missed out both on dinner and on playtime with Faleel. She was livid.

"You were sleeping so peacefully, we didn't want to disturb you. Anyway, let's go ahead and get some breakfast."

In truth, the other three had slept the afternoon through, so by the time evening came they were wide awake. Likewise, Faleel has slept all through her kidnapping, and was, by then, wide awake as well. Together the four of them had played the night through. Hearing this, Mile screeched in anger, but there was nothing that she could do about it now. All she could do was seethe and grit her teeth.

✧ ◈ ✧

Three days later, when they popped in at the Guild as usual, the members of the Crimson Vow were called to the guild master's office. Perhaps they were finally going to learn the results of the interrogation.

"First of all, your reward. Please take this," he said, taking two leather sacks from his drawer and placing them heavily on the desk.

Normally, the Guild used cloth sacks to save on expenses, but on more momentous occasions, or when a congratulatory mood was to be conveyed, they used leather, which felt more special. Today, they were receiving not just a payment for a job but a "special reward," so leather was the obvious choice...although Felicia was known to hand out leather sacks with reckless abandon, something that was no good for the Guild's bottom line.

"This is your bonus from the Guild, and *this* is your bonus from the palace. Unfortunately, some of the criminals were ones that we couldn't sell as slaves, so there's a separate amount from the palace's own coffers to compensate. And because even the enslaved criminals couldn't be given a lifelong sentence, just a set term, the price was less than usual. They aren't bandits, and they didn't kill anyone, so their servitude will have a limit, seems like. A few exceptions escaped even that much."

The exceptions that were mentioned probably referred to the mages, who could not be left unmonitored to the life of a slave, though perhaps there were some other extenuating circumstances, such as an intervention by some noble or person of influence on one of the criminals' behalf. Either way, it was really none of the Crimson Vow's concern. They were neither in a position to interfere with the administration of justice, nor interested in doing so.

Felicia, standing just behind the guild master's shoulder, took the two sacks and handed them to Mavis, who, as usual, appeared to be the leader of the Crimson Vow. Felicia seemed to have made the unilateral decision that anything to do with the Crimson Vow was to be within her purview and her purview alone, and of course, since there wasn't a soul around who would dare argue with her, the other guild employees simply accepted this as the natural order.

"Thank you so much!!!" they said all at once, bowing their heads courteously. Mavis then accepted the bags, and, as per usual, handed them straight to Mile to be stowed away, without bothering to look inside. Obviously, they would investigate the amount later, but this was not the time or place for such things.

Why was that? Well, it just didn't look as cool.

"So then, what were the results of the investigation?" Mile asked boldly, voicing the question on her mind.

"Ah, well, there were both countrymen and foreigners among the group, ranging from middle class to lower upper class. They're all fellows who fell under the influence of some heretical cult from somewhere. Apparently, the teachings originally came from some country to the east, but none of them could pinpoint just where."

"To the east...?"

The Crimson Vow had arrived here in the Vanolark by heading west from the Kingdom of Tils, the land where Mavis and Pauline were born and where Mile first became a hunter, and then further west still, through Mile's home country of the Kingdom of Brandel. As a result, they might conclude that this cult could not be from a neighboring nation, but somewhere much farther east still—in the completely opposite direction from the way they had been traveling. Heading back that way would be a huge hassle.

Well, all our current problems have started right here, so I guess we can worry about the east another time...

Mile was not terribly concerned.

"Plus, well, what they were really after was the summoning of a god, or rather, 'conducting a ceremony to welcome the god's descent.' They claimed that they had no intention of harming the girl but merely using her a vessel for their god, so it was ruled to be not an attempted murder, but merely a kidnapping. It doesn't fall under slave trading or illicit trafficking, either.

"Of course, kidnapping *is* a pretty grave crime on its own, and the victim was not a human but a beastgirl. There were also some apparently affiliated nobles and merchants who came to put pressure on the Crown. I suppose it doesn't look good for them to have their dependents labeled as felons or heretics..."

It was all a big, fat lie. Back at the clearing, the men themselves had said that Faleel had been intended as a *sacrifice*. They would never use what they considered to be an inferior life-form as the "vessel" of their beloved god.

However, this was not something for Mile and the others to decide. They had already given their own testimony, which had most certainly included the word "sacrifice." Plus, if the sentencing had been made with political considerations in mind, there was nothing that a group of mere C-rank hunters could do about it.

"Is that so...?"

Mile swiftly gave up hope of learning anything further. On top of all that, there was no telling how much of even what the guild master had told them was true. Asking anything more was pointless.

Of course, everyone else was merely glad that the matter had been settled. If the kidnappers had been punished, and they were assured that nothing like this would happen again, then that was good enough for them. Even if some bigwigs had stepped in, it was not as though the perpetrators were getting off scot-free. They were still receiving proper punishment due to abductors of a young girl. They had just dropped the whole "cultist" part.

Even the ones who escaped the fate of servitude were not being entirely acquitted. Whether it was serving a term in jail or paying an exorbitant sum in bail, they would be punished one way or another. Plus, an investigation was sure to be launched into all their cohorts who had not been present, as well.

Honestly, it was only to be expected that the standard procedures would not be followed when those apprehended were people of influence. And besides, they would be under scrutiny from there on out—if not from the authorities, from those nobles whom they might be troubling and their dependents.

Evidently, the Servants of the Goddess had already received their reward and their update. As far as the two parties were concerned, the matter was now closed.

"Well then, let's go find a normal job to do today!"

"All right!"

And so, they headed back down to the first floor to see what was on the job board.

✧ ◈ ✧

Rustle, rustle.

Late that night, when everyone was sound asleep in their rooms, one person remained awake, still slinking about.

Naturally, it was Mile. Thanks to the sound and vibration

barriers she had erected, no one noticed as she shuffled about on the top bunk of her bunk bed.

Though she had previously been sound asleep, the nano-machines had sent vibrations through her eardrums to murmur a morning wake-up call to her (though it wasn't exactly morning). The phrase they used was a peculiar one.

GOOD MORNING, MILE. IT'S TIME FOR YOUR DAILY BRIEFING...

Of course, Mile had instructed them to say this. And then, quietly, she replied,

"Okay! Let the 'Super Secret Agent Gambit' begin!"

Once again, Mile had something strange up her sleeve.

After stepping out into the hall and closing the door, Mile released her barriers. If she kept them up, the others wouldn't be able to hear thieves or invaders, which was a bit of a problem. For the same reason, using sleeping magic on them was out of the question. No matter how low the risk was, she would never put her companions in that sort of danger.

Then she slipped quietly out of the inn. Her destination? The palace. Where else?

As she neared the palace, she put up light, sound, and vibration-blocking barriers, and, just in case, she cloaked her scent as well. It was the palace, after all, so it was not entirely out of the question that there might be personnel with a beastly sense of smell in their employ. Even if the probability was fairly low, it was better safe than sorry. If she were caught, she would be in big trouble.

After making certain that her barriers were impenetrable, Mile snuck inside.

Hidden as she was, she could have walked through the front door without incident, but that wouldn't be any fun. And in truth, her head was running wild with thoughts like, *What if the guards actually* can *see me?* and *What if my barriers suddenly collapsed right in front of them?* She could not bring herself to be calm.

Thus, just on the off chance of something going wrong, she decided to move about as though she had no barriers at all. Furthermore, she was wearing not her usual garb but a clever disguise so that her true identity would not be revealed, even if she *were* caught.

She wore a mask upon her face and a headband with cat ears. As for her outfit, she wanted desperately to wear the sort of leotard that your typical female cat burglar would wear, but as she had never actually come into contact with the genuine article, she did not know enough to recreate one. Besides, when she considered how thin the material would be, she lost her nerve. Instead, she settled on something she was far more familiar with—a school-issue swimsuit like the ones from Earth.

Of course, such an article had never been proven combat-ready, and as a result, she was relatively nervous. Her bloomers would never fit underneath it, so she had to go without. At least to the people of this world, who had no concept of either leotards or swimsuits, she judged there was probably little difference between the two...which was true. Considering that both were equally absurd—equally shameless—it really made no difference which one she chose.

Location magic! Tell me where those criminals are...

Indeed, it was time for her to harvest a word or two from those kidnappers herself—that is, to speak to them directly, and in her own way.

They had probably already been through the wringer in terms of interrogation, including torture, but given that she couldn't buy what she had been told, their story as it stood was meaningless to Mile. So, it was time for some one-on-one, face-to-face questioning.

Honestly, it was a big pain.

Mile's plan was an absurd one, which, honestly, the men had no reason to go along with. However, Mile was never bothered by such little things. She was not in Japan, and she was not on Earth. Compared to that, all this was essentially trivial...at least in Mile's book.

All right, there they are!

Thinking that she might find herself in just such a situation, Mile had committed the criminals'—and particularly their leader's—body language to memory, and with that information, she was able to track them right to where the men were being held. Naturally, it was not some important part of the palace, but an outbuilding constructed specifically for the containment of criminals.

Hm. They're separated into groups, a few in each. Well, I guess that makes sense. No one here would be stupid enough to put all those dangerous mages together in the same spot. Plus, it lowers the chance of them corroborating each other's testimonies or scheming behind the guards' backs!

And so, with her barriers still up to protect her, Mile crept into the building.

"Good evening, gentlemen!"

"Wh-who's there?!" the kidnappers replied uneasily as the two soldiers who were stationed as lookouts suddenly fell into a deep sleep.

There were five men in this particular area, including the leader. It was only natural that they would call out in such a panic when suddenly addressed by a formless voice.

"A robber..."

There was no way that Mile could neglect to use her practiced phrase now.

"A-a robber?"

"Ah, no. I was just pretending to be a robber..."

If they thought that she really were a robber, the conversation could never proceed, and so she quickly corrected herself.

So that they could speak normally, she decided that it was time to reveal herself. No one would ever speak candidly to someone whom they couldn't actually see, after all. And so, she released the barrier.

"My name is Lady Cat's Eye!"

The name was a mix of several manga characters, and of course, it was a tribute to Faleel.

"Wha...?! I-It's..."

"A flattie!" cried three.

"A pervert!" cried the other two.

Horrendous. Both reactions were equally horrendous.

"Wha-wh-wh-wh..."

Mile was shaken at the utterly unexpected reactions and burned red in the face with anger. However, it was not as though they could help it. In this world, ladies wore bloomers. Compared to that, a swimsuit, with its stretchy, form-fitting fabric and high degree of exposure was about as close as one could get to being totally naked.

"A catgirl, is she?! I tell you, those beasts have no sense of decency..."

"Obviously! Can't expect a beast to understand virtue!"

"Honestly, have you no shame at all?"

"Whatever. I'm not interested in seeing some skinny little girl in the buff."

"Hm. That's not a bad look..."

So went each of the men's appraisals. The last one was probably the worst!

Nngh... I can't allow this. Forget my *reputation—I'm giving catgirls a bad name! I'll have to change my name... I can't be responsible for something like that.*

Mile whipped the cat ears off her head and stored them away.

"Huh? She took off her ears?" the men were stunned.

Mile thought quickly and then announced her new name: "You may call me Little Evil God!"

"What the heck is thaaaaaaaat?!"

A few minutes later, once the men had finally calmed back down, Mile introduced herself properly.

"Now then. I am the last survivor of the gods that came to this world from another in the distant past. After our companions retreated, those of us who valued our pride too much to flee in such a cowardly manner remained in this world. In the final battle, we persisted, blow-to-blow with the denizens of this land, and were nearly destroyed. Yet on the brink of death, I was sealed inside a holy barrier where I slumbered for eons. And then, when I sensed that a gate had been opened to my home world, I awoke..."

As far as the men were concerned, they had already been captured and said all that they had to say. As a result, there was really no point in anyone from the palace trying to deceive them, and even if they were, it wasn't as though they didn't know saying anything more would get them in a lot of trouble.

At any rate, it was absurd to think that this girl might be a spy or official from the palace. No such official agent could possibly exist. They were far more unassuming and reserved. Such a figure would be ridiculous even for a Miami Satodele novel...

Plus, given the fact that she had snuck into the building and knocked out the guards, it was clear that she was someone who was hostile toward the Crown.

Considering these points, the men's tension began to ease, though they were still not convinced that she was a "god from another world."

Mile then conducted a demonstration.

Twist, twist.

With her finger alone, she twisted the iron bars.

Fwoom! Sparkle!

Fire came from her mouth and strange beams of light from her eyes.

And then she took on her "Goddess" form.

The men prostrated themselves on the floor of the cell.

From there, they answered her questions frankly, though it was unclear whether it was because they truly believed that she was the final survivor of the ancient gods or simply because they were understandably frightened of this strange entity that had broken into the building and could twist an iron bar without effort—which had to mean she could easily wring their necks as well...

As far as Mile was concerned, the reason didn't really matter, as long as she was able to learn the truth.

What the men were finally able to tell her was the following:

The closest country to the east was the Kingdom of Brandel, Mile's home country. Further east still than that was the Kingdom of Tils, where Mavis and Pauline were from. (Because Reina had grown up as a traveling merchant, she had no idea what either of her parents' home countries were or even where she had been born. For some reason, her father had never told her.)

Much farther east than either of those, in some unknown country, a new religion had begun to flourish.

The teachings of this religion told of a war between the gods of this world and the gods of another world in the far distant past. Those who heard this story quickly realized that it resembled the legends told by the elves and dwarves.

That said, there were several important points where these stories differed. The most significant of these was that, while the stories of the elves and dwarves painted the gods of this world as "good" and the gods of the other world as "evil," this religion's view of the pantheon held no concept of rank or morality. Their view was simple: the gods of this world had abandoned them, so it was time to worship a new set of gods and receive their divine protection. Similarly, where the elves and dwarves' legends took the view that, "The elves, dwarves, humans, beastmen, and demons must all join hands to protect this world abandoned by the gods," these men taught that, "Only humans hold the power to worship the foreign gods. All other races are our enemies."

If you're trying to popularize a new religion, wouldn't it be easier to choose one that's accessible to all races? Why bother spreading one that's less accessible and encourages antagonizing others...?

Mile had her doubts, but then again, she supposed, most religions were not fully accountable to logic. She decided to think no more about it.

The legends of the olden days had been lost among humans, and so the stories, as told by the elves and dwarves, had generally been written off as having nothing to do with the human race. Why, now, had stories with similar origins—but completely different perspectives—made a resurgence?

The men seemed to have little idea. All they knew was that this new faith had spoken to their desires and to the promise of obtaining divine blessing through their deeds, and as a result, they had become believers. The teachings of this religion required no great sacrifices and did not demand they proselytize to others, merely asking them to pray for divine protection to save their own skin—and conduct rituals. The ritual they were attempting the other day was the greatest of these, one they had been preparing for and awaiting just the right moment to perform.

Indeed, it was a ritual to open a gate to another world and call forth its gods. If they could offer up a sacrifice from one of the aberrant races to one of the gods, their wishes would be granted...

So they were *trying to sacrifice her! Wait, no! I already knew that. The issue here is...*

"And who came up with the incantation for that ritual?"

"Ah, well. The spells were compiled by the late founder of the sect... They've been passed down faithfully, though admittedly, there are some parts that even we don't understand. Of course, the words aren't the only important part. It's crucial that you pray deeply to the gods while you say them..."

Hm, I think I get it now. I still don't know where it came from, but otherwise...

"Well, well. I see. Now that you have answered my questions, I shall be taking my leave. Farewell!"

"Oh! P-please wait!" the leader pleaded, as Mile, her business concluded, started to make her exit.

"What is it?"

"U-um, we're your believers, so please grant us your protection! Rescue us from this hardship!"

Receiving divine protection would prove that they were messengers of the gods. Instead of being treated as criminals, they would be lauded as divine messengers. What a total reversal of fate!

Apparently the men were so desperate for a miracle that they now believed this "Little Evil God" to be a true otherworldly deity—or at least, they were trying very, very hard to do so.

"There's no such thing."

"What?" the men asked in unison.

"If a pack of huntsmen came into the woods to hunt, and a jackalope said to them, 'I am your truest believer! Please grant me your favor, and place me and my brothers at the head of the forest hierarchy!' do you truly believe that the huntsmen would do so?"

"........."

"Of course, anyone other than myself would have already eaten them right from the start. Any foolish jackalope who would show itself right before a huntsman, that is!"

"........."

"Oh? Did you all assume that *this* was my true form? If you were to see my true form, it would shock the life right out of you... Do you wish to see it?"

Shfshfshfshfshf!

The men noisily shuffled back from the iron bars as quickly as they could, their backs up against the opposite wall.

All right! Home free!

Mile put her full range of barriers back up, just as they had been when she arrived.

"Sh-she vanished..."

Leaving behind the men, who were still on the floor, a mix of despair and relief upon their faces, Mile carefully walked out of the building.

Hopefully, they won't attempt to use that dimensional linking magic again after this. Fingers crossed, anyway...

The ritual was one that required the combined magic of a number of mages, something they had only been able to set into motion after gathering their numbers. Now that they would be scattered about, some of them imprisoned or enslaved, it would probably be impossible for them to attempt such a feat again. Once all their terms had ended, there was the possibility of them regrouping and attempting the ritual once more, but given that the eyes of the authorities and their relatives would be upon them, it would likely be very difficult to do so. If they were to try anything at all suspicious again, they would surely be dealt with by their own relations.

If it came out that one member of a family was a criminal— a cult worshipper, little-girl abductor, and would-be murderer— the young people of that family would never find anyone to take their hand in marriage, after all.

✧ ◈ ✧

Finally, without a sound, Mile slipped back into the inn and returned to the room she shared with the rest of the party. She released her barriers, a black cloak wrapped around her. She gripped the doorknob, gently turned it, and slowly opened the door...

"Eek!"

Reina, Mavis, and Pauline were all sitting in chairs facing the doorway.

"........."

Mile attempted to close the door again slowly.

Reina curled her finger, beckoning Mile. Resigned, Mile opened the door wide and entered the room.

"Care to explain yourself?"

"Um... Well..."

Reina narrowed her eyes angrily.

"How many times have we told you not to slip off on your own without telling us, Mile?"

"A...a lot..."

Mavis looked at her sadly.

"Seriously, again?! You were going to leave me alone again, Mile?!" Pauline looked about ready to cry.

"So, what did you run off to do *this* time, huh?! Didn't we say that we were gonna do everything together?!" Reina shouted, rising from her chair and stalking over to Mile, then shaking her by the shoulders.

The cloak slipped to the floor, revealing the swimsuit underneath.

"Actually," said Reina, "next time, just go handle your business on your own."

"Yep," Mavis agreed. "I'm good, thanks."

"That's even worse than that thing you made *me* wear! I'm good, too!" Pauline chimed in.

"Dismissed!" the three said at once, before dispersing, each snuggling back into her own bed and heading right back to sleep.

"Huh...?"

For Mile, who had been preparing herself for a stern dressing-down, this was something of an anticlimax.

"Huh...?"

And yet, somehow, she was not happy about this at all.

"Huuuhhh...?"

CHAPTER 59

Leatoria Returns

"YOU DECEIVED ME!"

One day, as the Crimson Vow headed into the guildhall to see what was up on the job board for the day, a little girl came rushing their way, red in the face and screaming.

"Oh, Miss Leatoria..."

Indeed, it was the young daughter of Baron Aura, Leatoria.

"You said that you were going to be my friend, so why haven't you come to visit me at all?! Plus, I heard that I could register as a D-rank hunter!"

"Oh no! She found out!"

"I registered as a hunter! I'm the D-rank magic war club wielder, Leatoria the Crusher! You better remember my name!"

"What the heck is thaaaaaaat?!?!"

A war club. It was a six or eight-sided rod, originally made out of a dense wood like yew but later covered in metal plates or made entirely out of metal. The all-metal versions were incredibly heavy and difficult to handle even for an extremely powerful wielder, so there were limits to how long or thick they could be. Yet somehow, the one in Leatoria's hands was made fully of metal, with a length and girth that was completely out of proportion to a small girl's hands, and countless hideous-looking bumps protruding from it.

Unconsciously, Mile suddenly began to sing to herself, as the theme song of a particular anime came to mind. "*Pi-piru, pirupiru...*"

Behind Leatoria was Bundine, his face looking utterly pained, along with a maid who was by all appearances a completely normal person, wearing leather armor that did not suit her at all and looking as if she was about to cry.

No, well, that was a bit of an understatement—she *was* actually crying. Under what looked like hand-me-down leather armor, she was still wearing the uniform garb of the Aura household, frilled headband and all, even as she held a staff. Perhaps she had some magical ability and so had been conscripted by the baron into accompanying his daughter—as someone who might take care of Leatoria's daily affairs, and, should it come down to that, serve as a human shield.

"That's terrible!!!" the Crimson Vow cried as this last thought occurred to them.

If the baron had indeed ordered the maid to accompany Leatoria, then that was clearly some sort of violation of contract.

However, none of them could imagine the baron actually doing such a thing, which meant that this young woman had probably volunteered herself—though whether she had truly volunteered of her own free will or had no choice but to volunteer was unclear.

No matter how good a person he might have been, a noble was still a noble. It was only natural that he would value the life of his own daughter over that of a peasant in his employ.

"If that's the case, then he should have just told his daughter to give up on it from the staaaaaaaaaaaart!!!" Reina shouted to the universe. Everyone in the hall who overheard her nodded in agreement—including Bundine the butler and the weeping maid herself.

"Leatoria," said Mavis, a serious expression upon her face, "there's something I would like to ask you. Do you mind?"

"S-sure. What is it?"

Silence fell across the guildhall. Mavis's voice rang out loud and clear.

"How did you get a nickname so soon after joining the Guild? Tell me!"

"What the hell kind of a question is thaaaaaaaaaat?!?!?!"

Several minutes later, Leatoria, Bundine, the young maid, and the members of the Crimson Vow sat in the Guild's snack corner. The seats around them were unusually full, and everyone was listening attentively rather than conducting conversations of their own.

"Anyway, if you don't want this maid to begin to resent Leatoria, I suggest you send her back home," finished Reina.

Bundine nodded and signaled to the maid with his chin. The maid rose and bowed her head respectfully to Reina and then flew from the room like a bat out of hell. Apparently, even Bundine thought that her presence was a tad unnecessary.

"So, what are you going to do now…?"

This was as far as anyone had planned.

"Well, obviously," said Leatoria, "I'm going to become a member of the Crimson Vow and work my hardest to be a strong hunter!"

"Ah, of course…"

The four members of the Crimson Vow were at their wits' end. If you counted Bundine, that made five people in this position, and if you added everyone in the Aura household, there were plenty more. And then, when you considered the trouble it would cause to send a noble's young daughter straight to her death, the number expanded to include every guild employee, from the guild master down to the clerks.

The whole debacle really had nothing to do with the regular hunters, though. Unlike Mile, none of them would even think to lay a hand upon the daughter of a noble. If any of them were to ever dare, heads would roll. And in this world, of course, such expressions were not figurative but quite literal.

Actually, if a noble's daughter were to join the Crimson Vow, it would make it that much harder for anyone to make passes at the rest of the party. That was yet another vexing aspect of the situation.

"But," said Mile, "we're a party from another country in the midst of a journey of self-improvement through other lands. So I mean, there's a chance that we'll be leaving this city—in fact, even leaving this country—fairly soon... I mean, I'm sure that the baron would never permit that, would he?"

Leatoria just smirked.

"My father has no power over me. He could never stand up to my secret technique!"

Mile reflexively looked to Bundine, who nodded, his brow wrinkled and a somber expression upon his face. By "secret technique," she surely meant *that*—the ultimate surprise weapon, which Mavis had used in the battle against her older brother. There was no mistaking the fact that it must be something along those lines.

The members of the Crimson Vow began to ponder other excuses. For one, there was the fact that they were a fairly exceptional party. No normal person would ever be able to keep up with them...but then Leatoria was by no means "normal," was she? So that was another argument gone.

"Well, I mean, what we're saying is, we're technically stationed back in the Kingdom of Tils, and we'll have to go back there at some point soon. You have a home and a family here, don't you...?" Mavis asked.

Leatoria appeared unmoved. "I have older brothers and sisters, so I might be married off to someone in another country anyway. And if making the acquaintance of you and Mile gets me closer to marrying into a noble household, then that's a cause for celebration! Otherwise, the third daughter of a baron who already has sons to inherit his title is no better than a commoner. It would be a step up just for me to worm my way into the arms of some influential merchant, bureaucrat or some high-ranking military officer. That's about as far as my station will carry me."

Apparently, she still had no idea of her true value. She was the beautiful daughter of a noble, and she could use combat magic. As she was even now, she could easily catch the eye of a count or even a marquis.

"........."

Leatoria was formidable. And by all accounts she had more or less made up her mind. Why was she so determined to join up with the Crimson Vow?

If she were a normal girl, it would be impossible. She would never be able to keep up with their traveling speed, combat ability, level of confidentiality... There really were a million and one issues. However, Leatoria had decent magical ability and apparently could use several different varieties of spells. Plus, for some reason, since her recovery from her illness, her physical strength and endurance had drastically increased, and if she wielded a weapon that required little finesse—such as something of the bludgeoning-type—she could be quite a formidable contender in close-range combat. It was also true that she would never break the trust of the Crimson Vow. They had saved her life, and being still as young and pure as she was, her pride as a noble would never allow for such a betrayal.

Nevertheless, the members of the Crimson Vow were not prepared to let her in just like that.

The Crimson Vow was a party of four bosom companions, joined at the soul—Mile, Reina, Mavis, and Pauline. That was something that nothing and no one could take away from them...

The four desperately wracked their brains.

Ka-cling.

Just then, the doorbell chimed and another rather unique party walked through the door.

"Oh, if it isn't the Crimson Vow! How have you all been holding up?"

"I mean...y'all know how it goes..." the members of the Crimson Vow casually replied.

Apparently, some of the language from Mile's strange stories was starting to rub off on them.

"Wh-what sort of phrasing is that?" The Servants of the Goddess appeared rather taken aback.

That's it!!!!

Suddenly, all at once, the four members of the Crimson Vow came to the same conclusion—a rather wicked one.

"Hey guys, I've got a proposal for you..." Mile said, rising from her seat and rushing over to the Servants, dragging them to a spot a short way from the snack corner.

"H-hey! Don't pull so hard! We're coming already!"

"Would you come here a moment?" asked Mavis, tugging at Bundine's sleeve.

"Huh? Wha...? What's going—?"

Reina and Pauline stepped in, keeping the apparently oblivious Leatoria distracted with a bit of conversation. She was an easy mark. Leatoria's eyes sparkled as the three of them had a lively talk concerning tips and tricks for new hunters.

"What is it?" Telyusia asked suspiciously.

"Actually, I think this should be a welcome proposal for you. The only mage you have among the Servants is Lacelina, right? So your back line is spread a little thin, isn't it?" Mile asked.

"W-well, I suppose that's true..." Telyusia replied, a bit hesitantly, glancing furtively Lacelina's way.

In their party of five, they had only one mage. Well, in fact, there were plenty of parties who had no mages at all, so to complain about having *only* one was in somewhat poor taste. The Crimson Vow, in which three out of the four party members were mages, was an anomaly. In fact, their front line was lacking, which put their balance way out of whack—or at least, it would have under any normal circumstances.

In any event, Lacelina, who was still a D-rank, was not that strong. As previously stated, she was what might politely be called an "all-purpose" mage, but she was utterly lacking in powerful combat abilities. Even if she only supported the others on a utility level, the danger of her overusing her magic and running out was far too high. Yet without Lacelina's assistance, the combined strength of the Servants of the Goddess, who were not particularly strong as individuals, would drop immensely. They were all aware of this particular weakness of theirs.

However, no matter how aware she was of this fact, Telyusia kept her words non-committal, not wanting to say anything that would imply that Lacelina was anything less than capable...

"What if I were to tell you there was a lovely 14-year-old mage who just became a hunter but was allowed to skip to D-rank... And in fact, since she's proficient in several types of combat magic, her ability is more on par with a C-rank hunter. She also has a fair bit of physical strength for a mage, so she can both serve as a porter and contribute to close-range combat. She has a house in this city, and her family has already recognized her desire to be a hunter... Might you have any use for a girl like that?"

The response from all five was emphatic and loud:

"We'll take heeeeeeeeerr!!!!!"

Meanwhile, Mavis gave Bundine the rundown on the Servants of the Goddess.

They were a party of all women who had clawed their way up from E-rank, never once losing a person to withdrawal, injury, or death in their whole run so far. There was a D-rank mage who was likely close to Leatoria in age, and the others were not much older, so she would fit in swimmingly.

Unlike the Crimson Vow, the Servants were a reliable, more orthodox sort of party, so traveling with them would be far safer—and far more beneficial to Leatoria's development—than traveling with the Vow.

And, above all, the Servants were a stationary group, firmly settled in the capital...

Bundine already thought very highly of the Crimson Vow's abilities, but no one outside of the Guild yet knew of the incidents with the demons and the kidnappers and such. Moreover, he had yet to witness their combat strength with his own eyes. Thus, while he found their knowledge, wit, and sense of justice to be incredibly admirable, he had no way of knowing how that very particular knowledge translated to their skill in battle.

Plus, even if he did know how strong they truly were, Bundine still thought of Leatoria as a weak and sickly young maiden, and he worried that, should she end up surrounded by individuals much stronger than her, she would be crushed by her own sense of helplessness.

Compare this to the prospect of an all-female party with plenty of experience who always protected their allies, had a mage at the same level as Leatoria, and moreover, were stationed here in town. As far as Bundine—nay, the entire Aura household—was concerned, the choice was obvious.

The idea of Leatoria joining a party that included men and sleeping out in the open, in a coed environment, was something that the Baron could not abide. As a result, both he and Bundine had thought it would be preferable for her to go out in the company of the trustworthy members of the Crimson Vow—however, considering how much the Vow moved around, the Servants of the Goddess really were a far better choice. If every member of the Vow gave the Servants their endorsement, then surely they must be equally trustworthy.

"They're a good bunch," Mavis explained. "They took on the job of rescuing a young girl with only one silver as pay, and their leader even put herself in front of a magical attack to protect our Reina."

Bundine was shocked. That wasn't good-heartedness—it was practically stupidity. But even so, no one had been killed or seriously injured.

The Crimson Vow had come into town just the other day, so this incident would have to have been very recent. And yet, there did not appear to be any casualties among the parties—not even minor injuries. Which meant that they were strong enough that even a magical attack was nothing to them.

The Servants of the Goddess had defended the Crimson Vow easily! *What an incredible party!*

"If you can ask them," he replied, "please do so!"

"...And, their leader, Telyusia, is incredible. She's so mature, and a wonderful person. She saved my life! I think that their mage, Lacelina, is the same age as you, too. I'm pretty sure she's a D-rank, the same as you, too. Of course, she had to work her way up to that rank from the bottom. Hmm. Actually, mages usually get to skip a rank, so if she didn't start as a D-rank, I suppose that means she began at E?"

Reina recounted as much of their recent adventure to Leatoria as she could without lying. Naturally, Pauline chimed in as well.

"Wow, they sound amazing!" Leatoria said, audibly impressed.

Reina and Pauline looked on with smiles...wide, wicked smiles.

Mile and Mavis then brought both the Servants and Bundine back to the corner and pulled together the neighboring tables and chairs so that they could all speak as a group.

The hunters seated at those neighboring tables picked up on the situation and quickly cleared the space.

"You're Miss Leatoria, correct? We're the C-rank party, the Servants of the Goddess. I'm Telyusia, the leader. Nice to meet you!"

"Y-yes, I am! It's lovely to meet you!"

Leatoria's voice rose unnaturally. Of course, she couldn't help it when she suddenly found herself sitting before a powerful hunter, the leader of a party who had been so talked up by Reina and Pauline.

Mile had already shared quite a bit of information about Leatoria with the Servants. She rattled off a number of details and then explained that she had not yet suggested to Leatoria that she join up with them, since it would be more natural if the invitation came from the party in question.

Of course, she also explained to them that Leatoria really wished to join the Crimson Vow and offered some ideas about how the Servants of the Goddess might cajole her.

"You see, our party already has three mages, with only Mavis on the front line..."

"Ah..."

The Servants of the Goddess understood at once. No one had ever heard of a party with four backline mages and only one frontline fighter. Not that a party with a three-to-one ratio was any less unprecedented, of course. But at any rate, there was no doubt in any of their minds that a hopeful young newcomer could not possibly join up with the Crimson Vow.

And so the battle for the future of the Crimson Vow and the Servants of the Goddess—and the peace of mind of the Aura household—began.

"So, Leatoria, I hear that you just recently registered as a hunter?"

"Y-yes! I got to skip, so I'm a D-rank! The officials told me that even though my skill as a mage was on par with a C-rank and my close-range combat ability with my war club is C-rank as well, I don't have any of the knowledge or sensibilities that a hunter would. Without any experience fighting monsters or people on the battlefield, I had to start off as a D-rank..."

At this, the eyes of four of the Servants sparkled wildly. They had already heard this much from Mile. Leatoria was without a doubt, quite the delectable prize...er, party candidate.

"This really takes me back. I remember when we first registered as hunters and formed the Servants of the Goddess..."

Telyusia had deftly managed to transition the conversation to a self-introduction. Through one anecdote after another, she told of the party's strengths, naturally conveying their group's appeal.

That's an older person's wisdom for you!!! thought Mile, Mavis, and Pauline, all quite impressed.

Reina, meanwhile, softly said, "That's big sis for you!"

Aghast, the other three exchanged looks, wondering, *Who the heck are you?!?!*

When the time finally seemed right, Telyusia let loose the decisive phrase:

"Leatoria, won't you join us, the Servants of the Goddess?"

H-here it is!!!

The Crimson Vow watched nervously, wringing their hands. Leatoria was speechless at this sudden, unimaginable invitation.

"Huh? Well, I'm really glad that you would want me, but I'm going to join up with my friends, the Crimson Vow..." she replied as she came back to her senses.

Naturally, Telyusia was prepared for this reply. She looked to the Crimson Vow, and with a smile, she asked, "Won't you let us have Miss Leatoria?"

"She's all yours!" they all said.

"Huh...?"

Leatoria seemed a bit taken aback at this reply. Quickly, Mavis provided an explanation.

"Ah, well, uh, you see, three-quarters of our party's already made of mages, right? If you joined, that'd make four mages, with me as the only swordswoman, which is kind of, yeah..."

"Nnh..."

Leatoria, who had no idea that Mile formed a part of the front line as well—and who still had yet to confirm whether she would truly be able to contribute as a melee weapon wielder beyond simply a "mage who happened to be able to hold a blud-geoning weapon"—was unable to provide a rebuttal.

Honestly, the only value of her war club-wielding ability was pure destructive power; she hadn't the slightest fraction of actual technical skill. She had smashed through her sparring opponent's practice sword and struck them down. She had crashed into another's shield and blown them away, striking them into the wall.

A win was a win, but she still could not think of herself as particularly adept with a weapon. Even Leatoria herself recognized that the war club was nothing more than a means of self-defense.

Reina and Pauline went on to explain that the Crimson Vow were going to be traveling across the land after their stop here, whereas the Servants were going to be staying in this town, meaning that it was probably better for Leatoria to choose the group that would allow her to stay close to her family. And then, Telyusia landed the finishing blow.

"Leatoria, you wanted to join the Crimson Vow so that you'd have friends, right?"

"Y-yes. They're my first ever friends, so..."

Telyusia smiled wide. "It's true that if you joined the Crimson Vow, you would have four friends. But, if you joined up with us, you would have *five* new friends who would always be by your side. And the four friends you had before would still be your friends, too. Plus, you could stop at home whenever you like..."

"Oh..." Leatoria's jaw hung wide. She was utterly lost for words.

She's good!!! The members of the Crimson Vow and Bundine were all astonished at Telyusia's skill.

As far as Leatoria was concerned, the members of the Crimson Vow were her benefactors, the ones who had cured her of her illness. However, it had really only been a few days since she had first met them, and they had spoken no more than a total of several hours in total. Anyway, it was not as if they had even ever done anything together beyond sitting on beds and chairs and talking.

Sure enough, while she thought of them as her "first ever friends," in truth, they were merely the first girls her age whom she had gotten to sit and talk with. Thus, it wasn't as though the whole thing was *really* a matter of Crimson Vow or bust.

Lacelina gently reached out her hand and grabbed Leatoria's.

Tasha smiled.

"We need you, Leatoria…" Willine whispered sincerely.

"Stand by our side and become the pride of our land, your family, your companions, and all those who live under the Baron's rule!" said Philly, giving a big thumbs-up.

"I… I-I-I…"

Do it do it do iiiiiiit!!!

The bystanders, who had been watching the proceedings with interest, could practically hear the hearts of both parties screaming.

"I'll do it! I'll join the Servants of the Goddess!"

"Welcome to the party, Leatoria! We're so happy to have you!!!" they all shouted.

"Hooray!!!" the Crimson Vow cheered.

"Yeah!!!" cried the hunters and guild employees who had been listening in, the whole room raising their voices joyously in unison.

The guild staff were particularly overjoyed to see this young noble joining a party that would be free from the worries of coed living and one in which the danger of a newbie dying an early death was as low as it could be. It was an exceptional load off of their minds. Behind them, Bundine was nodding emphatically as well.

Mile seemed to be joyful for a slightly different reason. *Thank goodness she fell for it!*

Mavis was thinking something cruel. *All right! We got away!*

We let a real moneymaker get away here. This seems like a bit of a waste... Pauline was her usual self.

The Servants really are the much better party for Leatoria's sake. As long as Telyusia's there, there's no doubting that...

For some reason, Reina was the only earnest one.

All the loose ends were tied up nicely. This was a good result for everyone—no one got the short end of the stick. *If only everything could go this smoothly*, Mile started to think. But just then...

"Oh yes! I forgot to tell you!" said Bundine abruptly. "We're holding a celebration in honor of Lady Leatoria's recovery! We would like for you, the Crimson Vow, as well as Lady Leatoria's new friends, the Servants of the Goddess, to be in attendance..."

That was the promise made to the citizens who had lent Bundine money—and besides, people would be seeing a lot more of Leatoria, happy and healthy, around town from here on out. Plus, between starting work as a hunter, and the many hats that the daughter of a noble was required to wear, she was only going to get busier and busier. If such a celebration were to be held, there was no time like the present.

Provided she was not bedridden with illness, the daughter of a noble was, in fact, quite busy with a variety of tasks—so much so that one might call it a career. She was expected to study a variety of disciplines, memorize the histories and coats of arms and other miscellany regarding every noble household in the land, learn the names, lineages, and hierarchies of every royal and noble, pursue general studies, and become accomplished in the arts... and she was expected to master each of these pursuits perfectly.

Fortunately—or as fortunately as could be under the circumstances—Leatoria had had plenty of time to study while stuck in her room as a result of her illness. Thus, her skills were already well beyond what was expected of her age. Then again, a noble's work was never truly done...

"Hm? Leatoria, you were sick?" Telyusia asked worriedly.

Flustered, Leatoria quickly waved her hands in front of her face.

"No, no, it's fine! I'm completely cured now! We know the cause, too, so there's no chance of a relapse. I'm fit as a fiddle! And it's all thanks to the Crimson Vow!"

"Oh, is that so? That's go...od..."

Telyusia trailed off, her expression suddenly going dark.

"You were cured by the Crimson Vow...were you?"

Indeed, she remembered hearing a story like this very recently.

"D-d-d-d-don't tell me. She's..."

The cat's out of the bag, Mile thought. The illusion had been broken.

"Yes. You are speaking to Lady Leatoria von Aura, the daughter of Baron Aura."

"Whaaaaaaaaaaaaaaaaat?!?!"

Indeed, up to this point, the Servants of the Goddess had no idea that Leatoria was a noble. They had just missed meeting the maid, and while her appearance clearly gave the impression of a well-off young maiden, they had merely assumed that Leatoria was the daughter of a middle-class merchant or something along those lines. Even then, they would have guessed she was nothing more than a third daughter or perhaps the daughter of a mistress—someone who would rank fairly low in the line of inheritance. If she wasn't, there was no way that her family wouldn't have put a stop to her dreams of becoming a hunter. In other words, the Servants had assumed she was a child who her family could have easily been able to spare.

And since she was, of course, a beauty, they had assumed that there must be some other factors that further offset her value beyond simply her rank. Was she perhaps a bit soft in the head or...?

For a hunter, the advantages of a party was such that one member might make up for the shortcomings of another, so as long as you were skilled in combat, you were fine—within reason, anyway. However, for the daughter of a merchant, even the slightest flaw might be the kiss of death.

Anyway, no one would ever imagine a noble daughter in existence who could wield an all-metal war club. And so, the Servants of the Goddess had assumed Bundine must be merely a retainer or a clerk who had come along to accompany the supposed merchant's daughter.

Now, it was all becoming clear. A butler would never accompany a daughter of a mistress. Leatoria was the Baron's legitimate daughter.

"Y-you set us up..." Telyusia said, glaring at Mile, who had purposely failed to offer up any information regarding Leatoria's family.

At the same time, Mile had not told a single lie—and it remained true that Leatoria possessed all of the elements that the Servants desired. Therefore, the Crimson Vow felt no guilt in the slightest. Even if Mile had told them who Leatoria was from the start, the Servants probably still would have taken her in. They were just that sort of party, after all.

And so, Mile merely whistled, averting her gaze from Telyusia's glare...

✧◈✧

Several days later, a celebration of the recovery of Leatoria von Aura was held at the Aura family's capital residence.

Besides the Crimson Vow and the Servants of the Goddess, the invited guests included a number of commoners—in other words, the people who had donated money to Bundine back during the incident with the merchant. They had been promised as much, after all.

Normally, the family would have been making preparations for Leatoria's proper debut into society: her debutante ball, which was already a year late. They would be inviting acquainted nobles and sharing the good news of her restored health. However, under current conditions, if word of her combat magic ability, her health, her enhanced strength and stamina, and her pure and innocent beauty, on par with that of a goddess (her father's assessment always added about fifty percent) started to get out, nobles of influence would come breaking down the doors to force proposals on her, and the moment she turned fifteen, she would doubtless be whisked off into marriage. Frightened of this prospect, the Baron had firmly declined to introduce her more widely.

And of course, there was not a single person in the Aura household who objected to this approach.

So that these commoners, who had little concept of what went on at noble gatherings, would not find themselves lost, the Baron had suggested that they include only things with which their guests would be familiar. However, Bundine refused. These commoners were expecting to experience a noble's celebration— something new and exciting. What did the Baron think would happen if they didn't give them what they wanted to see?

Bundine was right, of course, so the Baron consented and set about preparing a party fit for nobles.

"Whoooooooaaaaaa!!!"

The invitees, who included the owners of businesses both medium and small, raised a cry of astonishment at entering the ballroom of a noble household, the likes of which they had never seen before, and taking in the sight of the splendid dishes that were lined up upon the banquet tables.

Among nobles, a baron was more or less the lowest of the low—and in fact, the food that he had put out was still cheaper than what would normally be served at a party. Yet there was still a clear enough difference between these dishes and the food of a commoner's banquet for them to be surprised.

That said, a real party thrown by nobility would also feature plenty of nobles talking and laughing and dancing, so the ballroom, mostly empty, was really little more than a big and fancily decorated room filled with lots of gourmet food. One simply could not think of inviting commoners to a party that was truly meant for other nobles. Honestly, what would the other noble families have thought?

"Thank you truly, all of you, for lending my daughter, Leatoria, your strength..." said the baron's wife, lifting the hem of her skirt in a curtsy, followed by her eldest daughter, which was echoed by her second daughter, and then her third daughter, Leatoria herself. The baron's eldest son offered a noble greeting as well, though the baron himself stood apart, smiling from a short distance away.

Even so, for a commoner to be greeted by the wife, son, and daughters of a noble in such a manner was unthinkable. This was literally a once-in-a-lifetime experience, the first and last time they would ever witness such a scene. The invitees were all trembling with emotion.

"It seems to be going well..."

"Yeah, Lady Aura and the others are really giving it their all."

"At this rate, I'm confident that the house of Aura will come to be thought of as good nobles, who are sincere and keep their promises even with the common folk. Plus, tales of this day are going to be told over and over again, all over the place. Nothing like this has ever happened before, so the rumors are sure to spread widely. Which means that, one of these days, the rumors that the Aura family are allies of the common man might even reach the palace..."

Indeed, just as Mile implied, the growing reputation of the Auras as a family who truly valued common folk might in fact prove to be of use to them someday. After discussing this with Mavis and Pauline, she decided to go and convey the sentiment to the baron, his wife, and his children.

The Auras truly were thankful for all of the people who had helped them out in the incident with the medicine. As such, hosting this party was both in their own self-interest and a genuine act of gratitude.

"Thank you so much, everyone! My good health is all thanks to you!" Leatoria said warmly, shaking each of the guests' hands.

Secretly, the baron was very reluctant to go along with this, but he plastered a forced grin upon his face as he stood watching.

After all, no father in the world would be happy to see his daughter holding hands with strange men.

"You all really did it this time, huh?"

"Hm? We never lied to you, did we? This all turned out to be quite the boon for you, didn't it?"

"Ngh..."

Later, the Crimson Vow and the Servants of the Goddess chatted with one another, stuffing food from overflowing plates into their mouths.

The Servants had already made their introductions to the Aura family. Naturally, there was no way that the family could entrust their dear girl to anyone without scrutinizing them first. However, it seemed like they had safely obtained the family's approval.

Of course, Bundine had already told the family what he knew of the Servants, and a background check had been conducted via the Guild. The Baron was exactly the sort of father who would hire a private eye just to learn more about his daughter's associates.

The hunters could talk Leatoria's ear off at any time they pleased, so for today, they left her to the other guests, content to chat among themselves as they scarfed down the delicious provisions. Leatoria had been informed of the same and instructed to give her all in entertaining the invitees. Without such instructions, she probably would have stuck to the hunters like glue.

Still, Leatoria was no dummy, and she knew that she would have plenty of opportunities to spend time with her new friends from now on, so she dutifully followed her orders.

Now, while the Servants of the Goddess talked among themselves, the Crimson Vow huddled in together as well, discussing in hushed voices.

"It looks like we've cleared all the side quests in this town now..."

At this point, the others understood perfectly well what Mile meant by "side quests." They had gotten the general idea from the recurring elements that tended to pop up in her Japanese folktales.

"Yeah, you're right," Mavis agreed. "Guess we should be rolling out soon."

The Crimson Vow was still a party on the move. It wasn't as though they were hurrying forward, though they did strive for continual progress. If they didn't take the time to stop and learn about each country they passed through, they would be little more than tourists. Thus, it made the most sense for them to stop and stay a while, understand what they could of the land, take on some exciting jobs, and build their reputation—not among the common folk, mind you, but among the guild staff and local hunters, at least.

However, this still did not mean that they could stay indefinitely. If everyone in the region at least got to know them well enough, their reputation would remain, and they would be known as young hunters off on a journey of self-discipline.

For these reasons, Mile and Mavis were beginning to suggest that it was time to go.

"Oh?" Reina tittered. "I'm surprised, Mile, I thought you'd be all, 'But, the catgirl! Let's stay here a bit longer—scratch that, let's stay forever!'"

Pauline giggled in turn. "I was thinking the same..."

"Wh... Well *I* was thinking that *you* would be saying, 'Oh, but I can't leave 'big sis' behind!'"

"Wh-wh-wh-wha...?" Reina went red in the face at Mile's unexpected retort.

"Got something to say?!"

"Do you?!"

"Gnrrrrrrrrrrrrgh..."

"Okay, okay, okay, okay!"

Mavis hurriedly intervened. Naturally, as a daughter of a noble family, Mavis's sensibilities would not permit such an argument to unfold at a formal party. The only area in which Mavis was lacking was when it came to things that were common knowledge to the masses. At least as far as most nobles would be concerned, she was a perfectly sensible individual—except, that is, for her exaggerated impression of the abilities of mages and knights, which had been shaped by various legends and the hyperbolic boasting of her brothers.

As the party slowly separated into three groups—the commoners and the Aura family, the Crimson Vow, and the Servants of the Goddess—everyone talked, ate, and drank their fill, and the rest of the celebration went off without a hitch.

Yes, as long as the invited guests got to speak with the daughter of a noble—and as long the two hunting parties got to eat delicious food until their bellies were bursting—everyone was happy.

✧◈✧

I still don't know if I'm happy about this...

As Leatoria spoke cheerfully with the merchant guests, a mildly troubling thought crossed her mind.

She really had wanted to travel with the Crimson Vow. Thanks to her illness, she had thought that she was going to live the whole of her short life as a caged bird, and they were the ones who had come and flung open the doors, letting her fly out into the big, blue sky.

I bet they spend their days on strange and exciting adventures—things that other hunting parties could never even dream of, she thought. *They're a mysterious, wonderful party.*

I wanted to be a part of that. I wanted to travel with them, to be a member of that strange and marvelous party...but alas, that's impossible.

Among the four of them, there isn't a niche for me.

Plus, for someone like me, who can't possibly abandon their home and family, there's no benefit to my trying to go with them. Someday soon, I'll be married off into some other household some-where, so for the few short years that remain until then, the greatest freedom I can have, and the most valuable thing I can do, is to work from home as a commuting hunter.

That's why I decided to go along with their charade and join the Servants of the Goddess. It's what everyone wants, and the most valuable choice that I can make right now.

There's no other path for someone without any special abilities— someone like me.

Besides, it's not like I hate the idea of joining up with the Servants.

Unlike the members of the Crimson Vow, they're all normal girls, doing their best, just like me. They're a wonderful party.

I have to make the most of these next few years. I have to give it my all and have lots of fun. And then, someday, when I meet up with the Crimson Vow again, I can tell them all about what the adventures of a "normal girl" are like...

And so, the tale of Leatoria von Aura, a young noble maiden who thought of herself as a "normal girl," began...

CHAPTER 60 |

The Girl with Seven Faces!

"WE HAVE A SPECIAL REQUEST we would like you to take on."

When the Crimson Vow next stopped in at the guildhall, they were beckoned over by Felicia, the clerk, who then escorted them up to the guild master's office on the second floor. The moment they stepped through the doorway, they were hailed by the guild master, who spoke the words above.

"Huh? Well, um, I mean, we can't accept it without knowing the details..." said Mavis, the leader, seeking an explanation.

Even if it was the guild master who was doing the requesting, they were not going to accept any outrageous jobs. It would be no different if it had been a noble or even a member of the royal family. That was a rule that they had decided upon when the party was first formed.

Of course, "outrageous" for the Crimson Vow did not mean "difficult" or "dangerous." Such conditions were of little relevance to the girls. For the Crimson Vow, "outrageous" meant jobs that asked them to do something they didn't agree with or ones that someone with influence had pushed through on the strength of their own power alone.

"I suppose that's fair. I mean, most people would accept a direct request from a guild master without a second thought, details or no, but I do believe caution is the key to a long and healthy life..." he said with a wry smile before launching into the details of the job.

Apparently, there was a spot near a town about four days from the capital where travelers were being attacked with some frequency. The brigands would target any traveler who appeared to have a bit of money about them, whether they were traveling by carriage or on foot. The men and the elderly would be killed, the valuables and cargo stolen, and the women and horses spirited away. Perhaps because they would be too easy to track, the carriages were usually left where they were. With a cart, the brigands wouldn't be able to go far from the road, and even if they were to sell it, a little bit of investigation would reveal the cart's origin, which meant that was out of the question as well.

If it were merchant caravans or commuter carriages that were being attacked, the local lord would have to step in. After all, such a thing could have huge effects on the economics of the region. However, travelers who were merely passing through were none of the lord's concern. People who didn't think to hire a sufficient guard force reaped what they sowed. In fact, if the brigands sold their stolen goods off for cheap within the territory, it was actually an economic boon. There was no reason for the lord to bother with something as foolish as setting aside the budget for hiring more soldiers to guard the roads, and furthermore, allotting funds to treat any injuries that might arise when the soldiers fought against the brigands.

Of course, no truly noble lord would ever abide by such logic, but if every lord in the land were wise and just, then such suffering as this world saw would never have existed in the first place.

Even if the brigands' victims were not citizens of the town, the people of the region could not simply let things be, so the local Merchants' Guild had gathered up the funds to hire on hunters. Yet no matter how they searched, they could not find the bandits.

They had tried hiding hunters within traveling carriages departing from the town, but for some reason, these carriages had entirely failed to attract the attackers. Since the attacks had yet to stop, the townspeople were still quite vexed.

That was when the townsfolk finally realized why it was that the brigands attacked only travelers and not the people of the town. The bandits had realized that, should they attack the townspeople, an extermination force would quickly be organized. They would face soldiers hired by a wary lord who feared reprimand from the crown for not upholding his basic duties of collecting taxes and protecting the populace—and by hunters, hired by the families of their victims and any merchants whose businesses had been hurt...

How could the bandits tell? How could they be certain that the people they were targeting were travelers and not townsfolk—and only travelers with valuables on them, no less?

It was because they had an inside man. In other words, someone had infiltrated the people going in and out of the Hunters' Guild, thus protecting the bandits from being fooled by the disguised hunters.

With this assumption in mind, this time, the local Merchants' Guild had decided to place a request not with their own Hunters' Guild but with the capital branch. And so the bandit-hunting request had been made.

"Is that so?"

Thanks to the guild master's thorough explanation, the Crimson Vow now had the gist of things. They also understood why this was a job being assigned to a group of newcomers like them.

First off, all they would have to do would be to change their clothes, and no one would have the slightest clue that any of them were hunters. Second of all, no one in the town would be familiar with them—hunters and guild staff included. And thirdly, they were more than strong enough to wipe out any bandits.

The four looked to one another and gave an emphatic nod.

As one, they said: "We'll do it!"

"Um…" Pauline then continued, "Will you be providing us a stipend with which to purchase disguises?"

When the guild master insisted that the fees for necessary expenses were included in the reward, Pauline cajoled him into footing the bill for their disguise purchases at a clothing store, arguing that women's clothing, particularly that of a rich young lady, was quite expensive. The guild master fought back tooth and nail, insisting that the Guild would only finance clothing purchased from a secondhand shop. It was a knockdown, drag-out defeat.

"We'll be heading out tomorrow, so today is for preparation and relaxation!"

Starting the next day, they would be walking for four days, so for now, it was best to let their feet get some rest. However, before that...

"Now, it's off to the clothing store!"

"Okay!!!"

Even if they were only buying secondhand, going clothes shopping was still fun. And going clothes shopping on someone else's dime was all the more exciting.

A few days later, when the guild master received the bill, he went wide-eyed with shock.

"Damn it! If I don't handle this right, it looks bad for the Guild, but if I just go along with this and pay the bill, people are going to start getting carried away..." the guild master grumbled, gripping the paper in his hand.

A nearby female guild employee looked over the paper. "Oh? But that's rather cheap... Sir, you have no idea what the typical prices of women's clothing are, do you?"

"Hm?" he replied. "I-Is that so? Wait, is women's clothing really *that* expensive?!"

"Well, I mean, not necessarily for normal clothing, but slightly nicer garments, stuff like this—it does cost a bit more."

"………"

The guild master, who had three daughters, all still young, was aghast.

"I better start saving up..."

✧ ◈ ✧

"Just a little further," said Mile.

"Yeah, we should be seeing it pretty soon," Mavis agreed.

Just as the two suggested, their destination, the town Zarbef, was just a little farther down the road. For normal hunters, it would have been about a four-day walk, but for Mile and the Crimson Vow...it took about four days as well.

Had they gone into "sonic speed" formation, their swords and staves stored away in Mile's inventory, it would have taken them no more than three and a half days. But for some reason, Reina, Mavis, and Pauline had insisted that they all carry their own weapons and luggage—not the extra-light, false gear that they normally used, but their actual, fairly heavy gear and canteens.

At first, Mile couldn't comprehend their reasoning, but as she thought about it, she concluded that this was welcome practice for them. This was how would they have to travel if she were not around, and since it would have taken regular people four days to make the journey, it was just fine. For once, they decided to be normal.

They changed into their disguises on the morning of the third day. They didn't want any of their acquaintances from the capital to view them in their new garb, so they hadn't changed anywhere around the capital. However, they also couldn't let anyone see them dressed as hunters anywhere near their destination. Therefore, they decided that it was safer to change somewhere around the midway point.

The outfits—or rather, the roles—that they had assumed were as follows:

Mile: The daughter of a low-ranking noble household.
Mavis: An apprentice knight and bodyguard.
Pauline: An attending maid.
Reina: A traveling peddler, serving as their guide.

Honestly, they were in rather shabby form for a noble maiden's entourage, but there were a lot of different types of nobles and a lot of different types of maidens. She could be a fourth daughter, or a fifth daughter, or a daughter born to a mistress or concubine. Furthermore, even among those, there were plenty of girls who had the sort of qualities that meant their families would rather see them disappear—after all, this had been Adele's position back in her family home.

Even if this maiden did have a bodyguard, it was not particularly strange that the bodyguard in question couldn't protect her from any harm greater than petty crooks and pickpockets in town. Plus, even if the bodyguard were only an apprentice knight, anyone who practiced the sword in earnest would put their blade and their life on the line to protect their master, meaning that no two-bit crooks were likely to come sticking their noses in. Knights were often an ill-tempered bunch, drawing their swords to cut an offender down at only the slightest provocation.

Mile had donned a fluttering, frilly dress, and Pauline was in a maid's outfit, though she had no apron or frilled headband. Such things would only be in the way on a long-haul journey, so they had left out the excess items. Even secondhand, such things were fairly expensive.

Mavis and Reina were in their usual clothing and gear. Even if she were not a mage, it was not particularly strange for a young lady who was traveling by foot to be carrying a staff or rod with which to fend off kobolds and goblins and such. Thus, her weapon alone was not enough to expose Reina as a magic-user. Of course, she would still stow her staff away before they entered town.

Incidentally, while the two of them *were* still wearing their usual garb, they had in fact been allotted the funds for four outfits. As a result, the party had purchased additional wardrobe items for Mavis and Reina on the Guild's dime and stored them away in the inventory for later.

Finally, the town of Zarbef came into view.

"All right! Let's do this!"

"Yeah!!!"

And so the curtain was raised on the stage that was Zarbef, where the traveling actresses of the Crimson Vow were about to make their debut.

That Mile... What a scary girl!!

So as not to blow their cover, the four of them decided to stick as close to the actual truth as possible—without revealing the fact that they were hunters. Mavis's role remained more or less true to reality, as did Reina's, leaving out the fact that she was a mage. Pauline was, of course, not actually a maid, but she played the part flawlessly. And as for Mile...

"There's no point in you even acting. Just be yourself!"

"Wh-what? How rude! I'll have you know that my family often said that I was 'quite the actress'!"

As a red-in-the-face Mile screamed at Reina, Mavis muttered to herself, "Somehow I don't think they meant that as a compliment..."

Incidentally, the role that Mile had chosen to embody was that of a low-ranking noble girl from a foreign land who was largely disregarded by her parents and admired hunters enormously. This would make it all right if she accidentally said hunter-ish things. People would most likely take her for nothing more than a young noble playing make-believe. As for her magic, Mile decided to pretend that, for some reason, the only thing she was good at was storage magic. That way, they were sure to entice the bandits, and they didn't have to hide Mile's storage abilities, which made things easier for everyone in general.

The others had decided that they would carry their own things, so as not to rely on Mile too much, but her storage really was too handy to give up entirely.

Finally, the Crimson Vow arrived at the hill overlooking the small country town of Zarbef.

"All right! From here on out, it's time for us to really embody our roles. We never know when someone might be listening in, so we can only discuss Vow affairs when we're outdoors and can see what's around us or when we're inside one of Mile's barriers. Anywhere else, we need to speak as our characters would and can only have normal, everyday conversation! Got it?" Reina directed.

The other three nodded in return.

"Crimson Vow, roll out!"

"All right!!!"

As the group triumphantly descended the hill toward the town, Mavis spoke in a forlorn manner, almost to herself, "Guys? Can we at least *try* to remember that I'm the actual leader...?"

✧◈✧

Ring-a-ling.

As always, the guildhall had a bell attached to the front door. These were put in place so that guild employees could look and tell at a moment's glance whether or not whoever had just entered appeared to be a troublemaker. Having a fight occur while they weren't paying attention was not a possibility to be taken lightly, especially if that fight resulted in crossed swords. Thus, if someone who appeared to be a troublemaker entered, the employees would make a note of that person immediately.

That said, the group who entered now looked like the sort who would cause a commotion for a wholly different reason.

When someone new entered the hall, it was not only the staff who looked over to evaluate them but the gathered hunters as well. As was their habit, everyone in the hall had done so, and in this case, guild staff and hunters alike came immediately to the same conclusion:

They're sitting ducks!!!!

There was a girl who appeared to be a low-ranking noble, with an endearing appearance but a rather vacant look on her face.

There was a large-busted maid.

There was a fierce-looking redhead.

And last, there was a gallant, but rather meek-seeming young swordswoman.

It was plain to anyone that the four of them would be easy marks. Obviously, they had come here to place a request for an escort. With a young noble maiden like that, so oblivious to the world, one could probably get her to cover all sorts of additional expenses along the way, if one played one's cards right. Obviously they couldn't overdo it while on a request placed through the Guild, but should the girls happen to place any "additional requests" along the way, why, then that was another matter entirely. Thinking this, some ill-behaved C-rank hunters ogled them, eyes glinting. For some reason, however, instead of walking straight up to the request counter like the hunters thought they would, the girls walked toward the job board and halted before the information board beside it.

"Mistress, it seems that bandits have been preying on the travelers in this area. Perhaps we should hire on an escort here," the swordswoman proposed.

The hunters watched, grinning.

However, the noble maiden then replied, "Oh? But shouldn't you be able to handle a few bandits? If we were to hire someone, wouldn't you be ridiculed as a coward?"

No way no way no way!!! everyone retorted in their hearts.

The maiden then turned to her maid and said, "Besides, Pauline, I know you've been training in the yard with mops and brooms during your breaks and on rest days. With that 'Maid-Style Killing Arts,' or what have you..."

No way no way no way no way no way no way!!!

What the girl was referring to was probably some sort of calisthenics or game. Internally, the hunters and employees immediately rejected the young maiden's logic, though they could not voice their objections aloud. For some reason, the maid seemed rather proud of herself.

"What are you all carrying on about?!" asked the redhead suddenly. "The master of the house placed me in charge of this team, so I'm the one who will be making decisions about our travels!"

There was no way that a girl of no more than twelve would have been placed in charge in lieu of the seventeen or eighteen-year-old swordswoman or the fifteen or sixteen-year-old maid. The girl had to be much older than she looked, the hunters thought— maybe an elf or a dwarf, most likely. The total washboard that was her chest confirmed this. Actually, as she was not short and stubby in the manner of dwarves, it was far more likely that she was an elf, or at least someone with elven blood.

At any rate, it seemed that the noble maiden had hired someone with sense as her guide for this expedition. So, everyone in the room thought, one could expect that she would have had the sense to hire a guard for them as well. However...

"Like I'd waste our money on something like an escort! I get to keep a third of any money we save, and we aren't going to throw it away on something like that!"

Whaaaaaaaaaaaaat?!?!

Their leader was valuing her own profits over the group's safety—in a situation where her own life might be at stake! Hunters across the Guild were flabbergasted.

"Whatever. It doesn't look like there's very much good information here. Let's get going... Oh!"

Midway through urging the group on, the redhead looked as though she'd had a sudden change of heart.

"We're running low on money. Milady, get over here!"

Though she addressed the young noble with an honorific, there wasn't a hint of respect in the redhead's tone. It was plain to see where the true power lay in this team...

The group of girls then headed to the game exchange counter.

"Bring it out!" ordered the redhead to the noble.

Honestly, it was becoming less and less clear which of them was the mistress and which the servant.

"Ah, o-on it!"

However, the noble maiden complied without complaint, as though this was how things always were between them.

"C'mon out, orcs! Let's go!"

Boom!

Suddenly, two orc corpses appeared before her.

"Whaaaaaaaaaaaaaaat?!?!" A cry rang through the room.

"Sh-she's got storage magic... And such a large capacity..." one of the hunters stuttered out.

Indeed, the fact that this girl could store not only one orc, but two, put her in the upper echelons of storage magic users, a quite sparse group to begin with. Even if she were a powerless, utterly useless girl otherwise, the fact that she could rival the carrying capacity of an entire wagon on her own more than made up for any other flaws. Even for a merchant or noble, the uses of such a girl were endless: she could hide away confidential documents or cargo when suddenly set upon by tax inspectors, she could smuggle illicit goods...

Once again, a thought occurred to everyone in the guildhall at once:

A golden goose...

"Is it possible for non-hunters to sell things here, too?"

Misrepresenting oneself to a guild employee was a punishable offence. However, Reina was not telling a lie—she had merely asked a question, never implying that she herself was not a hunter.

"Y-yeah, that's fine."

Normally, the one in charge of the exchange counter was some gruff old man, and this Guild branch was no exception. If a woman were put in charge of the exchange counter, as with the other stations, you would start getting idiots who came in trying to intimidate a higher exchange rate out of her. Therefore, the job was usually entrusted to some tough-looking old fellow who had retired from hunting due to age or injury. Even so, no matter their age or health, such men would have no trouble putting a greenhorn in line with a little short-term violence—in fact, this was a prerequisite for the position. No hunter would ever dare oppose or disrespect the chief of exchange.

Plus, hunters never knew when they themselves might fall victim to injury, and someday, they would all grow old. Even the roughest of ruffians would put on their best sweet-talking act before the influential employees of the Guild, who might some-day see to their own reemployment.

That said...

"Yo, old-timer, how much can ya give us for... Ngah!"

"Pardon us, might we ask you to assess these?"

Even if it was merely an act, Mavis could not abide Reina being so grievously rude to the man and hurriedly clapped a hand over her mouth.

"Oh please, Mister, you'll give us a good price for these, won't you?" Pauline's flattery was blatant, but if it was for the sake of fattening her purse, she'd slap on a false smile in a heartbeat. However...

"P-please, Mister!" Mile said, attempting to wink, though as she was unaccustomed to such a gesture, she ended up closing both of her eyes. Indeed, she had done exactly the same when attempting her "Angel's Wink" lightning magic.

"No need to overdo it there," the old man said, grimacing. "You're really somethin', though. I've never seen anyone who could hold that much in storage before. Plus, it looks like y'all got these orcs' heads off in one clean shot, with no other damages..."

"Ah, well, we bought them for cheap off of a hunter who was in a bind. He had killed three of them, but couldn't carry them all," Mile quickly explained.

Most of the price that an orc fetched stemmed from the difficulty of transporting it from the hunting grounds back to town. That fact alone made her argument a persuasive one, almost ridiculously so. The bulk of the hunters who overheard this began to lose themselves in wild fancies, imagining what their own profits would be if they could get their hands on someone like Mile. Of course, it would be one thing if she were a rookie hunter, but even low-ranking, she was still a noble, so the chances of something like that actually happening were more or less impossible. Still, it was fun to indulge in the fantasy.

"All right," said the old man, "This is what the evaluation comes to. That fine with y'all?"

Surely enough, the coins that the old man heaved onto the counter were the standard payment for two orcs in good condition. Reina nodded, and Mile waved her hands over the coins to store them. Obviously, such a gesture was not actually necessary, but it certainly looked attractive. There were plenty present who had never actually seen storage magic used in person, so she thought it nice to put on a bit of a show for them.

"Well then, let's go find an inn," said Reina. "Tomorrow at the second morning bell we'll set out for the town of Caldile."

"Yea... Yes, ma'am!"

The other three began their usual boisterous agreement and then quickly corrected themselves to a more proper manner of speech.

Their plans now loudly and clearly announced to everyone, the four then left the guildhall to seek an inn. Once they had cleared out, a hush fell over the room. Among the quiet figures were those who were taken aback, those who were uneasy...and those who were greatly concerned.

"So, do you think that did the trick?" asked Reina afterward.

"Hm, I wonder if we overdid it a bit," said Mavis.

"Actually, I think that was just about right for 'idiot daughter of a backwater noble and her team,' wouldn't you say?" asked Pauline.

"And just who are you calling an 'idiot daughter'?!" Mile raged.

The four talked among themselves as they walked casually down a side street.

"It's important that we pick the right inn, too," said Reina.

"You're right," Mile replied.

Naturally, the Guild was not the only place where they needed to purposely leak information. If someone was going to pray on travelers, then the places that travelers frequented, such as inns and restaurants, would be the most likely places for them to go.

The level of danger varied little by inn. No matter how high-class the establishment, it was impossible to vet every single employee and their external relations. So why would the girls go out of their way to pick a mid-sized inn on a side street?

"Please try and pick the cheapest place possible," Pauline implored.

Indeed, it was nothing more than a matter of expense.

"I'd like it if we could find another one with a catgirl..."

"You shut your mouth! If you start creeping on some other beastgirl, I'm going to tell Faleel! I'll tell her that you have indiscriminate taste, and that as long as there's a beastgirl, any inn's good enough for you," threatened Reina.

"Oh! You wouldn't!" Mile panicked.

The childish, greedy behavior that Mile displayed the day of Faleel's rescue from the kidnappers had started to seed doubt in the young girl's heart, but when her mother and father explained to Faleel later on that Mile had been instrumental in her rescue, the girl finally began to understand. When, thanks to an explanation from Reina and the others, Faleel came to realize just how big a role Mile had played, she embraced her all the more tightly.

Mile, assuming that the only reason Faleel had clung so closely to the Servants of the Goddess was that she was glad to see them again after so long, began to spend more and more time in Faleel's company. By cajoling her father, who was not a man of strong will, by reminding him of her role in rescuing his daughter, she found herself with more and more one-on-one time with

Faleel—the highlight of Mile's young life. It was as though she was trying to force herself to forget that they would very soon be parting. Thus, she could not bear the idea of Faleel thinking poorly of her in any way.

Besides, it wasn't like some little country town was likely to have an inn with a beast-eared girl in it, in the first place.

All the fight suddenly gone out of her, Mile fell to sulking, leaving the choosing of the inn entirely to the other three.

"I guess this is the place, then," said Reina, as the Vow stood before their chosen inn.

There were not a lot of inns in town to begin with, so it was not as though they had very many choices. Plus, comfort was not their priority this time. They would be staying for only one night, and picking the most questionable place they could find was best for the job they were currently on.

"Yeah, this should do the trick," Mavis agreed.

"It looks cheap and pretty shady... Perfect," said Pauline.

"It really wouldn't matter anyway," said Mile. "Good enough!"

The decision was unanimous.

"Shady" had probably been a bit of an overstatement. Yes, the place was a bit dirty, but it wasn't as though there were any criminal types coming in and out of the lobby. It was merely that the place was a bit crude compared to the Crimson Vow's usual choices of lodging, which were inns that were tidy, seemed safe for a group of young girls, and were cozy, even if they were a little pricey. This inn was the sort of place that any normal group of travelers would lodge at for cheap, so there was really no issue here.

"Welcome! Will you be staying the night?"

At the counter sat a precious young boy of around seven or eight. Mile's eyes flashed, and she was immediately drawn to him.

In her previous life, Mile had always wanted a little brother. She wanted an older brother too, but that was a physical impossibility. Well, technically, if her parents had separated, and one of them got remarried to someone who already had kids, then perhaps she would have still had a shot, but there was no way that a couple who were as in love as those two were would ever grow apart, and she certainly was never going to say to them, "Hey, can you get divorced so that I can have a big brother?"

Therefore, she had settled for wishing for a younger brother, but around the time she reached high school, she had given up on that dream as well.

In fact, Mile's true weakness was not cute little girls but cute little boys. Seeing how quickly she now perked up, the other three looked on wearily...

"I swear, Mile!"

When they entered their room afterward, the exasperated comments began immediately.

"You can't be so boy crazy! Have you no shame?!"

"What will people think about us for being with you?!"

"You do realize that with a boy that young, it'd be a crime..."

Even Pauline and Mavis went in on the attack this time.

"I-I-I-It's not like that!!! I just love to dote on little boys…"

"I… I can't believe it… Mile, you really are—"

"A pervert!"

"A pervert…"

"It's not like thaaaaaaat!!!"

"So…when are you going?" asked Reina.

"Going where?"

Mile did not catch Reina's drift.

"Honestly! Hurry up and go bring that kid up here!" the mage impatiently demanded.

Mile looked to Mavis and Pauline to see two more hopeful faces staring her way.

"Seriously, what is with you guuuuuuuuuys?!?!"

Indeed, even more so than Mile, Reina, who was an only child; Pauline, who was nostalgic for the days when her brother was little; and Mavis, who was the youngest of her line, were all starved for the affections of an impressionable younger sibling.

"And you all thought you had the right to criticize *me?!*"

Of course, not even Mile had the courage to bring a boy up to their room. It was one thing for a girl, but four young ladies bringing a boy to their room was bad no matter how you looked at it…

At dinner, the four continued to talk loudly about their plans for the following day.

"So, tomorrow at the second morning bell, yes? We'll head straight to Caldile and reevaluate our schedule once we arrive."

Reina's voice carried easily, so the other guests and the employees of the inn were certain to hear them. By conveying their departure time and their destination so concisely, they made themselves easy prey for any spying bandits. It made ambushing them more efficient, which meant less wasted time. They were doing the brigands a great service.

After they returned to their room, Mile snuggled into her bed, ignoring the lingering gazes coming her way from the others, who silently implored, "Are you sure you won't go fetch him?" The rest of the party, lacking the courage to do anything about it themselves, gave up on the venture and went to bed as well.

They had another four-day journey to prepare themselves for, after all, and this time they were carrying all their own gear, so the rest was all the more necessary. And so, the sounds of peaceful snores came quickly after that.

✦◈✦

"Okay, let's head out!"

"All right!!!"

Apparently, the Crimson Vow had already given up on the whole "Yes, ma'am" business. When children went about pretending to talk like hunters, the adults usually went along with it. Thinking that their behavior would be interpreted in this manner, the members of the Crimson Vow opted to go with their usual reply rather than an unfamiliar, more conspicuous turn of phrase.

"Let's walk at a normal pace today," Reina suggested, earning nods from the other three.

This time, there was no telling when they might be set upon by hidden assailants, so except for Mile, who was playing the role of the young noblewoman, they were all equipped with their staves and swords. Besides some small canteens, the rest of their gear was stashed away in Mile's storage. Now that they had revealed her ability publicly, it would be more unnatural for them *not* to be utilizing it. Thus, they could very easily move more quickly than normal hunters. However, that might put a hitch in any attackers' plans. They had to proceed at the pace of any normal group of non-hunter ladies with a child in tow, just as the attackers would expect.

Of course, there was also the possibility that rather than being ambushed, they would be tailed. The whole thing would be moot if they left their pursuers in the dust.

"We should be seeing them soon," Reina said, as the sun began to set.

The only people who were attacked on leaving Zarbef were travelers, not townsfolk. This implied that the bandits were lurking within Zarbef, or at the very least, that they had informants who lived in the town. In order for them to relay information back and forth quickly, their stronghold could not be anywhere that far out—particularly not if they were actually town residents.

The casualties that had occurred thus far had, furthermore, all happened at places one or two days' walk from the town. If they attacked too close to town, it would be easy to hunt the bandits down, so that particular distance had certainly been taken into account, too.

Well, speak of the devil, and he appears. Surely enough, not long after Reina spoke, five men appeared ahead of them from behind a rocky formation on the side of the highway. They all appeared to be in their thirties or forties, with decent-looking hair and garments.

"I doubt they've set up shop right there. They probably go back and forth from the town."

"It does seem that way..."

It was likely just as Reina and Pauline said. If they lived as far out as this, their hair and beards and clothing would all be in a bit more of a "bandit-y" state. It didn't look like there was anywhere the men could wash up around here, after all.

"There are three behind us, too," Mavis announced. "Standard practice."

Indeed, another trio had suddenly appeared at their rear, drawing nearer with wicked grins upon their faces.

"Stand back!" Mavis declared to the men. "If you should come any nearer, you will be considered brigands, and I, as the guard of this daughter of a noble household, shall deal with you accordingly! Should it come to that, I take no responsibility if you are injured or killed. And, if you should happen to survive, you will be apprehended and taken to the authorities, where you shall be handed over to the city guard as criminals by way of the Hunters' Guild!"

Naturally, such a threat was not enough to convince the bandits to stand down. This was nothing more than standard proceedings to create a situation where Mavis could fight them without holding back. This way, the men could not later backpedal and say that it was a "misunderstanding" or that their intentions had been misconstrued.

"Heh heh heh," chuckled one of the men, "better settle down there, little lady. There's eight of us, and, from the looks of ya, only one of you's gonna put up any kinda real fight. You can fight us all ya want, but all yer gonna do's end up hurt."

"Very well," she replied, "I will take that as confession of your banditry, your intent to do harm, and an official threat! Let the battle of justifiable self-defense begin!"

"What?"

The chief bandit was suddenly quite puzzled. Not only was their quarry not quaking in her boots, the young lady was now spewing off all sorts of phrases he had never even heard of, still cool and collected.

The Crimson Vow swiftly moved into formation. Against the five bandits at the front were Mile and Pauline. Against the back three were Mavis and Reina. Pauline and Reina had their backs up against each other.

"Oh? Dunno what you gals're playin' at here, but tell me, what exactly's a little maiden like you gonna do against us emptyhanded?" the leader asked with a sneer.

"Hm?" said Mile. "Empty-handed? What are you talking about?"

"Huh???"

The bandits in front did a double take. Sure enough, this noble maiden, who had been empty-handed until just moments ago, now held a sword in her right hand.

"Wh-when did she... That's right! Storage!"

That confirmed it: they were affiliated with someone in the Guild. There hadn't been a chance to talk about Mile's storage magic at the inn, and it would have clearly been unnatural to go out of their way to bring it up. It would have been incredibly hasty of the brigands to leap to the conclusion that a young noble-woman would have storage magic, a very rare thing. Usually one would think, "She must've been hiding that sword somewhere!" or something along those lines.

"Heh! If little girls like you start playin' at swords, all's that'll happen is yer gonna get hurt!"

The leader's words were directed at Mile, who stood in front of him, but behind her, Mavis, who was facing the rear group with her back turned to the man, suddenly flinched.

"Little girls like you can practice with a blade all you want— it don't mean nothin'! Why wouldja even bother?! If you just stayed at home playin' princess like good little girls should, you wouldn't be endin' up in situations like this! Gyah ha!"

Crack!

"What did you say? What did you just say, you bastard...?" came a low voice.

"She's snapped!!!" the other three gasped.

Yes, Mavis had well and truly snapped.

"Heheh. Eheheh. Eheheheheheheh…"

"Oh my god!!!"

Mavis was laughing. The other three began to tremble. This was Mavis, who was always courteous and kind, considerate to a fault. Her will was so strong, no one could even imagine what would possibly ruffle her feathers.

But of course, Mavis did get angry sometimes, just like anyone else. And what made her angriest was a personal insult, such as an attack on her family, her honor, or her tireless pursuit of her own dreams.

Ka-chk.

Reina and Pauline could not see it, but Mile, with her dynamic field of vision, noticed Mavis rotate the hilt of her sword in her hand.

What is she doing?

The utterly meaningless maneuver left Mile perplexed.

And then, Mavis shouted, "Don't worry! I'll only strike you with the back of the sword!"

"They'll die!" Mile suddenly screamed out. "Mavis, you'll kill them!!"

A Japanese-style sword was one thing, but rotating a Western-style sword, with a cutting edge on both sides, was summarily pointless. Apparently, even in her haze of rage, Mavis still hoped to end the battle without a fatality. She had remembered a technique mentioned often in Mile's Japanese folktales—the reverse-blade strike, which could be used to fell a foe without killing them. What she had forgotten, however, was that the katana used in these stories and the double-edged blade in her own hands were not the same thing.

That said, even a single-blade katana, used in reverse, was still a metal rod, and being struck hard with such an instrument could result in broken bones, internal injuries, and if one was not careful, death...

"Reina!" shouted Mile, "Please save those bandits!"

"What the heck?!?!"

Reina was thrown for a loop at this outrageous instruction, but in truth, she had already grasped the situation herself. She was prepared to kill without hesitation if she had to, but even she knew that a situation like this, where they had plenty of leeway, was not the time for that.

"Ugh, guess I better..." she grumbled, quickly and quietly beginning an incantation.

The three rear bandits, not hearing Reina's incantation, and thinking Mavis and Mile's conversation merely that of a pair of fanciful young ladies, paid them no mind, until...

"Firebomb!"

Ka-boom!

As Reina's spell went off, the three men were blown backwards. She had purposely aimed it away from them, so while they might end up a little singed and a little bruised, there would be no fatalities.

Seeing that Mavis was displeased that her quarry had been driven away, Reina nodded to herself. "Protecting them by attacking them... This must be what Mile meant when she once said that, 'The best defense is a strong offense...'"

...No, Reina, that was not at all what the phrase meant.

"Wh-wh-wh-wha...?"

The men had assumed that, besides the swordswoman, these were all normal little girls, but suddenly here was a combat magic wielder—a fairly skilled one, at that. The boss found himself panicked at the realization that three of his men had just been blown away in an instant, but when he turned his fretful eyes to the young mage, he saw that she was not looking his way but walking slowly toward the three she had just attacked. Perhaps she was moving to finish them off so that she would not be attacked from behind while she was not looking.

In any event, this gave the bandits the perfect opportunity to capture the other three while her back was turned, and take them hostage. If they could nab them all...

There was a noble maiden who could use storage magic and a combat magic user—and both of them were young and pretty to boot. Even the well-endowed maid and the swordswoman would fetch a fair price on the black market.

The men in the front faced the noble, the maid, and the swordswoman, who had now turned their way. Of the three of them, two appeared to be complete amateurs in combat. Those forces were up against five ruffians. Capturing the girls would be like taking candy from a baby. First, to strike down the swordswoman...

Smack! Clatter!

And so, the sword was struck down...*the bandit leader's* sword.

"Huh...?"

He looked down, stunned, at his suddenly empty hands, then abruptly fled to the rear.

"Get 'em!"

She had closed the gap and struck down his sword before he could even react—this woman was dangerous! The leader suddenly valued his safety over the prospect of capturing Mavis unharmed. There were still three other girls, after all, and the swordswoman would probably fetch the least of the bunch anyway, so it was a small loss.

At the leader's command, two of the four remaining subordinates headed toward Mavis, while the other two went for Mile and Pauline, respectively. Even if Mavis was a sword wielder, she was still a young woman. Two of them should be more than enough to keep her in check. And, while she was down, all they would have to do was thrust their swords at the noble who employed her and the maid, and the fight would be finished—all before the mage girl could turn back their way.

Smack! Smack! Thwump! Thwump!

Indeed, the bout was over in an instant. Mavis struck each of the two men with the flat of her blade, in what could perhaps be called a "side-strike" style, knocking them down entirely. Apparently, she had cooled down a bit since her initial burst of anger, so Mile stood back and left her to it. Mavis, in her right mind, would never kill anyone senselessly.

However, in that same moment, the remaining two men were still gunning for "the noble and the maid."

Gotcha! the leader thought, when suddenly, the head of the bandit who was facing the maid suddenly caught alight.

"Gaaaaaaaaaah!!!"

The man cried out, dropping his sword and writhing, his hands clutching his head. The other man, however, had seized the noble maiden around the waist and now had a sword held to her throat.

All right, that's it!

The leader was a little bit shocked to see that, somewhat improbably, the maid was a mage as well, but it was not as though people who could use at least enough magic to light small fires were rare. Now that they had the maiden as a hostage, this was little skin off of his back, anyway.

A satisfied grin on his face, the leader began to issue a decree of surrender to the young women.

"All right, ya little bastards! If y'all wanna see yer precious little mistress make it outta this alive, then..."

Just then, the captured maiden gripped the blade at her throat with the thumb and forefinger of her left hand and casually bent it away. *Crack.* The blade snapped off with a soft pop, a few inches from the guard.

"Huh?!"

The bandit hurriedly moved to draw his back-up dagger when Mile gripped the wrist of his right hand tightly.

"Owwwwwwww! Stop it! Lemme go! You're gonna break iiiiiiit!!"

After twisting the arm that was wrapped around her away

from her body, she casually landed a blow to his gut, and the man crumbled to the ground, unable to breathe.

The mage, meanwhile, had been busy beating the other three men with her staff, incapacitating them with physical power instead of magic. Then, she began walking the boss's way.

The maid had a wide, dangerous grin upon her face.

The noble maiden held her sword in her right hand, the thumb and pointer of her left hand opening and closing like a crab claw.

And the golden-haired swordswoman, who still appeared unsatisfied, swiveled her sword in wide circles in one hand.

"I surrender! I surrendeeeeeeerr!!" the leader shouted.

"Aw…" the four girls sighed.

"Wh-why do y'all sound so disappointeeeeeeeed?!?!"

"Now then, you're saying that this is only the second time you've ever attacked anyone?"

"Y-yes'm! I swear it to the Goddess!"

There were no gods or goddesses in this world, really, but their influence remained strong in the minds of individuals who did not know this. Accordingly, most soldiers, hunters, bandits, and anyone else whose lives depended on the whims of fortune were—in direct contrast to their speech and manners—actually quite devout. At the very least, praying to the divine gave them peace of mind free of charge, so there wasn't any harm in their believing—it wasn't even as though they needed to donate to any church.

"What do you think?" asked Mavis.

"Hmm," Reina thought. "All their previous victims have either been killed or sold off to places, so we have no way of confirming either way. But, I mean, a bandit's a bandit, and they'll be sent off to the mines all the same. So, why don't we just say it was these guys?"

"Wait! Waaaaaaaaaait!!" the bandit leader frantically interrupted their exchange.

The punishment mentioned was not, in fact, "all the same."

If a man had been a bandit his whole life, then he had likely committed the act around thirty times in his life before sentencing. As a result, he would probably be sentenced to hard labor, in the harshest environments possible, for the rest of his life. Of course, for better or for worse, that life would not be a very long one...

However, if he had committed the act only once before, and the victims were not killed but only sold off, still alive and able to be rescued—and if the man was able to provide tips on the illicit slave trade, then he would be assigned to jobs with far fewer hardships with a potential term of only thirty or forty years.

"It's true! There've been so many bandit attacks lately that we figured if we just did it once or twice then it'd all be blamed on those guys! But you can't pin everythin' those guys did on *our* heads! I'm beggin' ya!"

Mavis was bewildered at the man's excuse. "I can't help but wonder if the other guys were thinking the same thing..."

"No, but seriously! We've got an alibi! Most of the other attacks happened while we were on jobs or drinkin' at the pub! Even if ya turn us in, it's gonna be obvious there's still plenty of other bandits out there. Plus, even after we're captured, the attacks aren't gonna stop, so folks are gonna figure it out real quick!"

"I-I see. I guess you're right..."

She had no choice now but to accept his explanation. If they were to call the job finished here, and the attacks still continued afterward, they'd be in a bit of a pickle. Of course, they could truthfully say that they had captured some bandits, so the job would be counted as complete, but that was not a result that the members of the Crimson Vow themselves could be satisfied with.

"Let's continue!" said Mile, to nods all around.

✦◈✦

"I think this should just about do it," Mile declared.

The other three shrank back slightly but nodded.

Before them were eight bandits buried up to their necks in the dirt. As usual, they had been bound entirely with fishing line and then buried into the ground, the dirt magically packed in around them. They were then gagged and blindfolded, and their ears were covered. Thankfully, Mile had at least had the forethought to leave them a bit of a gap around their chests so that they might be able to breathe.

Before covering their ears, Mile had firmly warned them that if they should scream too loudly, their throats would dry out, and they would perish of thirst before the girls returned to collect them. Plus, if they made too much noise, beasts or monsters might hear them and come prowling. Also, as she had placed a wooden sign behind them, labeling them as bandits, they might be killed by any travelers who came upon them... And so, she posited, it was best that they kept quiet and saved their breath until the Crimson Vow returned.

The men all nodded in agreement, their faces pale; as their mouths were already stopped up with the gags, they could not respond verbally.

Just in case, she had also cut down some leafy tree branches, which she placed over their heads, and put up a barrier. Their voices and smells would be isolated, but air could still come through. Granted, as soon as Mile left, the barrier would dissipate, but it at least offered her momentary peace of mind.

"Well then, shall we be going, Mistress?"

"Indeed, let us proceed!"

"...We're still doing that?"

"You're the one who said we should..."

And so the journey of the noble maiden and her servants continued.

✧ ◈ ✧

"End of the road, girls!"

"Here we go!!!" the Crimson Vow chorused.

(As per usual, Mile's line of thought was a complete non-sequitur, as she was suddenly reminded of an old commercial for a brand of chocolate.)

This time, four men had appeared in front of them. They looked back, but there were no men behind them.

"Another miss?" asked Reina.

"Looks like it..." said Mile.

Indeed, it did seem like another miss. For as much as they had seen, it was difficult to believe that four bandits alone could have been responsible for all of the attacks that had happened up until now. It was equally difficult to believe that a larger party would not have surrounded them from behind. In other words...

"All right there, ladies, give us all yer cash!" the bandits said, grinning.

Hm...?

The Crimson Vow found this peculiar. Normally, the standard procedure here would be to capture the girls and drag them back to their base and then rob them of all their possessions at the bandits' leisure. There was no way they would let a group of pretty young girls, who would fetch a good price, slip out from under their noses, and if they intended to carry them off, then there was no reason to do something as futile as robbing them where they stood. Though bandits were not the brightest of the bunch, the men now before them appeared to be pros, so they had to know at least that much.

Plus, all they were doing now was standing before the girls.

They were not approaching, and they had left a wide gap. There was clearly something fishy going on here.

"C'mon now," said one of the men, "Give it up and do as you're told."

However, he made no moves to do anything about it. It was almost as though...

"Are they stalling?" Mile asked quietly.

"I swear," said Reina, "Why is it the wheels in your head only get turning at times like this?"

"That's Mile for you," said Mavis.

"It'd be nice if you could break that out all the time," Pauline agreed.

Apparently, the three of them had all come to the same conclusion as Mile had.

The standoff had dragged on for around ten more seconds, when suddenly, there was a strange voice from behind.

"Hold it! Hold it right there, you bandits!!!"

The Crimson Vow turned to look, and saw four more men approaching quickly from behind them. These men appeared to be hunters.

"Looks like we've got trouble," said Reina. "If we let them steal our prey, it's gonna make things more complicated. Mile, Mavis, handle this!"

"On it!" the two acknowledged.

They rushed forward, striking down the bandits in an instant. Naturally, they struck the men with the flats of their blades, just as they had with the bandits before. If they killed them, they wouldn't be able to sell them off for a reward—and besides, it caused all other sorts of issues... Er, well, they did it because it was the humane thing to do. Probably.

"Fiendish bandits! We, the Soaring Twin Dragons, shall... Uh?"

When the hunters finally made it to the scene, they found four girls standing nonchalantly before them and four bandits writhing on the ground.

"How...?"

It should have been obvious what happened, but if no one said anything, it seemed as though the frozen hunters might never move again. So Reina offered an explanation to the stunned men.

"I get the impression that you gentlemen were trying to save us. For that, you have my thanks. However, this sort of thing is barely notable for us. We'll be fine so, please, feel free to carry on your way."

The four men were stunned silent, troubled looks upon their faces.

"N-no, we couldn't possibly do that! They might try to launch a counterstrike! We will escort the bandits from here!"

"Are you trying to steal our quarry?!" shouted Pauline. "Or are you going to try and extort an escort fee out of us? You've just seen that we're more than capable of handling these men, so we have no need for your assistance! We will transport these men, and *we* will turn them over to the Guild!"

She could not forgive anyone who would try to muscle in on their hard-earned profits. There was no one who could bend the aspiring merchant's iron will when it came to such matters.

"Ngh... W-well in that case, to eliminate the danger, we should kill the bandits where they stand! C'mon!"

At the instructions of the man who appeared to be the leader, all four of the hunters drew their swords, walking toward the bandits. They then thrust the points of their swords down violently at the men, who were still prone on the ground.

Ka-clang! Clang, clang!

"Huh...?"

The four men were speechless. Though no normal hunter could have been expected to make it in time, two of the girls had deflected the men's swords, leaving them to look on, once again awestruck.

"What in the blazes do you think you're doing laying a hand on our quarry like that?!" Pauline raged. "If you kill them, *their price will go down!*"

"........"

With Pauline already having done the shouting, the other three had nothing to add, though they were thinking to themselves how peculiar it was that these hunters would be so hasty in trying to muscle in on someone else's prey.

That's suspicious...

Indeed, it was highly suspicious.

These hunters were malicious thugs if they would interfere with another hunter's quarry unprompted. If the Guild caught onto such a thing, it could be ruinous for your reputation—you could lose your qualifications as a hunter, or, should worst come to worst, be sentenced to several years' hard labor on top of that. Normally, the only sort of people who were driven to such acts were old men at the end of their wits, not young twenty-some-things like this party who still had long lives ahead of them. This was on top of the suspicious behavior of the bandits just before...

Reina turned her back to the men and gave a quick glance to the others, moving only her eyes. It was one of the signals that the group had previously established. It meant, *They might be enemies. Be on your guard.*

Seeing this, the other three moved their eyes quickly downward as surreptitiously as Reina had. *Roger that*, said their silent reply. It was subtle enough to avoid setting off alarm bells in an enemy's mind.

"What're you all looking at? Hurry up and move along," said Reina, but the men showed no signs of moving, and Mile and Mavis remained in place between the hunters and the fallen bandits. It was a natural stance to take as the men still had their drawn swords in hand.

When the men realized that the two girls' eyes were still upon their blades, they hesitated briefly. Then one of them put his sword away, and following his lead, the other three sheathed their weapons as well.

Seriously, why were they hesitating?! the four girls thought.

The bandits were all defeated and unconscious, so there was no need for these hunters to keep up their guard, weapons bran-dished. They could always draw their swords again if there was any sign of the enemies regaining consciousness. There was no way that anyone would be able to launch an immediate attack from a prone position on the ground. And yet, there they had stood, swords still in hand.

It seems like they were trying to decide whether to attack us...

Reina's train of thought was indeed not unfounded. However, though it seemed that whatever they had initially intended to do had not panned out, the men did not seem prepared to continue to force the matter. Of course, doing so would reveal them as bandits rather than the hunters they had presented themselves as since arriving on the scene.

"A-anyway, we'll go ahead and transport those bandits. It's still quite a ways to Caldile, and for four greenhorns like you to have to transport bandits that far alone would be..."

"Oh? Still on about that, are you? Awfully rude of you... The 'Soaring Twin Dragons,' was it? If you're going to continue to threaten to interfere with our hunt, we'll be reporting your attempted poaching to the Guild!"

"Er..."

That would be rather inconvenient for the men. It would be one thing if they had participated in the battle, but for them to show up after the fact and try to meddle... If they were hunters, they would face punishment for the crime of poaching prey, but civilians would be treated as plain old bandits.

"Plus, why in the world would you take those men all the way to Caldile? As you implied, it's still some days away. There's nothing but tiny villages in between here and there, with nowhere to turn them in. Wouldn't it make more sense to take them back to Zarbef, which is only a day's travel from here?"

"Er..."

For the last minute or so, the men had only been able to stammer wordlessly. Surely, they were thinking that, on a journey that took days, with several nights of camping, there were plenty of chances for them to claim, "They slipped away when we weren't looking." Of course, there was no way that the Crimson Vow would have agreed to traveling along with them in the first place—not as companions, anyway.

As captive prey, however, that was another matter...

While Reina was speaking with the men, Mile had busied herself binding the bandits. As always, in her practiced style, she used her thin and sturdy fishing line. Mavis was holding herself in a battle-ready stance, her blade ready to be drawn at any moment, and Pauline held a spell ready to fire, both prepared for an enemy strike at any moment—the enemies being not the bandits but the suspicious hunters, of course.

Mile then withdrew some smelling salts from her inventory, pretending to produce them from a pocket, and held them under the bandit leader's nose to rouse him. She had prepared an ammonia-like medicine, in case of just such an occasion.

"Uh... Ugh..."

The leader awoke, groaning.

"Wh-where am I...?"

"You're on the highway, where we just captured you and the rest of your bandit group. We're very grateful to you lot—you're going to make us a lot of money and then work in service of the country doing hard labor for the rest of your life."

"Wha...?" The man slowly processed Mile's words, seemingly still in a daze. "Wait! Wait just a minute! We ain't bandits! We were just asked to..."

Suddenly, the man noticed the four hunters and shut his mouth.

"What sore losers you all are. You can't try and tell me that after you were clearly performing bandit-like acts. You're just lucky we didn't go ahead and kill you right off the bat, like these hunters over here urged us to do."

The hunters, to whom Mile gestured, suddenly began to go pale. And so, of course, did the bandit leader.

"Wh-wh-wh-wh-what did you say?!" he screamed in disbelief. "Y-you backstabbers!"

Just as planned. Mile spoke again, to be doubly sure.

"Just before, while you were unconscious, those men tried to stab you right through, but luckily we stopped them! My, that sure was risky! We stopped them, like, just in the nick of time—for real!"

"Y-you bastards..."

The hunters unconsciously retreated a few steps as the leader glared daggers at them.

"Well, it seems there's been some kind of setup here," said Mile. "As it stands, I guess you'll all be facing a nice long life in the mines. Still, is there anything you'd like to say in your defense? We'll listen."

Faced with the prospect of a life of hard labor, the leader's lips suddenly loosened.

"We aren't bandits! We're just humble woodcutters! Those men there hired us on. They told us, 'There's a group of defenseless and stupid young girls trying to leave town without hiring an escort, so we need you to intimidate them into hiring someone. It's an act of mercy.' It seemed like all they really wanted to do was promote themselves for the job, but we figured that, being that there really have been bandits around, it was in your ladies' best interest. Plus, we were gettin' paid for it, so it should've been a win for everyone involved... They told us that the only one in yer group with any kind of battle sense was an apprentice knight—they never said anything about y'all having the skill to defeat us all in the blink of an eye!"

The hunters fell silent as he stared them down.

"Is all that true?" asked Mile. "If it is, and there's really no evidence that you were attempting to act as bandits—and furthermore, that you were merely trying to do a job out of goodwill, with no ill intent—then this will probably just end with these men here getting a good scolding from the authorities... Assuming we don't press charges, that is. However, if you're lying to me, you'll end up in the mines for the rest of your life. So, give it to me straight: is all that true, every word?"

Hearing Mile's speech, the hunters now saw that they had a chance of being pardoned for their charges of banditry, and their eyes glistened hopefully. The man who seemed like the leader began to frantically offer his petition.

"I-It's true! You all said that you were going to be traveling on a road where bandits had been appearing without hiring an escort, so we wanted to persuade you to hiring someone for your own safety! I'm not lying, I swear to you!"

In fact, the man probably *was* telling the truth. Even if they intended something sly like ripping the girls off by charging a higher rate for an emergency on-site job or trying to get them to tack on some additional services later—or even if they thought they might try and persuade Mile and her storage magic into their party if possible—none of that would directly contradict the appeal that the men had made. If all they truly intended from the outset was to intimidate the girls into hiring an escort, not actually steal from them, then the offense was mild enough as to not break Guild regulations or bring criminal charges.

Of course, pretending to be bandits in order to intimidate the girls was still a bit out of line, but they probably assumed that so long as they were not discovered as accomplices while doing their "gallant rescuers" act, then they would be fine.

"Deceiving you girls as we did was unforgivable, of course, but we were prepared to get our hands dirty if it was for your safety. We thought that the ends justified the means and that the Goddess would forgive us. You all would agree, wouldn't you?" prattled the leader, looking self-satisfied.

"Hmm, I suppose you might be right. That's not an unnatural course of action to take, if you were worried about us... Very well. We will put in a good word for the men who were playing the bandit role so that hopefully they'll be dealt with more leniently."

"Thank you so much. You're really helping us out of a tight

spot here. Now, we'll all travel back to Zarbef with the woodcutters, and there we'll go our separate ways..."

"Hm? What are you talking about?" Mile asked suspiciously. "The woodcutters were simply pawns in this scheme, but we're still taking *you* in as criminals and handing you over to the authorities via the Guild."

"Huh? I mean, I know it was rotten of us to deceive you, but you do understand that we did it from a place of good will, right? Plus, we never intimidated you or raised a sword against you ourselves—we acted as your allies from the very beginning. If you've already forgiven us for lying, then what's the problem here?" the leader petitioned frantically.

Mile casually replied, "Yes, well, that is indeed true in regards to your actions toward *us*, but you did try to murder those woodcutters to silence them, even knowing that they were not actually bandits, but in fact people that you yourselves had hired to complete a job. The way you were thrusting those swords, if Mavis and I hadn't stopped you, you really would have struck and killed those men. In other words, you attempted murder. Anyway, trying to kill someone you hired just to save your own skins is an incredibly malicious act in and of itself... A felony, in fact."

"Ah..."

The hunters swiftly saw their error, but it was too late to make amends now.

"You all do appear to be hunters, so I'm sure you'll be receiving punishment from both the Guild and the town guard. Now then, if you'll just keep calm, and..."

"Now!" cried the leader.

"Okay!" replied the other three.

And with that, they all drew their swords.

At this rate, after all that they had done, the best they could hope for was merely to have their reputations ruined. They might be stripped of their qualifications as hunters, likely sentenced to serve ten or twenty years in hard labor as penance for their actions. The way things had turned out for them, they would have been better off turning to banditry for real, capturing the girls, and selling them off to another country. Not only were the four of them an attractive set, that set included a young noble maiden who had storage magic of a ridiculously high capacity. They would be certain to fetch an immense price on the black market.

Besides, the hunters could count on their friends, the idiotic woodcutters, to take all the blame. If they killed the men and buried them here, people would assume that they had taken to banditry, kidnapped the girls, and fled the country with them. That would be that. It was possible that the woodcutters might not even be tied to the crime, and the whole thing could be passed off as the work of normal bandits.

All these assumptions made, the hunters now brandished their blades for the sake of their lives and their livelihoods.

"Ah... There's the chink in the armor," Pauline said, brandishing her staff with a sinister grin. "When you all tried to plunge your swords into those men, your movements were far too swift, too coordinated. And here again now, when you drew your swords, not one of you hesitated for even a moment. Normally, among a group of four, there would be at least one or two who would hesitate to murder a group of mock bandits who they themselves had hired or balk at the idea of turning their swords on a group of innocent young ladies who were not even hunters. And yet, none of you even batted an eye... This isn't the first time that you all have attacked civilians, is it?"

"Sh-shut up! What the hell are you implying?! Whatever. It's not like any of this changes how things are gonna end up for you all! And here we thought you'd be good little girls and hire us on, but I guess you're too stupid for that. We thought we might be able to get Little Miss Storage there to join our group, but it looks like we're gonna have to just sell her off somewhere now. A bit of a shame there, but I guess we've got no choice..."

They probably intended Mile's 'recruitment' into the group to be compulsory. There was no other way that they could have managed to bring a girl of noble birth into their party. Of course, what they had intended to do with the other three was anyone's guess...

Apparently, these men were even more malicious than the Crimson Vow had initially supposed.

"Well, I guess that's how it's going to be, then. Miley, Mavis, if you would."

"On it!"

The men seemed not to have been paying very close attention to what had happened when the girls struck down the woodcutters. They were still a short distance away at the time, and Mile and Mavis had moved too quickly to track. Therefore, all they knew was that the woodcutters had been defeated—a fact that, in and of itself, was not particularly surprising. They may have been pretending to be brigands, but they were still just woodcutters, total amateurs in battle. Even if she were still at an apprentice level, it was clear that a trained knight would have no trouble defeating a group like them. Of course, they had also assumed that the young lady had been hired on as a ward against attacks and that an apprentice knight would not deign to challenge four bandits all alone, of her own accord. Besides, they never thought that the woodcutters would actually try to attack or harm the girls on their own.

Finally, the men had assumed that they should be able to maintain eye contact with the woodcutters for the scant seconds that it would take them to come running, so there was no worry of the plan going askew. They never suspected that the knight would challenge an enemy four times her own number without waiting for the rescue that was already on its way.

At any rate, they had still evaluated that the only enemy worth considering was the apprentice knight, not taking into account either the noble with the sword in her hand or the staff-wielding child and maid. Surely, as C-rank hunters, they would be stronger than the knight, and there were four of them to boot. So really, why *should* they have worried?

"Mavis, Mile, finish them!" Reina commanded.

"Okay!"

"On it!"

The command that she had just unleashed was very much like that which might be issued by one of the figures that appeared in

Mile's Japanese folktales, such as Lady Penelope Creighton-Ward, or Freiza, or Doronjo. It was a phrase that they had heard so often that by this point it had been drilled into the other girls' heads. Following that command, Mile and Mavis drew their swords.

Cling clang! Smack! Smack!

The sounds of clanging metal rang out in concurrent sets of two, and suddenly the four hunters collapsed to the ground. Naturally, they had been struck with the sides of the girls' blades, so their lives were not in danger.

With some rare exceptions, Western-style swords were a lot sturdier than swords of Japanese make, so even if they were used in an unorthodox manner such as this one, there was little chance of them breaking—particularly if they were enhanced by nano-machines, such as these were.

"All righty! Time to go ahead and bury them," said Reina.

The other three nodded.

✧ ◈ ✧

"It's just one false lead after another..." Mavis grumbled.

"Well, to be fair, if we ran into those guys *after* we'd dealt with the real ones, it would be a problem for our reputation. People would doubt whether we really had handled the problem, y'know? So really, it's better that we tie up all the loose ends beforehand," said Reina.

Mile and Pauline nodded in agreement. If there were two groups of bandits, and they dealt with one group while the other was still active, people would most certainly doubt their capabilities. *Did they actually exterminate those first bandits?* other hunters would wonder. *Did the bandits actually let some innocent people get captured in their stead?* And so on and so forth.

As they had initially planned, the girls continued on toward the town of Caldile, leaving the second group of offenders trapped in dirt, just as the first group had been.

The woodcutters were buried alongside the hunters. They still needed to be handed over to the authorities for a scolding, and even if the girls were to ask their names, the men could give them false identities. This was the natural course of action. Of course, the woodcutters had already given their side of the story, but as far as legal proceedings were concerned, at the moment they were still as good as bandits, and their claims were the protests of criminals. It was not out of the question to deal with them accordingly.

Plus, even if the Vow would testify as to the extenuating circumstances involved, it was not up to them to decide on anyone's punishment. The men were not hunters, so while they would not receive any penalties from the Guild, the town guards would sentence them, and as such, their punishment had nothing to do with the Crimson Vow.

That said, the Vow had at least covered their victims' heads with a metal cage this time, so that they would not be killed by beasts. Naturally, a barrier spell had been furnished as well. That would be enough to keep them safe for at least a little while.

After the girls had been walking for about ten minutes...

"Halt!"

A man who appeared to be a traveler had been resting atop a boulder on the side of the highway. Suddenly, he stood and held up his hand, and a crowd of vulgar-looking men appeared from around the bend behind him.

The fish were really biting today. Must have been some pretty tasty bait...

"Well now, here comes another one..." said Mavis.

A Pnumekin?

As always, Mile's mind conjured up a reference that no one else could possibly hope to understand.

They look back to see a number of men piling up behind them also. There were ten-odd men in front and five or six behind. These numbers were roughly comparable to what they had guessed, based on the reports of the attacks so far.

"Looks like these guys are the real deal," said Reina, and the other three nodded. It was highly unlikely that multiple bandit squads of this number would all be launching attacks in the same place.

It was quite fortunate that they would be able to wrap this up on the very first day—fortunate for all the buried men, that was. If they weren't dug up soon, they might just take root and start to grow. Or start rotting away. Well, first an eye might sprout up and then some teeth would grow, the nose would blossom, and then... Mile suddenly realized that Reina had made a joke along very similar lines some time ago, back when Mile had gone to investigate the fallen golem. It would be one thing if she were doing a parody or an homage or respectful nod, but Mile would not tolerate herself stealing someone's thunder with wholesale plagiarism.

We should probably get back and retrieve them before worms start crawling out of those blossoming noses, anyway...

Unfortunately for the men, Mile, in all of her genius, had neglected to consider what effects their imprisonment would have on their physiology...

"Insolent whelps! You must be well and truly addled!" Finally back in the moment, Mile spewed out a speech fit for one of her folktales. "Have you any idea what greatness stands before you?!"

At her words, Reina and Mavis were spewing internally. Some two-bit daughter of a poor noble household could hardly refer to herself as a thing of "greatness." If she were a princess, it would be another matter, but a princess she was not. Luckily, this was all a part of Mile's plan to determine just how much information the bandits had about them.

"Tch, some low-class nothing like you, *great?!* Don't make me laugh! If yer travelin' around without even so much as a guard then I bet your family don't care anythin' for you, storage or no, little Missy. We've got a much better place ready for you!"

Mile was frozen in place, mouth half-ajar at how utterly simple her own intelligence-gathering had been and how comprehensive the information was. Just like that, they could confirm that the men were aware of everything that they had said back in the guildhall. The other three grimaced.

There was no need for the Crimson Vow to investigate the method by which the men had come by the information. That was something for the bandits to give up on their own once they had been captured, and extracting that information was a job for the Guild and the guards. All the Vow had to do here was to apprehend them. Ascertaining the source of the leak would be nothing more than a bonus service, a way to safeguard themselves for the future by learning where any remaining forces might lurk. Thus, the only choice here was to take out every last one of them.

"Now then, shall we?"

"Yeah!!!"

"Now now, little ladies," said one of the bandits, "ain't no point in resisting here. Just be good and surrender. We won't do anything bad to ya. We won't hurt or kill ya. In fact, we're gonna send you ladies off to some folks who'll take nice, good care of ya."

"That's plenty bad enough!!!" the Vow chorused in reply.

Mile folded her arms and nodded in approval at their beautifully coordinated rebuttal. The fruits of conditioning the others with her Japanese folktales were finally starting to ripen.

"Enough of yer grousin', just hurry up and..."

"Firebomb!"

Ka-boom!

"GYAAAAAAAAAAAAAAH!!!"

"Ice Storm!!!"

Blamcrackleshinkshunkbambambam!

"WAH! GYEH! GWAAH!!!"

Reina's explosive fire crashed into the bandits from the front while Pauline's ice attack showered the men from behind. While Pauline's favored area attack was the "Hot" spell, it was not the only trick up her sleeve. She could use water, wind, and fire magic to various degrees; it simply happened that, unlike Reina, she was better at water magic than fire. Furthermore, this time they were not on their home turf, and she was using her spell against a number of people who were going to be questioned later, so it was more prudent to put aside her unique spell in favor of more standard ice and wind magic.

Numerous fist-sized balls of ice were whipped up into a maelstrom on magical winds. In this pattern, the ice would not pelt the men once, but again and again until the ice melted, or the magic stopped... Even if the ice were to break on impact, meaning that damage from each individual hit might decrease, the chunks of ice that would hit the bandits would then be twice as many.

Next, Mile and Mavis rushed in. Mile went to the front, while Mavis took the rear. Reina had limited her attack on the men at the front to a power level at which they would not be killed or injured seriously enough as to lose any limbs, and so, only about a third of them were unable to fight. The other two-thirds were in various conditions: some unhurt, some limping, and some with their arms dangling numbly.

It was highly unlikely that any bandit crew would include mages who were skilled enough to use their magic in battle, so for this group to pit themselves against the Crimson Vow, who had three mages in their group, was reckless. Well, really, even if the bandits had *ten* mages, their efforts would have been equally futile...

Meanwhile, the men at the back were still standing, but they were all equally bedraggled. Pauline's ice had effectively engulfed everyone standing within its radius. Thanks to this, all of the men's battle capabilities had been significantly compromised—though, honestly, this made little difference to Mavis and her True Godspeed Blade. A normal C-rank hunter could handle perhaps two bandits, but Mavis could take down five or six bandits in top form as easily as swatting a fly. By nature, bandits tended to favor an indolent, carefree life. Lacking the diligence to become a soldier, the sincerity and patience to become a merchant or artisan, and the skill to become a hunter, they were typically negligent in both effort and training.

After all, if they were actually strong, they would have at least become hunters, not bandits. The bar to enter the Hunters' Guild was incredibly low.

And so, the battle—or rather, the one-sided massacre—was over in the blink of an eye. All it had taken was a few strikes from the sides of Mile and Mavis's blades to strike the men down. After the opening blows, Reina and Pauline's job was done. Then all they had to do was sit back and watch.

Of course, Reina was still holding an attack spell, and Pauline a healing one, just in case. The healing spell was for the bandits, in case Mile or Mavis "accidentally, unintentionally" overdid it. And yet, the confrontation was over, and the bandits were successfully apprehended without the opportunity for Pauline to use her healing magic ever arising.

This time, Mile bound the men not with fishing line but with normal rope. There were a lot of them, and she got the feeling that they might resist being forced to migrate, so she was worried that if they struggled too hard within the fishing line, their fingers or even their heads might pop right off.

They'd fall like ripened fruit. That's so grooooooooosss!!!

Mile was truly a girl of many worries.

Soon it would start growing dark, but they could not make camp now. Still, there was no way that they could make it back to Zarbef tonight, especially given the matter of the men entombed along the way. Naturally, Mile had no intention of making them spend the night like that. She didn't mind if they ended up a bit perturbed over the experience, but it would leave a bad taste in her mouth if they were attacked and killed by wild animals, and it would be creepy if worms started crawling from them...They would probably smell pretty bad, too.

Therefore, Mile proposed that they at least get back to the spots where she had buried the men, a proposal to which everyone agreed. After Mile applied her smelling salts, Mavis used a judo-like resuscitation technique, and Pauline and Reina kicked them in the sides repeatedly, all the unconscious men finally awakened. The men who had not passed out looked on, their faces drawn.

"Now then, let's get moving! Hurry up and follow me!" Mile said, pulling the rope holding the bandits behind her. However, the bandits did not seem particularly interested in complying with her instructions.

Of course, this was no surprise. When they arrived in town, what awaited them was a lifetime of servitude, probably in the harshest locations possible. It was only to be expected that they would waste the girls' time by grousing, hoping to invite negligence or give them time to launch a counterattack and escape. No matter how strong these girls might be, they were still just four little girls. Even with their hands tied, if the men rushed them all at once at a short enough range as not to grant their captors time to incant a spell or draw a sword, or if they pulled the ropes free from the girls and ran in different directions all at once, there was still a chance that they might be able to do something. Their feet were not tied, after all.

Thinking this, the bandits made the unilateral decision not to walk. However...

Drag.

"Huh?"

Drag drag drag...

"Whaaaaaaaaat?!?!"

The bandits suddenly found themselves being dragged along the ground by the rope in Mile's hand.

"Oww! That huuuuuurts!!"

Even if the road was not paved with asphalt, the packed dirt still had rocky portions, pebbles scattered here and there. It was a bit like getting dragged along a cheese grater. Straight away the bandits found themselves scraped and bleeding.

"Wait! We'll stand up! Please just wait!"

The bandit's sudden fearful cry came less from a place of being shocked at the superhuman strength Mile must possess to drag all of them on her own and more at being unable to bear the pain of being dragged violently across the ground.

Still, there was no use in showing kindness to thugs like this. Even after standing, they did not seem particularly inclined to walk, so Reina hurled a firebomb beside them.

"Gah!"

"Wh-what're you tryin' to do?!"

It had been a small firebomb, using the bare minimum of her power, but if it had hit the men head-on it would not have been pretty. They would not have died, but losing a limb or two would have been unavoidable.

The first bomb had struck into the ground about a meter from the bandits, but then there came a second at 60 centimeters' distance, then 30, inching closer and closer by degrees. And the fourth would...

Frantically, the bandits began to walk.

Still, given that it did not appear they would be camping for the night, the men were probably already scheming, planning what they would do during their march the next day when they were nearer to town. If they dragged their feet enough, they might not make it to town the next day, either...

Realizing this, a look of utter boredom spread across the Crimson Vow's faces.

No matter how skilled they might be at battle, there was no avoiding menial tasks such as this one.

✧◈✧

"Huh, there's two riders coming up, moving at high speed. Let's clear the road!" Mile announced.

For once, she had learned this not with her surveillance magic but with her own two eyes. They pulled the roped bandits to the side of the road to open up the path.

"Oh hey, those guys are probably heading toward Zarbef, too! Why don't we ask them to forward a message to the Guild? They'll probably be making camp soon, but they'll still arrive in town well before we do tomorrow. If we play our cards right, we might even be able to get the Guild to send out reinforcements..."

"Hm, I wonder..." said Mavis. "They seem like they're in a hurry. If they're knights or high-speed couriers or something like that, they'll probably just ignore us..."

"Still," said Pauline, "no point in giving up from the start. Never hurts to ask."

"Seriously though," chimed Reina, "we have no idea if they'll even stop for us to begin with, so let's not hem and haw over it now. It's not like we can block the road and force them to stop, anyway."

The girls all fretted, waiting to see if the riders would even stop to speak with them. The two riders approached and then halted as they reached the girls and the bandits, before they even had a chance to pass them by.

"Just who are you lot?!" shouted one of the men.

Judging by their dress, the riders were not knights or couriers but hunters.

Mile casually replied, "Oh, we're just travelers. We captured some bandits who attacked us, so we were planning on taking them back to Zarbef in the morning. We were hoping that, if you all are going to Zarbef, if you would put in a request for the Hunters' Guild to send out some reinforcements...?"

"Hm...?"

The riders appeared perplexed. There were seventeen or eighteen men attached to the ropes and four young women, two of whom still appeared to be underage. The riders were frozen in place, eyes wide and jaws slack, as they took in the whole scene.

When the men finally recovered, the members of the Crimson Vow were able to speak with them and learned that the two men were the advance scouts for a party of hunters who had taken a job escorting a merchant caravan, riding ahead to make sure that there were no enemies lying in wait. Naturally, it was prudent of them to come and investigate the group of around twenty people who had been spotted not far ahead of their party.

If they saw anything suspicious, they were to turn around just before they reached them and go back to tell the others, but as this did not appear to be a bandit ambush in the making, they had approached, ready to turn around and ride back at any time, if necessary.

If possible, the merchants were hoping to reach Zarbef tomorrow while it was still light, so they intended to travel a bit farther tonight, even after sunset, to cover a little more distance and save time the next day. Traveling through the woods in the dark was its own matter, but traveling along the highway in the dark was no big deal, really. Of course, they still could not push it *too* far, as traveling in the pitch-black raised the risk of the horses slipping and hurting their legs.

After the Crimson Vow explained the situation, the riders were surprised, but they agreed to the party's request before riding back to the rest of their troop.

"Don't you think they bought that a little too easily?" asked Mile as the men rode away. "If we were allied with the bandits, we could just wait until the merchants showed up and suddenly have the bandits slip out of their ropes, drawing concealed swords or something. They didn't even consider that..."

"Don't be a dummy. If we were trying to deceive them, do you really think we'd tell them some tall tale about four civilian girls capturing nearly twenty bandits all on our own?" replied Reina, shooting Mile down. "If we wanted to deceive them, we'd have to tell them a bit of a better lie than that. This isn't one of your Japanese folktales, after all..."

A short while later, the mid-sized merchant caravan finally arrived from behind them. There were twelve wagons with two riders on horseback at the front and back. Naturally, they could be expected to have ten or more other guards, at the very least, within the wagons themselves.

The caravan caught up with the girls and then stopped. A man who appeared to be a merchant, along with an elderly hunter, disembarked from a wagon that was near the center of the lineup.

Judging by the circumstances, these two appeared to be the representative of the merchants and the leader of the guards.

"Greetings," said the merchant-looking man, "I am Cerivos, representative of this caravan. On behalf of everyone, I extend to you our deepest thanks for capturing these bandits, the most dire enemies to our trade... That said..."

Cerivos looked over the bound bandits, clearly stunned at the circumstances.

"Honestly, I can't even believe my own eyes..."

His surprise was to be expected. The other guards, descending from their wagons, were similarly wide-eyed and paralyzed with shock. If ordinary girls like these could wipe out a group of bandits all on their own, then what place did guards like them have in the world?

Still, there was little chance of this caravan, with its four guards on horseback and ten or more riding in the wagons, being attacked by some bandit army of four-score men; such groups scarcely existed in the first place. There were rarely targets that would fetch that much of a profit this far from the capital, on the roads near some backwater town, and such activity would warrant the attention of the local lord—or even the Crown, if the bandits were particularly unlucky.

Therefore, given that there was such a small chance of this particular caravan getting into any scuffles with bandits to begin with, the thanks that Cerivos offered was not on the behalf of their group specifically but on the behalf of merchants as a whole.

"It seems like a huge bother to transport all these men with just you four—and dangerous, to boot. We would like to do everything that we can to help. We'll camp the night here with you," Cerivos proposed.

"Oh, thank you so much!" Mile happily replied. "This is a huge help! We do need to travel just a little bit farther before we make camp, though..."

From the get-go, Cerivos had already intended to travel a bit farther before nightfall, so he had no objections. And so, with the bandits lashed by their necks to the wagons, forcing them to walk at the wagons' pace lest they be strangled, in the "Pauline bandit-transporting style," the newly formed party proceeded down the road.

✧◈✧

"........."

The merchants watched, eyes filled with dread, as the Crimson Vow magically excavated first the second group of attackers, the mock bandits, and then the first group, the newbie bandits, from their dirt prisons. Cerivos and the three merchants, twelve drivers, and sixteen guards (including the two original riders) all stood, wide-eyed and wordless, at these scenes.

To leave someone not only buried in the dirt up to their neck but with the dirt around them magically packed in, leaving them utterly defenseless to the wilds in the middle of the forest on the side of the highway, was a hellish act, the horror of which was beyond the pale of the imagination. What if wild beasts or monsters found them? What if they were left there and help never arrived? It was too frightening to think about.

Plus, even if the men *were* found, who knew how much time it would take to safely excavate the magically packed dirt? It was highly unlikely that any traveler who chanced to pass by would just so happen to be carrying a hoe or a pickaxe. More than likely they would simply give up, saying, "I'll inform the Guild when I reach the next town!" and run away as fast as they could.

And of course, even in that scenario, the men did have signs beside them proclaiming, "These guys are bandits," so their prospects were rather dim.

The biggest problem here—though, of course, it was not really a *problem* per se—was the fact that the immensely strong individuals, who had captured three separate groups of bandits without so much as a scratch, were four little girls who appeared to be nothing more than average civilians.

"The meat's ready! The soup is done, too!"

The noble girl had produced everything from ingredients to cookware to tableware, all from her storage.

Her maid had not only used magic, the likes of which they had never seen before, to cleanse and purify the clothing and bodies of the bandits who had soiled themselves, but she had also healed one of the drivers' wounds instantaneously when they stopped to repair a wagon wheel.

The apprentice knight had prepared the kindling for their bonfire in the blink of an eye, not by gathering it—oh no, but by chopping a fallen tree into logs with her own blade. Normally, swords capable of performing such a feat were not forged, and even if they were, no mortal who possessed the power and skill to complete the task existed. Or rather, they *should* not have existed.

At least, the redhead who had lit the fire felt normal. In this, the caravan group found their one, sole comfort.

It was better that they were unaware of the truth. What they didn't know couldn't hurt them...

✧◈✧

"Breakfast is ready!"

The next morning, Mile furnished breakfast for the caravan, just as she had with dinner the night before, a meal that had been sumptuous, full of fresh meat and vegetables. They had only just departed Zarbef the previous morning, so it was believable that they would still have fresh ingredients in storage and equally feasible that if they were turning back toward town anyway, that they would rather use these ingredients up before they went back. However, the amount that the girl had stored was, in and of itself, still flabbergasting.

The four merchants, including Cerivos, looked at Mile with an envious gaze. The hunters, who had seen her pull out an entire orc the night before, had their eyes peeled also.

Once they had finished breakfast, Mile raised a request to Cerivos. She wished for him to send one of the riders ahead to the Guild, carrying a letter she had penned the night before.

"Of course!" he replied. "Leave it to us!"

The thought that Mile and the others might be plotting something did not cross the man's mind once. Having just one fewer guard present out of over a dozen made little difference to their defense. With the fighting force they currently had among them, it would take many scores of bandits to bring them down.

The captured bandits' physical states and the ropes that bound them had been double-checked when securing them to the wagons. The almost fanatic way in which they had been bound was not something they would be able to worm their way out of anytime soon.

Plus, there was no reason that a group like these girls, with their excessive storage, healing magic, and swordsmanship, would ever have to turn to a life of crime just for money. Cerivos would stake ten gold on that.

At some point, shortly after noon, a number of riders on horseback appeared from the road ahead, stopping just before the caravan.

"I am the guild master of the Hunters' Guild of Zarbef!"

It was obvious that if one requested assistance from the Hunters' Guild on such matters, one would generally receive it. What was more surprising, however, was that the guild master himself had arrived on the scene.

The guarding hunters and the merchants relaxed, and the caravan halted. The newly arrived riders approached, all of them climbing down from their horses in front of the Vow, who were still on foot.

"I presume you all are the ones who sent this letter? Well, judging by what I can see here, it's pretty clear you weren't deceiving us..." said the guild master, looking warily over the leashed bandits.

Though the girls had never seen this particular guild master before, as usual, he was an older man, middle-aged, perhaps approaching elderly. After all, it normally took about that long to acquire the skills and knowledge that such a position required. It wasn't a job that any young whippersnapper fresh out of D-rank could do.

"So, there are three bandit groups here," Mavis explained in her capacity as leader. "One is the real group, and the other two are just small fry. Please see to it that the arrangements are as we wrote."

"Sure thing," said the guild master with a nod. "Good work here. You can leave the rest to us."

Of course, the wagons that would transport the bandits moved slowly. Until they could all be assembled on site, the group would have to continue the way they were for a little while longer. After speaking with the merchants briefly, the guild master, two of the men who had accompanied him, the chief of the real bandits, and two of his subordinates, all clambered into the first wagon. The guards who were riding in that wagon climbed out, and three of them took up the horses that the guild master's crew had rode in on.

The reason for this soon became obvious, as a short while after the caravan began moving again, there rang a bloodcurdling scream from within the first wagon. However, none of the rest of the party paid it any mind... At least, none of the merchants' group or the men who arrived with the guild master.

Yes, the only ones who showed any distress were the other bandits and the members of the Crimson Vow.

Sometime after that, they rendezvoused with the transport wagons. After seeing that all of the bandits were loaded in and issuing a strict gag order to the merchants, the guild master left the transport to his subordinates and started his own ride back to Zarbef.

✧ ◈ ✧

"We shall now begin the official inquiry regarding the bandit activities occurring in the vicinity of the town of Zarbef."

It was three days later, in the manor of the lord who governed the territory in which Zarbef was situated. Within the grand hall, which usually housed balls and parties, something akin to a trial was now taking place. It would be a great bother to examine each of the three bandit groups one by one, so they had all been gathered in the same place.

The officials present were as follows: the prosecutor (a retainer of the lord), the chief justice (a retainer of the lord), and the presiding judge (also a retainer of the lord). None of these men were specialized in their positions; they were merely vassals of the lord who had been temporarily appointed to these roles. In terms of legal counsel—there was none. Thus, this was a perfectly fair and honest trial (or something like it).

A trial of this scale was a rare thing to see in a backwater fief like this, and so the usual courthouse was far too small for it. Normally, petty criminals would just be handled in the military barracks, but for this occasion they chose to use the manor proper. Within the lord's domain, all branches of power—legislative, executive, and judicial—lay within the lord's hands. The bulk of the questioning had already been completed before the event, so this was merely for the sake of making a formal and public announcement of the findings... Or so it would be, normally.

Because a portion of the defendants in this case were members of the Guild, the guild master and several other guild employees were present in the gallery, along with the master and several employees of the Merchants' Guild. Also present were two B-rank parties from the town and about ten other citizens. Even if they already fully expected the sentence the lord's men might hand down, they were poised and ready to protest any punishment that they found to be outrageous—a role that they could not neglect. The fact that they were allowed to do so was proof of the fact that the lord was a just man.

The lord himself could not influence the trial, but as he appeared to have great interest in this particular one, he sat to the side in a special seat that had been furnished, watching.

After a brief confirmation of the charges, the announcement was made first to the main bandit crew.

"You have all been issued an A-rank lifetime sentence of hard labor."

The bandits were stoic and unflinching. Reacting would have

achieved nothing. There could have been no other sentence for them, and considering the circumstances, what difference did it make if they were sentenced to a term of life or of 800 years? It was improbable that anyone would take extenuating circumstances into account in the case of such a blatant offense. The fact that they were not given capital punishment was something they should be grateful for.

Unless there were no other options, criminals were not usually sentenced to death. The only individuals to receive a sentence of execution were typically those who might refuse to labor seriously out of defiance, as well as bloodthirsty fiends, mages (whose escape would be difficult to prevent), and those who committed crimes against nobles or royals—individuals of particularly malicious intent.

Naturally, the fact that mages had so very many avenues by which they could make ends meet contributed to why there were so few magically adept criminals. However, the fact that they were so much more likely to be sentenced to death if caught also played a huge factor. Even if one were to bind and gag a mage upon capture, there was still the chance of them suddenly attacking with a wordless spell, so many, fearing this, were not particularly inclined to grant them any leeway.

Indeed, most mage criminals, when caught, were dispatched immediately at the scene of the crime—even if they were not particularly competent or the crime they had committed was relatively trivial.

The sentencing continued.

"E-rank hunter, Ivick, you are sentenced to death. Hunters' Guild employee Dallam, you are likewise sentenced to death. Furthermore, Dallam's family will be sentenced to twenty years of hard labor."

"P-please wait! I don't care what you do to me, but, my *family?!* My wife and daughter?! They have nothing to do with what I've done here!!!"

The judge who had announced the decision brushed off the protest without so much as a reply. No voice was raised from the gallery either.

The fact that Ivick was registered as a hunter did not mean that the Guild was cooperating with the bandits, but rather, that one of the bandits had secretly registered as a hunter. His role was to gather information and forward the intel he got from Dallam to the other bandits.

The Hunters' Guild was an organization whose trade was built on reputation. They were an international enterprise, spanning across borders. When their rules were violated, they were not a group who let bygones by bygones. They did not have the authority to directly interfere with the official decision, but they carried enough clout that it would be easy enough for them to put pressure on the lord. That said, it was not something that they would go out of their way to do, and a capital punishment was more than customary in cases such as this one.

Then, there was Dallam, the guild employee who had raised the objection.

According to his interrogation, the bandits had threatened to harm his family, and this much did appear to be true. However...

He had betrayed the Guild. That fact was not something that could be undone or ignored.

If he was being threatened, then he had a duty to report it to the guild master. As it stood, not only had he not reported this, but he had dutifully obeyed the criminals, forwarding information that had led to the murders and kidnappings of countless innocent travelers. Furthermore, though the money was only a pittance, it appeared that he had been paid for the intel he provided.

So that no one in the future would ever think to do the same thing "for the sake of his family," none present could bring themselves to excuse his relations. Thus, the logical argument would be that, even if he was merely following orders, he had still damned his own wife and daughter, and that the only correct choice in his position would have been to report the matter to the authorities immediately.

Dallam was an accomplice to countless murders, and if his family was his reason for this, then by extension, his wife and daughter were guilty of the same crime. In Japan, such reasoning would be utterly unacceptable, but in a civilization where order was weak and recognition of human rights was slim, such measures were necessary to ensure the safety of the general populace.

Of course, in the past on Earth, there were also places that utilized a similar system of guilt by association. In some nations, this persists even to the present day. Likewise, in this world, it seemed it was only a matter of course that Dallam was inviting trouble upon the shoulders of his family by granting them a direct connection to his crime and putting them in a position where they benefitted from his actions. The fact that no one observing the proceedings, save Dallam himself, had made so much as a peep, was a testament to that.

Ivick the infiltrator and Dallam the traitor.

The Crimson Vow had been summoned by the guild master before the caravan had arrived in town, with the express purpose of allowing him to extract the true identities of the two and apprehend the two before they had a chance to flee. Within that first wagon, he had tortur—er, *questioned*—the bandits for the identities of their two accomplices and then returned to town to arrest them, arriving back before the caravan had arrived.

For the bandit leader, a life sentence of hard labor was as certain as his capture, but the off chance of him receiving a death sentence was not entirely out of the question. Therefore, all it took was a little bit of pain to make him talk. Really, the fact that he did not squeal immediately was merely a bit of posturing, for the sake of looking good in front of his subordinates.

Up next were the rookie bandits, the first to have been captured.

"C-rank hunters, the 'Hurricanes of Flame.' As you have committed the act of banditry twice, it has been judged that this was not an impulse but something that you intended to make a habit of. However, we have taken into consideration the fact that in truth, there is only one set of victims of your crimes. You killed no men, merely selling all your victims into illicit slavery, from which they can be recovered. Thus, you have been sentenced to a B-rank lifetime sentence of hard labor. Furthermore, if all of the victims are able to be recovered safely with your cooperation, your sentencing shall be reevaluated and reduced to a C-rank sentence, or your term of service diminished appropriately."

The C-rank hunters of the 'Hurricanes of Flame' bowed deeply, tears welling in their eyes. Their sentencing had been far more generous than expected, given that their heinous crimes—banditry and human trafficking—were two-fold. Given how much the trafficking had been emphasized, however, it was clear that the fact that they had not killed the men of the party, who were troublesome and would sell for very little, had left quite the good impression, showing that they were still decent men, at least in some sick, twisted way...

A C-rank lifetime sentence of hard labor was really not such a bad thing at all. The work would not be so unbearable, and there was little chance of being killed on the job. They might be provided with ale now and then, and while it was rather rare, if luck was on their side and their behavior was good, they might be awarded a clerical position. Better yet, if they could be upgraded to a term sentence, while they would still have no freedom and would earn no money, they wouldn't be treated terribly, and when the appointed day came, their emancipation was assured.

If they had not acted as reasonably as they had, they might have been facing an A-rank sentence. Their tears of joy were inevitable.

After each party received their sentencing, they were escorted to the next room. The guild officials and hunters in attendance only nodded sagely, apparently having no objections to raise to any of the decisions thus far.

Finally, they came to the last group, the four woodcutters and the four hunters, the Soaring Twin Dragons, who had been apprehended second. The judge read out the decision.

"The four woodcutters are found innocent of the crime of banditry. However, impersonating bandits and threatening young girls for your own gain, an act committed of your own volition for the sake of profit, is still an illicit act and shall be strictly punished."

The woodcutters, who thought that the court would go easy on them because they had been deceived, went pale.

"You are hereby sentenced to one hundred lashes each and to work diligently at your own jobs, aware that you will face no such kindness next time. In fact, the only reason we are granting you such lenience now is because of a direct request from your victims. Truly, you ought to be sentenced as the allies of bandits and punished accordingly!"

Hearing this, the woodcutters all bowed their heads deeply.

Receiving one hundred lashes was no light matter. It was not like being swatted on the behind as a child—they would be struck on their bare backs or buttocks with a whip or a rod of bamboo with a fringed edge. This punishment, which could only be administered by a professional so as not to break anyone's bones or damage their internal organs, was one that petty criminals feared; not only was the pain unbearable, but the aftereffects would last for a while longer, leaving them unable to even sleep face-up for some time.

That said, after hearing the sentences of execution and enslavement handed down just before, their punishment was as good as a godsend.

Finally, the proceedings came to an end with the "kindhearted" party who had concealed their identities.

"C-rank party, the Soaring Twin Dragons. You are sentenced with an A-rank lifetime term of hard labor."

"Wh—?! That's absurd! We were merely trying to rescue a young noble and her party who were being assailed by bandits! I'm not saying we deserve a medal, but what is the reason for such harsh punishment?!"

Obviously, the young men were grasping at straws. If they were bandits, their punishment would be unavoidable. Thus, they had insisted all the way through three days of interrogation that the woodcutters truly were bandits, and that those men had merely been spewing lies upon their capture, trying to get the hunters embroiled in their crime.

"Yes," said the judge, "but it was not only the woodcutters who attested to your crime but the victims as well. Deny it all you like, but it does not change the facts."

In this world, the veracity of a charge was decided at the presiding judge's discretion, whether or not there was any evidence to prove it. That meant that even without hard evidence, if there was any circumstantial evidence, or something else that was sufficient to support the decision, that was enough.

Conversely, it was quite the tricky feat to prove that one was innocent even *with* hard evidence.

"Those fine ladies were merely misled by those woodcutters—nay, those *former* woodcutters, who have now fallen into a life of crime! They blocked the road and attacked those girls, and we rushed in to try and save them. We would never try to alter that fact!"

"What?!?!" the woodcutters cried, but the leader of the Soaring Twin Dragons did not appear to give a care.

A traveling noble would have no reason to care about the bandits, nor any reason to go out of her way to make a prolonged stop in some nothing of a country town. She and her party had not once looked in during three days of questioning and would have already left the town long ago. She could not have afforded to make such a stop without reason. To detain a selfish traveling noble was to invite grave trouble. If things went poorly, heads would roll...literally.

However, if they were able to pin all of this on the woodcutters, perhaps they might be able to get out of it, thought the leader. Thus, his insistent raving continued.

"Those bandits saw that they were at a disadvantage and tried to drag us down into their sins when we moved in to stop them. They were able to easily deceive that young maiden, who is lacking in experience and ignorant of the ways of the world, in order to make her believe that *we* were the bandits! That is what happened here. You can ask the Guild—we are upstanding hunters! They can offer you ready proof that we left town but shortly after those young ladies did!"

The attending hunters looked conflicted at this statement. There was in fact nothing so peculiar about the young man's claim. The bandits had attacked the young girls, and a group of local hunters had rushed up from behind to save them. There was nothing odd about that.

No matter what objection a perpetrator might raise, the judge was the voice of the law, and the decision he handed down was clear. However, there were many guild associates and hunters in attendance, and one would not lightly pass a sentence without everyone present in agreement. And so the presiding judge was troubled...*not*. In fact, he looked concerned for only the briefest of moments before his mouth twisted into a cruel sneer.

Just then, a voice rang out from beside the chief justice.

"*Objection!*"

"Huh?"

This phrase was one unknown even to many people on Earth; on this planet, it was utterly unheard of... Lawyering was not an occupation that existed here, and no such role was allowed within the courtroom.

The voice had come from an area to the side of the officials, where four young girls suddenly emerged from behind the group of gruff-looking hunters.

"Y-you all..."

Naturally, the reason that the Soaring Twin Dragons' eyes were as wide as they now were was because their old friends, the Crimson Vow, now stood before them. Reina and Mavis were still dressed as they had been at the time of their meeting, which is to say that they were clad in their normal garb. However, Pauline was no longer in her maid outfit but in her usual attire. Mile, meanwhile, was wrapped in a large cloak, which concealed her body.

"We were not deceived. Furthermore, you all clearly confessed back at the scene of the crime, did you not? You thought that you could capture us and sell us off to somewhere far away... It should be clear to you that we are not some simpletons who can be easily tricked. Your lies are no exception," said Mile, an aloof expression upon her face.

The leader glared at her.

"Y-you little..."

A party who everyone thought had left the town already had suddenly appeared. The leader of the Soaring Twin Dragons, disgruntled at Mile's unfavorable testimony, began to shoot back insults—but then recalled that this was now a debate, a battle of words. If he could talk them down and sway the judge to his side, there was a chance that they could turn this around still. They were local hunters, with a good reputation, while the others were just some young ladies who were passing through. Their testimony was far less reliable. Thinking this, the leader decided it was time to risk it all.

"Surely you must have been addled, hearing the bandits' claims before. This happens often with laypersons lacking in worldly experience—particularly young ladies. Furthermore, we already apologized for being a bit harsh in our attempts to admonish you for being so foolishly optimistic and getting yourselves into danger.

We truly regret that we seemed to be trying to intimidate you. It fills me with the deepest sadness that you would still treat us as bandits, even after that."

"Oh my, but you do know that providing false testimony is a crime, don't you?! Could it be that you were purposely hoping to entrap us, so as not to have to pay the fee for our rescuing you? And that you furthermore wished to reap the rewards of our being sold into slave labor? If you do not admit that you were mistaken, you might find that *you* will be the ones charged as criminals here!"

Indeed, it had been impossible to deceive the young ladies, which was why the hunters had bothered to breathe word of their malicious intent in the first place. However, the ones who they needed to accept their story were not those young ladies but the judge. Thus, the only choice he had now was to frame the young ladies as liars.

Presently, a commotion began to arise among the attending hunters. Each of them surely had plenty of bitter memories of clients embellishing the truth or using falsehoods against them.

Now!

The leader held tightly to this lifeline, the only thing saving his party from tumbling straight off the edge.

I suppose it's about 8:45, isn't it... Mile thought to herself.

Indeed, they had reached the final act. Naturally, Reina and the others, who had now been conditioned by Mile's Japanese folktales, were thinking something similar.

"Please don't fret for us. We are hunters who came here from the capital on the request of a job placed by the Merchants' Guild of Zarbef. We are already fully aware of the rules of this region, so..."

"What?"

A cry of surprise rang through the room, not only from the Soaring Twin Dragons, but also from the people in the gallery. However, none of the judges nor the lord who was watching over them showed any signs of shock. Apparently, this much had already been explained to them beforehand. The "Your Honor, if you would!" event flag had already been rendered moot.

"Then," cried the leader, "you're guilty of presenting a falsified identity! People associated with the Guild have certain obligations to fulfill! So, if you concealed the fact that you're hunters, then that means..."

"Hm? I don't recall us ever once saying that we were *not* hunters. Is there a rule that says that you have to declare, 'I'm a hunter! I'm a registered hunter!' every time you walk into a guildhall?"

Mile looked to the guild master, who grimaced and shook his head.

"But then there's the matter of nobility! You never directly represented yourself as being a noble, but your dress and manner and speech clearly gave the false illusion of your being one! Doing such a thing is considered to be falsifying one's status and impersonating a noble, a crime to be severely punished! Ha! Looks like the cat's out of the bag. You all are the criminals here! Guards, hurry up and apprehend them!"

If Soaring Twin Dragons could denounce the noble travelers, or rather, the hunting party from the capital, as criminals, then that would render their testimony against the offending hunters invalid. Staking everything on this hope, the leader called out triumphantly, his fellow party members swept up in the moment and cheering him on.

All right, time for the clincher! Mile thought as she signaled to the others with her eyes, walking confidently forward.

"Once, I was the daughter of a viscount. Once, I was an academy student pretending to be a commoner. Another time, I was a rookie hunter. And yet another time, I was the daughter of a viscount..."

Ignoring Reina's insistent whisper that she was repeating herself, Mile continued her speech.

"However! As I stand before you now, I am..."

Mile whipped the cloak from off of her body, exposing her standard hunter's gear beneath.

"A disciple of truth and justice! C-rank hunter Mile of the Crimson Vow!!!"

"Mavis von Austien, likewise!"

"The Crimson Reina, likewise!"

"Pauline, likewise!"

"We are four allies!"

"Bound by an unbreakable friendship!"

"At our very souls!"

"And our name is..."

"The Crimson Vow!!!"

Ka-boooom!

A dazzling display went off as they finished their catchphrase in unison; of course, as they were indoors, they were framed only by audiovisual effects, lights of four colors dancing behind them.

"........."

The four girls held their practiced poses until their muscles began to tremble, giving everyone in the room a chance to collect themselves...

"Well, if your party has two nobles, including yourself, then I suppose that does not count as misrepresentation... Now then, as previously announced, the four members of the Soaring Twin Dragons will be sentenced to a lifetime term of hard labor. Furthermore, we shall be noting in the court record that they appear to be malicious individuals who would attempt to incriminate others in order to save their own hides without any hint of remorse. I'm sure that this will see that the appropriate workplace is arranged for them. Guards, take them away!"

The judge, who had clearly recovered from his surprise, announced this decision, and the four hunters—no, the criminals formerly known as hunters—were dragged from the room.

"Oy, there!"

There was silence from the Crimson Vow.

"I said, oy!"

"Y-yes, sir!"

The master of the Hunters' Guild was calling to them, looking displeased. Though they had tried to ignore him, it did not look as though there would be any escaping this.

"Why didn't you tell me?"

When penning their letter, the Crimson Vow had insisted that the guild master tell the absolute minimum number of people possible—and only those in whom he had absolute faith. Even when collecting the bandits, they had insisted that he borrow carts and riders from the town stables instead of the Guild. However, they had not once informed him that they were hunters on an official job. True, he had some mild suspicions. The instructions tendered were rather unbefitting of some idiot daughter of a noble and her cohorts.

Reina prodded Mile forward again until she had no choice but to be the one to answer.

"Well, um, the ones who placed the job order were with the Merchants' Guild, and we were asked not to tell any unrelated parties about the job, so... Plus, there was the possibility of a traitor within the Guild. We couldn't possibly contact the guild master without an introduction, and there was the chance that the traitor might be the clerk who helped us or an employee we relayed a message to."

"I understand. I'm sorry to have been so cross. That's completely understandable. You managed to clean up after *our* mistake. Thank you."

The Merchants' Guild in their own town had passed over the local Hunters' Guild in favor of the hunters of the capital.

Normally, this would not be a particularly strange thing. The hunters of the town, none of whom were above a C-rank, were not suited to more difficult jobs. Still, the jobs did usually at least go *through* the local Guild. The fact that the guild branch had been bypassed entirely was a huge loss of face for them. It was an affront to the guild branch itself.

However, now was not the time to be raising complaints about this. Just as the Merchants' Guild had feared, there was a traitor in the midst of the Hunters' Guild. Two of them, in fact, one of them an employee of the Guild, no less. The fact that the individuals who had been able to capture the bandit gang—something that the Guild had been unable to do up until now—were a group of four tender young ladies, half of them not even of age, just added insult to injury.

To complain about this would bring them more shame upon shame. The Guild would be the laughingstock of the town. Ridicule would spread like wildfire through the other guild branches and the country beyond. They had to do something...

"W-we would like to offer you a reward as well!" the guild master squeaked out.

"Huh? Are you sure?!"

The Crimson Vow grinned widely. They were not hurting for money but receiving a reward personally from the guild master was different from normal payment—it was a mark of the guild master's high esteem. It would bolster their reputation, and naturally, it came with a heaping helping of contribution points. In this case, it was the guild branch's final chance at redemption, by showing that they would pay their dues to the people who assisted them, even if their own reputation had been dragged through the mud. The proposition was a mutually beneficial one.

Of course, it was not that the guild master himself had never suspected the possibility of a traitor among his own staff. However, as he could not cast doubt on any of his subordinates outright, he had been hoping to conduct a quiet investigation without raising suspicions. In the meantime, the Merchants' Guild, tired of waiting, had been forced to take action.

We messed up...

The guild master was unlikely to lose his position, but his reputation was sure to be irreparably tarnished. He would have to work hard in order to recover from this failing. As he watched the Crimson Vow, who were shaking hands with the master of the Merchants' Guild and seemed to be receiving an invitation to dinner from their lord, the master of the Hunters' Guild's shoulders slumped.

Behind him the hunters of the two local B-rank parties, who had been in attendance to ensure the appropriate treatment of the hunters who were on trial, stood stunned.

"Man, are there really that many nobles among the hunters in the capital...?"

"M-more to the point, is it really possible for four rookie C-rank hunters from the capital to capture almost twenty bandits single-handed...?"

"The capital's a scary place..."

The hunters of the capital were getting quite a reputation.

Didn't I Say to Make My Abilities Average in the Next Life?!

CHAPTER 61

The Tale of the Wicked Maiden's Foiled Engagement

IT WAS WELL AFTER the Crimson Vow had returned from their journey of self-improvement to work in the capital of the Kingdom of Tils, their original home base, when one day, upon arriving at the Guild to receive a mark for a newly finished job, they were hailed by a guild employee.

"Oh, Miss Mavis! There's a letter here for you."

Mavis received the letter and turned it over to see who the sender was, then immediately stowed it away into her breast pocket. It was unthinkable that anyone besides her own family would be sending her letters, and she wasn't about to go opening a private communication in a wide-open room, surrounded by strangers, after all.

"........."

After returning to their inn, Mavis pulled the letter out and read it, then froze in place. Her eyes were wide and unfocused, and did not appear to be following the letters on the page at all.

"Hm? What's wrong, Mavis?" Mile asked, concerned.

As Mavis turned to look at her, one could practically hear her now-frozen joints creaking.

"Th-there's going to be a wedding..."

"Oh, one of your brothers is getting married? That's wonderful news! Though I'm sure it's a bit of a shock for a bro-con like you, isn't it, Mavis? But still, it's not *that*..."

"No...it's..."

"Hm?" Mile asked, unable to make out Mavis's whispered reply (which had seemed to utterly ignore Mile's implication of a brother complex).

This time, Mavis answered clearly.

"Apparently, *I'm* the one getting married..."

"Whaaaaaaaaaaaaat?!?!?!"

Lacking the willpower to even explain the situation, Mavis merely held out the letter and slumped down into a chair. The other three took the note and read it over...

Evidently, a marriage proposal had come suddenly from the second son of the family of some marquis. Even if he was the second son, his family still ranked highly, and furthermore, the boy's own father was ranked second within their family. That made the father a viscount, a station that this second son would inherit. In addition, the family was of good standing within the Austien family's personal faction. The young man was a perfect match...as far as Mavis's family was concerned.

Apparently, Mavis's own opinion of him did not factor into this in the slightest, but then, well, that was rather standard for the marriage of a daughter of a noble household, wasn't it?

"Congratulations, Mavis!"

Smack!

Mile's stupid joke immediately earned her a smack to the back of the head from Reina—a very hard smack, which made a rather splendid sound.

"So, what're you going to do?" asked Reina.

Mavis was silent, unable to reply. According to the letter, the Austien family, given their alliances and social standing, was not in a position to refuse this proposal. And of course, as much as her father and brothers said that they would never give her up to marriage, it wasn't as though they intended to keep her forever, forcing her to live her life as an old spinster. Being the wife of a viscount within the family of a marquis was actually quite a promising prospect. Thus, while her brothers were probably still grousing, her parents were surely eager to see this marriage take place.

"Could you just ignore them and skip out on the meet-and-greet?" Pauline proposed.

"If I did that, it'd be like spitting in the face of the man I'm supposed to meet, and the house of Austien would fall into ruin. It would be trouble not just for our family but for all of our followers and retainers as well..." Mavis answered sullenly. "As it stands, my father has already received the formal proposal, which means that this second son and I are now as good as husband and wife. Even though his acceptance is only provisional—even if we had no reason to accept the proposal—it's not as though we can really refuse. My opinion doesn't factor into it in the slightest..."

Mavis's shoulders slumped. The other three were silent.

Situations like these were not ones that could be altered by a noble daughter's will alone. Moreover, as the family's honor was on the line, Mavis's father could not excuse her from this role, no matter how much she might be the apple of his eye. And of course Mavis, the daughter of a noble who loved her own family just as dearly, could never simply run away and ignore her duty. More than aware of this, the other three girls wore dark expressions.

"So, you're saying that it's already too late for the Austien family to refuse?" Pauline confirmed.

"Yep..." Mavis replied in a sullen voice. "As the daughter of a noble household, it's only natural that my betrothal would be arranged for the sake of my family. Even if it's a mistake, I can't allow anything to happen that would cause trouble for my family or other relatives. This is the duty borne by all those in a noble household. It's the price we pay in exchange for the luxuries we enjoy and the world-class education we receive.

"And so, even if I've never met the man, even if it means giving up on my dreams, I must be wed, and bear children, and look after the estate, and bear more children, and mingle at parties, and bear more children, and think about all the dreams I was never able to...a...chieve..." A soft trail of tears dripped down Mavis's cheek as her voice petered out.

After a few moments of silence, Pauline spoke up again. "In that case, we have to force them to retract the proposal—or make something happen that makes it okay for your family to refuse!"

"Huh?"

Dark laughter began to bubble from Pauline's mouth. Reina and Mile began to grin also.

"If we can't pull our friend out from between a rock and a hard place—"

"Then what are allies for?! What are friends for?!"

"We are the Crimson Vow, allies bound at the soul!"

"And we're gonna smash that proposal to bits!!!"

✧ ◈ ✧

It was several days later, at the main estate of the Austien family, back in Mavis's home territory.

"Father, I have returned..."

"Oh, my Mavis! You've come back to us! Just as we planned, in two days' time we will be receiving a visit from your betrothed and his pare—Oh, you brought your hunter friends along, too?"

"Pardon the intrusion!" chorused the other three.

Apparently, the count had the wild thought in his mind that Mavis might simply abandon her party members and come home all alone. Once the first meeting with her betrothed had taken place, she would have to begin her preparations for marriage, so it made little sense to have them along. Surely, she did not intend to be going back with them...

"Since this gentleman is to wed our precious friend," said Reina, "we intend to make fully certain that he's worthy of her."

"Uh... Ah, I see..."

A commoner speaking so frankly to any noble, much less to a count, might be punished by death for such frankness. However, from hearing Mavis's tales of her family over and over again between their days at the Hunters' Prep School and now, Reina knew that the Count was not the sort of person who would do such a thing. She thought of him as her friend's father before she ever thought of him as a noble.

Of course, in truth, it was only by accident that she had slipped into her normal speech patterns, without thinking. Thus, the moment she stopped talking she slammed her mouth shut, with a face that said, "Oh crap!"

However, the Count had not been paying attention to what Reina had said at all. *Of course,* he thought, *it's dangerous for a young lady to travel alone, so they came all this way with her to see her off. What good friends you've surrounded yourself with, Mavis...*

Indeed, though they were rather shrewd as far as nobles went, the members of the Austien family were really not such bad people.

Mavis spent the two days until the meeting with her betrothed undertaking special lessons with a private tutor to remind her of all the etiquette she had begun to forget. Reina and the others meanwhile, with nothing else to do, toured the Austien family lands and further developed their schemes.

Naturally, they did not stay at the Austien family estate, but at an inn in town.

Mavis's family and the tutor alike had conspired to make Mavis wear a wig to hide her short hair. However, Mavis argued that the proposal had already been made with the knowledge that the Austiens were a martial family line and that Mavis had been making a name for herself as a rookie hunter for the past months. Besides, any sudden movement would dislodge the wig, causing their plan to backfire spectacularly. In the face of these protests, they all seemed to have a moment of clarity and abandoned the wig plan entirely. Once she had been all dressed up, Mavis was very pretty anyway, short hair or no.

✧◈✧

And then, the day of the meeting finally arrived.

Naturally, there was no reason for the other members of the Crimson Vow to be present. Attendance at this event was limited to the two key parties and both sets of parents. Brothers and sisters were not included under this umbrella, either.

"P-pleased to meet you... I am Jusphen, the second son of the family of Marquis Woitdein."

"And I am Mavis, the eldest daughter of the family of Count Austien..."

Jusphen was an earnest-looking young man in his early twenties. As far as looks went, one could do much worse. Considering the fact of his parentage, and that he was next in the line of

succession to a viscount, this really was an extraordinary pro-posal. For the Austien family, acceptance was the obvious course of action. Excepting the particularly rare girl who was aiming for crown princess or bust, a normal young noble to be leaping for joy at the prospect of a proposal from someone like him. In fact, leaping for joy would nearly be expected.

Unfortunately, Mavis was by no means "a normal girl."

As it stood, she valued self-improvement over romance. She wanted not a jeweled palanquin, but knighthood. When it came to marriage, she pictured a grand epic of being bound by deep and inseparable love to a fellow knight, alongside whom she rode in defense of the kingdom...

Mavis was a maiden of vast and wild dreams.

In fact, the first time Mavis had told the others about this dream of hers, the other three members of the Crimson Vow had felt their souls fly out of their mouths.

Mavis had no intention of purposely conducting herself in such a way as to make the young man hate her. She was fine with telling lies to deceive evildoers, but telling a lie in a situa-tion such as this would be in violation of her own personal code. Furthermore, to behave in any obviously boorish manner would only cause trouble for her family. It would mean trouble not only for her father's station but for that of her brothers, who would take up the family line after him.

Plus, Pauline had informed her that, "None of that will be necessary."

And so, Mavis greeted the newcomers like normal. Jusphen, who desired her mainly because of her status as the daughter of the house of Austien, was apparently also somewhat aware of her martial skill. It seemed he had met her once before, when she was around fifteen, and had become smitten with her, a girl who appeared at the time to be a slight and sheltered maiden, with long, golden locks. He had heard rumors that she had run away from home, registered as a hunter, and done all sorts of outrageous things, from the fights at the prep school graduation exam to the "red mark" jobs she had taken on. The more he learned, the more smitten he became...

He knew that she had fled from home, and that she was an egregious tomboy, and yet he still desired her as a wife... Lord Jusphen appeared to be skilled in many areas himself also. Truly, she could not hope for a better match...

The more he heard about the young man, the more enthused Count Austien became at the prospect of their pairing. As the conversation blossomed without a hitch, both sets of parents looked on, grins wide upon their faces.

Then, after a fair bit of time had passed...

"Well then, why don't we call it a day? You will join us for luncheon tomorrow, won't you?" said Count Austien, drawing the day's proceedings to a close.

Naturally, the Woitdein family had already approved this next meeting, which had been on the schedule from the start. Because first meetings usually involved a lot of awkwardness between both parties, the true event would begin with meeting for lunch the following day. And then, Mavis and Jusphen would have some time alone, just the two of them, before coming back together with everyone again for dinner. After that, they would all have some mild drinks and enjoy the easy atmosphere together. Because of this, today's meeting was to be short—just introductions, to take place around the second midday bell (about 3PM), and broken up before evening fell.

Mavis herself could not recall the party where the pair had met once before, a few years prior, but both Count Austien and Marquis Woitdein busied themselves with so many social events in the capital and gatherings at the palace that the fathers had become fairly well known to one another. They had even exchanged words now and then.

Then, just as the Marquis moved to stand from his seat...

"Um, if everyone would be so inclined, why don't we all dine together for supper tonight?"

"Hm?"

Both the Count and the Marquis found Mavis's sudden proposal suspicious. The Marquis and his family had already planned on taking dinner at a restaurant in town, thinking that too long a first meeting would put too much stress on the young couple, causing them to grow tired of one another. The evening meal for tonight was supposed to consist of both families eating separately, no doubt comparing notes on their own. The Marquis found himself thrown for a loop at this sudden change to the agreed-upon plan.

The Count, meanwhile, completely lost his cool at this new proposal.

"N-now, now, Mavis, suggesting such a thing out of the blue would be an enormous inconvenience to the Marquis' family, I'm sure. Besides, we haven't made any preparations..."

Indeed, extending an invitation to normal folk was one matter, but making preparations to entertain someone of a higher status than oneself, such as a marquis, took time. There was no way that they would have the suitable ingredients on hand nor the means to prepare them on such short notice. He was, of course, thrilled to hear Mavis making such a proactive suggestion of her own accord, but on a practical level, the notion might be a bit more trouble than it was worth.

"Well," Mavis continued, "we wouldn't have to entertain them here. The hunting party that I travel with accompanied me here to see me off, and I was thinking how desperately I wished for everyone to meet them... It would be at a low-class establishment, a restaurant frequented by commoners, but if you wouldn't mind that, then..."

Hearing this, the Woitdeins suddenly understood. *Ah*, they thought, *it makes sense for a young girl to want to introduce our son to her friends to reassure them, no matter who that son might be.*

They had heard that the other party members were all young ladies, and speaking with them would give the family a good idea of the sort of person that Lady Mavis was. Imagining this, the Marquis was happy to accept the proposal.

"Yes, of course! We accept!"

"Well, if the Lord Marquis agrees to it, then we shall as well..."

"Ah, actually... I was only inviting the Lord Marquis and his family. Father, Mother, you won't be attending."

"Wh...?"

Count Austien and his wife were lost for words.

"Well, you're already acquainted with my companions, aren't you, Father? Plus, I recall that you were rather displeased with the fact that I am a hunter, yes? That is why I'm only inviting the Lord Marquis and his family to this meal."

"B-but that's..."

The Count appeared distraught, but Mavis ignored him. Though she had returned to the mode of speech she used to use with him before running away from home, the Mavis she had become now was not the Mavis that she was back then, and she would not be moved by the tears glinting in his eyes.

"Now then, I shall lead the way. If you would come with me..."

After a short ride in the Woitdeins' awaiting carriage, Mavis arrived at what was one of the top three restaurants in the capital town of the Austien territory. Of course, even if it was a top-three restaurant in an important town, this was still the country fiefdom of a count. It could not compare to the sorts of restaurants that nobles would visit in the capital. Nevertheless, it was at least sufficient to entertain the nobility who might pass through now and then.

Mavis gave the receptionist her name, and they were led to a private room... Though giving her name was a bit redundant, as there was no way that anyone running a shop in the capital would not know the face of their lord's only daughter.

In the room they had been led to, they found three young

ladies awaiting them. Naturally, all three of them rose from their seats to greet the nobles.

"My, my..."

Because nobles only chose beautiful women for their wives and lovers, all noble women, from children to the elderly, were typically lovely creatures. However, to see such well-formed young women among a party of commoners surprised the Marquis enough that he unconsciously let a comment slip. It was not that they were impressively attractive as a set; though among the group was a girl with imposing, impish looks, a young and well-developed maiden who seemed gentle and kind, and a young girl who gave off a calming atmosphere—the sort of girl you'd want to protect. There was something about them each that one rarely saw among the daughters of nobles. Quite the fascinating bunch...

As the Marquis evaluated the trio, they each gave their greetings.

"I am Reina, a C-rank hunter," said Reina, bowing her head politely.

"I am Pauline, likewise a C-rank hunter, and eldest daughter of the Beckett Company," said Pauline, bowing her head.

"Likewise, I am the—never mind. I am Mile, a C-rank hunter and the only daughter of a viscount." Mile greeted them with a curtsy.

The Marquis and his family were speechless, mouths half-ajar.

Pauline was not especially worthy of note. Her family must be fairly successful as merchants to have their own company, but as far as the Marquis could observe, she was a commoner who had little money to her name. However, the sole daughter of a viscount was a different matter.

If she was the only daughter, and one were to take her for a bride, then one's child would inherit the viscount's title. In other words, the ranking members of each family line would be able to join forces, strengthening both factions. Plus, one could not underestimate the value of being connected to a noble from another country when it came to international negotiations or the off chance that one or the other might someday end up in exile. Furthermore, this girl had charming looks, seemed well mannered, and had a smile that put one at ease.

"Now, why don't we all rest our feet?"

"O-of course..."

At Mile's urging, the Marquis' party took their seats. As the food and drinks were carried in, the evening began.

"...And then, Mile blew the enemies away with an attack spell..."

"Hm? But I thought that Mile was a sword wielder?" Jusphen interrupted Reina's story.

Mile replied, "Yes, well, I'm actually a magic knight?"

"A magic knight?" the nobles echoed.

"Yes, I can use both magic and swords equally!"

"What???"

The nobles' eyes were wide. They had never heard of such a job title. However, hearing the explanation of Mile's position forced their eyes even wider.

As in the case of the Austiens, magic ability manifested only rarely within the Woitdein line. Even the ones who did happen to be born with the gift were not particularly skilled, able to use it only for practical conveniences. Furthermore, the rare few who did have more skill were still only good enough to become mages of a rather middling level.

Therefore, the idea of there being anyone reckless enough to try and master both the paths of magic and the sword was unthinkable. Mastering even one of these required a Herculean effort. Even this world had proverbs along the lines of, "He who chases both rabbits, catches neither." There were plenty of swordsmen who could use a little bit of magic and mages who could use a sword well enough to defend themselves, but no one had ever heard of a warrior who could use both magic and a blade capably in battle.

"I-I'd love to see that sometime..." Jusphen muttered.

"Oh, certainly. I'm free tomorrow morning, so why don't we meet somewhere where I can give you a demonstration?"

"W-would you?!"

Mile had him hook, line, and sinker. The Marquis looked to be brimming with curiosity as well.

The conversation continued on, but for some reason, the bulk of the Marquis' questions seemed to be directed toward Mile. Excluding the name of her family and the name of the country from which she came, Mile more or less answered his questions truthfully and directly. Indeed, she was quite frank about herself, and the fact that there were no civic issues within her lands, that they were currently being looked after by the king and queen, that she herself was the successor of her line, and that she had no fiancé...

Not one bit of this was a lie. She was in fact the successor—though she omitted the part where she technically had already succeeded her parents. She could of course, never tell a lie when it came to matters of peerage, as such a thing was considered to be a grave taboo.

Furthermore, while Mile was a bit lacking when it came to matters of common sense in this world, she excelled at matters that were "outside of common sense." Thus, she was able to speak eloquently on matters of agriculture, taxes, and commerce, topics about which she had a wealth of secondhand knowledge, thanks to all the books she had read in her previous life. Whether or not such ideas suited this world, and whether they could actually be implemented here, was a totally separate matter. But the Marquis was thoroughly impressed by her ability to even consider such matters.

Jusphen raised many topics with Mile as well, and Mile replied to each thread of conversation with a smile. All the while, the other members of the Crimson Vow continued to sing Mile's praises whenever they had the chance...

✧◈✧

The next morning, in the forest a little ways out of the capital, the Woitdeins and the Crimson Vow were assembled.

The Woitdeins had explained to the Count that they wished to take a morning stroll, with Mavis as their guide. The Count, thrilled to see Mavis getting along so swimmingly with the Marquis' family, agreed without a second thought.

"First off, I would like to show you my famous 'Copper-Cutting Trick,'" said Mile. "Could I ask you to throw a copper piece up in the air for me?"

"Ah, of course," the Marquis replied, drawing a copper piece from his purse and tossing it.

"Hup!"

As usual, Mile swiftly swung her blade in a cross-slash, and four equal pieces of the copper coin fell down into her palm, which she held out for all to see.

The Woitdeins were speechless.

Next up, she made light work of Mavis and her True Godspeed Blade in a sparring match. After that, she faced off against Jusphen and then the Marquis, at their insistence. Though she held back on them so that the matches would not be entirely one-sided, it was clear that the Marquis was holding back on her as well.

After that, she demonstrated how she could block an attack spell from Reina and how she could launch a powerful attack of her own without even an incantation, stunning the Marquis and his family all over again.

"M-Mile, a-are you certain that you don't have a fiancé right now?" asked Jusphen.

"Indeed, I have neither fiancé nor lover. My parents won't be pushing me into any engagements, so it's up to me to find a spouse on my own!"

Again, this was true. Both her parents had already left this world for the next, so they could not possibly force her to do anything.

Overhearing the exchange between Mile and their son, Sir and Lady Woitdein's eyes began to glimmer.

✧ ◈ ✧

After returning from their long walk, the Woitdeins declined Count Austien's invitation to tea, instead shutting themselves away in their guest room to continue a hushed conversation.

Finally, lunchtime arrived.

"We would like to shelve the matter of the proposal."

"What...?"

The Marquis' sudden declaration left Count Austien too stunned for words.

"I'm sorry! I'm so truly sorry, but we must ask you to humbly accept our withdrawal. Please excuse us!"

All three Woitdeins stood, bowing their heads.

For a brief while, the Count was frozen in place, until he finally stood up, red in the face, and shouted, "Don't toy with me! D-do you intend to make a fool of my daughter? Of the Austien family?!"

To speak to a person of superior rank in such an impertinent way was a rudeness of the highest order, but there was no one who would persecute him for it in this case. The one who had truly been rude here was the Marquis. His actions were an unforgivable slight against a fellow noble household.

However, the insult did not seem to be intentional, nor did the Marquis appear to bear the Austien family any ill will. Seeing how apologetic he was, the Count began to calm down—just a little.

"At least allow me to ask the reason!" said the Count, still red-faced and trembling.

However, the Marquis only bowed his head, again and again.

"I'm sorry, please forgive us! The blame here is all ours. You can scorn us as much as you like or disparage us as you see fit! But please..."

The Count's anger still had not subsided, but if the other party was no longer interested, then there was no point in continuing with the engagement. Even if he were to force the matter, it would not contribute to his daughter's happiness, and so, he had no intention of continuing the conversation.

"Please do not think that I will accept this insult to my daughter so easily."

"I'm sorry..."

The Woitdeins bowed their heads deeply again and then swiftly left the Austien residence behind. Mavis hung her head and returned to her room, shutting herself away.

"Mavis..."

Count Austien was in deep despair. Had Mavis's three elder brothers been present, the exchange would have ended in a far more heated manner. Truly, they would have had no choice but to slaughter the Marquis and his whole party. It was truly fortunate that they were all away, busy with their own careers.

Meanwhile, in Mavis's room, behind closed doors...

"I can't believe it! It's just like Pauline said! They broke off the engagement all on their own! I got off scot-free, and now the

Marquis owes us! It's just like magic!!! All right, now to continue as planned..."

"Father, you really did it!"

While riding in a carriage bound for the inn where Mile and the others were staying, the Woitdeins talked among themselves.

"Yes. What we've done to Count Austien and Lady Mavis is truly unforgiveable, but we shall think of some way to make it up to them soon. But more importantly, Lady Mile! We must absolutely welcome her into the Woitdein family!"

"Hear, hear!" replied his lady and his son in tandem.

She was the successor to a viscount from another kingdom. Besides the Marquis, who was the head of the family, the house of Woitdein also had a viscount of their own. Jusphen, as the second son, was already in line to inherit this title, but it didn't hurt for his wife to have her own noble rank as well. Even if it was a courtly rank from another country, if his wife had a title, that meant that there was something for their second child to inherit. Moreover, this meant that the pedigree of the Woitdein line would now include both the title and territory of another kingdom.

The chance to marry a young lady who was in line to inherit her own title did not come by just every day.

First off, there were very few family who had no male heirs. Second, among the families that did have only daughters, how many of these young women could be eldest daughters of marrying age who were not yet engaged? If such a girl existed, young people everywhere would probably come crawling out of the woodwork.

"It really is quite the miracle that Lady Mile has yet to find a fiancé... Actually, I bet you her parents decided on the excuse that she had to choose her fiancé herself so that she would not be inundated with proposals and then they made it impossible to meet with her! I see, I see..."

Based on what he had observed, the Marquis had no trouble coming to this conclusion.

"Well, she may have a title, but that's not the real gem here. If all she had was her inheritance, then there would have been no reason to practically spit in the face of the Austiens like we did. Here we were the ones to extend the proposal, and we acted in such a shameless manner, hurting even Lady Mavis... Yet Lady Mile is wise and knowledgeable. She has skill with the sword and with magic as well. We must induct her into our family. We need her abilities in our bloodline! Plus, of course, that wisdom of hers could help us develop our territory, her swordsmanship could be passed on to our elite troops, and she could help direct the mages... Blessedly, Lady Mile does not appear to dislike you either. Judging by the way she was with you last night and this morning, there's no worry of that. I wonder if that's because of my title, or because she's never been courted by a man before and so is weak to any attention..."

"Father, you could at least say that it's because of my charm!"

"Ha ha, let's say that it is, then!"

"Honestly, you two..."

"Wahahahahaha!"

Not once did the thought ever cross the Woitdeins' minds that Mile might turn down the proposal they were planning to make.

✦ ◆ ✦

"Think it's about time, then?"

"I'd say it's about time."

Just as Reina and Pauline weighed in with their predictions...

"Pardon me."

The Marquis and his family arrived at their room, escorted by an employee of the inn. Apparently, once it was known that one was dealing with a marquis, there was no question with checking in with the commoners being asked after to obtain their approval. The Woitdeins were simply brought in on the spot.

"Lady Mile, it is truly inexcusable for me to launch into this talk so suddenly, but won't you marry my son, Jusphen?!"

"Whaaaaaaaaaaaaat?!?!" the three girls cried out, their hands clasped to their mouths in shameless acts of surprise.

"B-but Sir Jusphen was going to marry Miss Mavis..." Mile pointed out.

"The proposal has already been dissolved," the Marquis replied, a bit guiltily. "So there's no problem now!"

"There's a *big* problem!" Mile cried back. "I would never steal someone away from my dear friend and party member! You don't expect me to betray Mavis, do you?!"

"No, but, we already got approval to retract the proposal from both Count Austien and Lady Mavis. Everything's fine!"

"Even if you don't have a problem with it, I still do! A huge one! Don't you realize how horrible that would make Mavis feel?! Plus, I'm only thirteen years old! I have no intention of getting married right now!"

Marquis Woitdein was shaken by this unexpected reaction. She had shown no signs of disliking Jusphen, and even if he was the second son, he was still the son of a Marquis. With the backing of the main family, their household could hold as much power as a count's. Plus, she had already heard the night before that Jusphen was poised to inherit the title of viscount. So it should have been clear to Lady Mile that they were not gunning for her simply because of her title. Considering all this, he had not expected her to refuse.

Even if he was a man of some years, the Marquis was still a noble, and thus had assumed that the notion of Mile choosing a spouse for herself was little more than a means of pest deterrent, never supposing that a viscount's daughter might possibly refuse a proposal from the son of a marquis.

The daughters of nobles married for the sake of their households, and even if she herself was the one to inherit, having a father-in-law, and then a brother-in-law, who was a marquis— even if it was in the peerage of another kingdom—wo uld raise her own household's status immensely. In the distant future, it would be quite the boon for her second son.

If her parents were present, they would have been certain to welcome this talk. With Lady Mile's abilities, it would not have been at all strange for proposals to come even from the offspring of a count, though according to the previous night's conversation, there were still few in her own country who were aware of the extent of her skill. It seemed that they would have to get an agreement from the girl herself. With this in mind, the Marquis pressed even harder.

"Well, of course, we would certainly need to meet your parents first and make an official proposal. If your parents were here, I'm sure they would…"

"But I haven't any!"

"What?"

The Marquis was dumbfounded at Mile's objection.

"I'm telling you, I haven't any. Neither parents nor grandparents. They've all moved on to the next world. Therefore, not only am I the successor of my family's title, but I have already succeeded them. I am the rightful head of my family. My family's lands are under the governance of the offices of his Majesty, the King, until I come of age."

"Whaaaaaaaaaaaaaaaaaaaaat?!?!"

Not one bit of it was a lie. After all, to lie about one's rank was a grave felony, punishable even by death.

"Therefore, I have the final say in who I will take as my companion. And furthermore, I have no intention of stealing away the fiancé of my comrade and dear friend. I will swear that to the Goddess!"

All the color drained suddenly from the Marquis' face.

Swearing to the Goddess was an absolute oath. Excluding extreme circumstances, that was a promise that one would not break, unless it was a matter of life or death. Naturally so—if one dared break one's promise and incur the Goddess's wrath, one had better be prepared for the divine punishment that would follow.

They had now lost all chance of Mile ever agreeing to the engagement.

"Please excuse us!"

The Marquis took his still-dazed wife and son by the arms and hurried out of the room.

And then, after a beat, Reina announced, "Let's roll out!"

"All right!!"

"F-father, where are we going...?"

"To the Austien residence, obviously! We'll get them to re-instate the engagement, even if I have to grovel in the dirt!" said the Marquis.

"........."

Did he really think that was going to work? His wife's and son's expressions were dark.

After they arrived at the Austien estate, following a rushed carriage ride, a butler guided the Marquis into an inner room where he bowed his head deeply to Count Austien.

"I'm sorry! You may redress me as harshly as you like, and if you would like me to get on my knees and beg, I shall! But I'm pleading with you! Please ignore everything that I said before, and let's continue discussing the engagement as planned..."

As the Marquis pleaded desperately, Count Austien made a pained face and pulled a single slip of parchment from his breast pocket, which he handed to the Marquis. Upon the paper was written the following:

I'm going on a journey for a while to heal my broken heart. Please don't look for me.

—*Mavis*

Surely, she would be traveling with her companions, so there was no need to worry about her. However, that did not temper the Count's rage toward the Marquis—particularly when the man had the impudence to offer up his proposal a second time. That was more than the Count could endure.

"You will pay a dear price for this," said the Count, with a voice that rang as though from the depths of hell.

The Marquis fell to the floor on his knees. He had not yet dropped into a full grovel, but it was still a pose that no Marquis should ever have to take in front of a Count.

"I understand," he said, groveling. "Not only will you receive a great sum as my apology, but any reports or proposals that you submit to the higher-ups, I will back. I will concede to those of your faction and any other thing you wish! I can never truly apologize for the harm done to Lady Mavis, but please, is there any way you can forgive me...?"

Even the Marquis, shrewd in the world of politics as he was, could only beg for an apology for wounding another family's daughter so badly that she would run away from home. After all, he had daughters of his own.

"Very well," said the Count. "What's done is done. We shall furnish your food and lodgings for the night and will discuss this further later. However..."

"However?"

"I will have to insist that you be the one to explain the circumstances of the situation to my three sons when they return home. Whatever punishment *they* see fit to give you, I expect you to sit obediently and take."

"I concede to your whims, good sir."

"Pauline, you're amazing! I can't believe we managed to break up that proposal safely without doing anything but being ourselves! Plus, since they were the ones to break it off, that keeps my father out of a bad position. On the contrary, I think they'll owe him a favor now. Just what sort of magic did you use?"

After reconvening at their agreed-upon location, the Crimson Vow were now heading back toward the capital.

The other three grimaced at Mavis's question. Even Mile, for once, had fully grasped the circumstances of the situation. Mavis appeared to be the only one who did not understand. In order to keep Mavis, who was bad at keeping secrets, from slipping up, Pauline had informed her only of her own role, not bothering to illustrate the full shape of the plan.

However, now that everything was over, and because it would be troublesome for Mavis if their stories did not align the next time Mavis returned home, she decided this was finally the moment to spill the beans.

"What? You're saying that the reason the proposal was broken off was that Lord Jusphen had his eyes set on Mile, and he wanted to go for her instead of me...?"

"Yes, that's correct. Thus, the Woitdeins were the ones to break off the proposal. Mile does give off a very similar vibe to the portrait of you from your younger years that your third brother showed us. Given that Lord Jusphen was smitten with that version of you, we thought that might be enough to attract him. Plus, she comes with a title, and there's the chance of her passing her sword and magical abilities on to her offspring... Furthermore, she has unique knowledge, and people find her pleasant. Honestly, she's got you beat hands down!"

"Wh...?"

"Ah, of course, we never lied to them, so this wasn't an entrapment. I mean, he's not necessarily a bad person, but the fact is he was taken with you after only seeing you one time, a long while ago, which means that he made his decision based only on your appearance, not because he liked you for your personality or anything like that. So really, he's a plain old garbage hound dog excuse for a man who judges women only by their looks!"

By now, Pauline had grown fed up with the disgusting men who could only stare at her chest when speaking to her, so she was critical of any man who would judge a girl's worth from her looks alone.

"Plus, we can assume that what they were really thinking about was the fact that you are the daughter of a count; that you are a skilled swordswoman who has made a name for herself; and that, since they are part of a martial line themselves, you would be valuable as the wife of their son. Right? All they care about is status and what abilities are most convenient for their own ambitions, don't they? Lord Jusphen was never smitten with Mavis, the woman herself, but with the abstract ideal of a woman who would be of practical value to him. And so, once we got his eyes to wander toward Mile, who has even more value to him, then hooking him was easy. He isn't the sort of person who would ever worry about your feelings or regret his actions."

Mavis seemed to be growing increasingly depressed, so Pauline tried to emphasize the fact that it was the Woitdeins, not Mavis herself, who were the bad ones, attempting to ensure her friend had no feelings of regret. However...

"You're saying that I have less value than *Mile* as a marriage prospect? So much less value that someone would toss me away, just like that? That I am *so much lesser* than Mile, with her *youth*, and her *height*, and her *body*, and that *vacant stare*, and that *complete lack of common sense?*"

Mavis stopped in place, clutching her head in her hands. She looked as though she was about to cry.

"M-Mavis, don't let it bother you! They don't know anything about either you or Mile as people! If they got to know each of you a little better, it's obvious who he would choose!" said Reina.

"That's right! It would...be...you..." Mile began to add, eager to comfort Mavis, when she suddenly realized just what the pair had been saying about her. "W-w-w-w-wait just a minute! What was all *that* about?! Just what is it you all think of me...?"

Mile was incredibly indignant.

"Come on! Answer me!"

"Errrr..."

"Mile, Mavis is in a delicate place right now. You need to leave her be!"

"Let's hear it from you then, Reina! Just which one of us is garbage on the inside?! Which one of us is the boor who no one would ever wed?!"

"I-I didn't say all that..."

"You didn't have to!"

"Now, now..."

Even with Pauline's mediation, it would still be quite a while until Mavis could recover, Mile's rage could subside, and the party could start moving again.

Didn't I Say
to Make My Abilities
Average in the
—— Next Life?!

CHAPTER 62

The Moment of Truth

"Now then, the moment of truth..." said Reina, casually. The other three nodded.

Yes, it was the moment of truth. The pivotal hour, when they would finally move on to the next town. They had already learned what the Guild was like in this city, completed a big job, and made a name for themselves. No matter how fond they had grown of the place, staying forever in one location did not a journey make. The day when they finally began to feel at home was the time that they should leave. Thus was the nature of a journey of self-improvement. It was *not* a journey in search of a place to put down roots.

Of course, there were plenty of hunters on such journeys who decided to settle down in some town that caught their fancy along the way, but the Crimson Vow still had five more years of obliged service to the Kingdom of Tils, and besides, they were far too young not to grow restless living in a country town. And they each still had their own dreams...

"Then it's settled. We'll make our report to the Guild, say farewell to the Servants of the Goddess and the Auras, and let the folks at the inn know that we're leaving."

Silence fell as strange looks spread across all of their faces. This town had its hooks in them, and yet they had to say farewell to everyone once more. Particularly to their precious cat-eared girl...

"Are you serious?! Well, actually, if you're on a training journey, then I guess that kind of makes sense..."

The guild master was quite understanding. However, understanding the situation and accepting it were two very different things.

"Still, are you sure you mightn't stay maybe just a little longer?"

If he didn't fight now, he was going to lose four hunters with very promising futures. These strange and wonderful girls had completed a whole succession of missions that anyone else would have thought impossible, without so much as a scratch.

You gotta staaaaaaaaaay!!! We need you here as our poster child! A party of smart and beautiful young ladies!!! Damn it, young men of this town, what are you doing?! If you would just get off your behinds and get these girls locked down... What am I saying? That's impossible...

In his head, the guild master toyed with wild fancies.

"No. We've already stayed long enough. The time is right for us to leave," said Mavis.

At this, the guild master thought of all the fun he'd had when he was a young man on a journey of his own—the sights he'd seen and the things he'd done as he traveled the land—and decided not to pester them about staying further.

Plus, there seemed to be some secret circumstances regarding the bandit incident that had just concluded, which left the party in a state in which they could no longer be publicizing themselves quite so much. Assuming that they wanted to get out before too much information started to get around, there was no use in trying to force them to remain. He was the one who had pressured them into taking that job, after all.

"I see. I hate to see you go, but I suppose you must. I will be praying for your success in the future. When your journey is over, won't you come back and see us again?"

"Thank you for everything," they said in chorus, "You've been a huge help!"

With their practiced sign of parting, the four left the guild master's office behind.

They really were a fascinating bunch. They were only here for a short while, blowing in like a storm, and leaving just as quickly... I wonder if we will ever see them again someday. The guild master was hopeful, though he knew already that even if they might visit again, this town was not a place where the girls would ever possibly choose to settle.

"We aren't going to tell any of the hunters besides the Servants of the Goddess," Reina declared.

The other three nodded.

The Vow, by now, had learned a thing or two—including the fact that, if you spoke on subjects you weren't good at, no good could ever come of it.

"So, we were thinking it's about time for us to move on to the next town..."

That evening at the guildhall, they caught the Servants of the Goddess, who were just on their way back from doing some daily requests, and led them back to their room at the inn. If they'd had this conversation at the Guild's dining corner, all eyes and ears in the room would have been on them, so they had little other choice. They couldn't use a restaurant for a conversation that they intended to be brief, and anyway, talking in a restaurant would be as bad as talking at the guildhall.

"I see. We've learned a lot from you all. Good luck on your journey," said Telyusia, leader of the Servants, with a smile. The other members offered their parting words one after the other.

And then, there was Leatoria...

"Please do your best out there! I look forward to the day when we can meet again, someday, somewhere. Until then, I'll work had to become a full-fledged hunter, too!"

Unexpectedly, she was acting like a completely normal person, not trying to chase after them, or even stop them...

"What was that all about?" asked Mile. "They were so attached to us before. Have we grown apart so quickly?"

"Maybe they had some—what was that you called it? 'Character development'?—while we were away?" Reina offered.

"I doubt that's the case," said Mavis.

As the three of them puzzled over the encounter, Pauline grinned.

"I thought that something like this might happen, so I made a request to Telyusia a while ago. I thought we should give it our all to put on a bit show for little Leatoria, of hunters on a journey, surprising friends one hadn't seen in some time and impressing those friends with how much she's grown in a moving scene of reunion..."

"Oh!"

The others understood immediately. This was a narrative pattern often used by up-and-coming young authors. Apparently Reina was not the only lover of these stories.

"Now then, it's off to the Aura estate!"

"It pains me to see you go, but this is something you must do for your own sakes. You really have helped us a great deal. If you ever have the chance, please stop by again someday. And, if you are ever in trouble, please don't hesitate to call upon the house of Aura. The payment and reward that we've given you is not nearly enough to truly repay you for all that you have done." The Baron continued, "Before you go, might I say one thing?"

"Yes, of course," Mavis replied.

The Baron took a deep breath and then screamed at the top of his lungs, "*Why did you have to make being a hunter sound like so much fun?!* Being a hunter is a wretched, miserable, garbage excuse for a profession! It's dangerous, you might die, and you'll always be hurting for money! How can you all look like you're having so much fun, always prim and proper, not even a scratch on you?! It's thanks to your stories that my precious daughter, my precious Leatoria is...!!!"

"W-welp, gotta go!!!"

The Crimson Vow ran as fast as they could, leaving behind the Baron and his tear-stained cheeks. Behind him, the rest of the Aura family and their staff bowed their heads and waved farewell to the girls.

"Boy, that was scary!" said Mile.

"I guess we got to see the Baron's true colors. Still, we did mess up, didn't we?" Mavis lamented.

Both of them seemed to share a sense of responsibility.

"None of our business though," said Reina.

"It's his own fault, really," agreed Pauline.

Neither of them felt any guilt at all.

Every man's problems were his own. Such was a natural philosophy for a hunter and a merchant. However, it was a concept that Mavis, who aimed to be a knight, and Mile, with her peculiar collection of philosophies, were unfamiliar with.

"Now, all we have to do is say our goodbyes at the inn and head out!"

That morning, a party of five hunters had set out, and that evening, only three of them had returned.

Another party had set out on escort duty, leaving their luggage, but their faces had not been seen on the day when they were scheduled to return, nor in the days that had passed afterward.

Such things were common. So, from a young age, many children of innkeepers developed a peculiar sense of life and death. Little Faleel was just one of those children.

"Are you all leaving now?"

"Y-yeah..."

She's gonna cry! Mile thought, unthinkingly throwing her arms around the girl. However...

"Is that so? Thank you for lodging with us. I hope you decide to stay at our inn again next time!"

"Wh...?"

Her response was businesslike and abnormally calm for her age. She did not appear to be moved at all.

"Whaaaaaaaaaaaaaaaat?!" Mile screeched, "Am I just chopped liver to you?! What about all that time we spent together, all those warm nights? Did that mean nothing to youuuuuuu?!"

"Can you not say things that sound so suspicious?!" the innkeeper shouted.

Smack!

Reina joined in on the scolding, chopping Mile right on the crown of her head.

"Don't go shouting things that make Faleel sound like damaged goods to everyone within hearing! What're you gonna do if people start spreading strange rumors about her?!"

"Huh? But those nights..."

"Those were the nights when it was too humid to sleep, so you stayed up late telling her bedtime stories, weren't they?!"

"B-but those steamy nights..."

"And it wasn't just the two of you! All of you were there! And it wasn't 'steamy,' it was 'humid'!"

The innkeeper, Faleel's father, seemed about ready to blow.

"A-anyway, thank you for everything!"

"Oh yeah, same here. I can't thank you enough for rescuing Faleel. If you ever pass through this town again, I hope you'll decide to stay with us."

"Thank you for everything!"

"See you again someday!"

"Farewell!"

And so the five girls each said their words of parting and bid farewell to the inn that they had called home for all those weeks, leaving the humble building behind.

"Now wait just a minute!" the innkeeper screamed.

"What is it?"

"Don't 'what' me! What do you think you're doing trying to whisk Faleel away like that?!"

Faleel, who had nearly been led over the threshold, one of each of her hands clasped in Mile's and Reina's, looked on blankly.

✦◈✦

"So, where to next?"

Mile, who had no understanding of the general layout of their surroundings, had left the route planning to the other three members of the Crimson Vow. Both Mavis and Pauline had a fair bit of knowledge, but in the end they had left the decision-making to Reina, who had actually traveled the countries of this region on foot alongside her father.

"Stopping through all the little towns and villages takes too much time, and they don't have a lot of value if we're trying to promote ourselves. The only time they're worthwhile is if there's some interesting job there. Our plan initially was only to travel between the larger towns anyway. The only places we should stop long-term are capitals or cities of comparable size."

This was fair. The other three nodded.

"Anyway, let's aim for the capital of the next country over. We'll stop at each of the little towns in between for just one night, check in at the Guild for jobs and information, and if there are no interesting requests, we move on. We'll plan on spending at least a few days in any larger towns. The length of time we stay will depend on the circumstances. We won't even bother staying in any villages—it's a waste of money. Instead, we'll just camp out."

With a nod of approval from everyone, it was settled.

Normally, sleeping outdoors was a far inferior experience to staying at an inn. Even with the latest advancements in outdoor technology on modern-day Earth, a tent that would sleep four would be incredibly cumbersome and heavy. In light of the much less-developed technologies of this world, a comparable tent set would be impossible to transport without a wagon. At most, one might be able to carry a bit of waterproofed canvas, and only one blanket per individual, and even that made it difficult to bring very much other luggage.

Furthermore, you had to sleep on the hard ground, do without heat, be swarmed by mosquitos and other pests, and worry about monsters. It was not the sort of luxurious stay that allowed you to kick back and relax until you were fully recovered.

Therefore, even if it was more costly, hunters generally chose to sleep at an inn, when given the opportunity. Letting one's health and form go to pot simply to save a bit of money, only to die on a job the next day because one was ill-prepared to fight, was a common rookie mistake.

Even if you were in the tiniest of villages, if it had an inn, you stayed there. If it didn't have an inn, one might beg to stay at the home of a local; even being given a barn to sleep in would be a big help.

And then, there was the matter of food.

Of course, a good night's sleep was one reason to stay at an inn, but the possibility of enjoying a wholesome meal was another important factor.

A good meal was one of the few pleasures in a hunter's brutal life. Out in the field, one had no choice but to eat whatever crude thing was lying around, so when you had the chance to eat something good, you took it. There wasn't a hunter around who did not feel this way.

It was for all these reasons that no hunter, except for those particularly hard up for money, would ever choose camping over an inn of their own free will...except in the Crimson Vow.

They had a large tent, which was already put together. They had more than enough blankets for each of them. They had cleansing magic and sometimes even the chance to bathe in a tub. They had food that Mile and Pauline cooked, with ingredients that were tastier and fresher than anything an inn could provide. They had insect-repelling barriers. They could roam freely in whichever direction they chose without having to worry about heading for towns or villages. They could travel the whole day through, until it was nearly too dark to see, which made them more efficient. And they didn't have to spend a single copper to get a good night's rest.

When, on the job, other hunters decided, "Let's stay at an inn instead of camping," to increase their chances of survival, the Crimson Vow might decide to lodge at an inn on the fly simply for the sake of intelligence-gathering, shopping, or sightseeing. There wasn't the slightest reason for them to stop by little hamlets where they would find no useful information, let alone stay there for the night. If they were going to stop in at all, the town needed to have a guild branch at bare minimum or there was no point.

"Say, can I ask you one thing?" Mile timidly asked.

"What's up?"

"Why are all of you dressed like that?"

Just as Mile had pointed out, everyone was dressed in the outfits they had purchased during the bandit-fishing job (on the Guild's tab, of course). Pauline was in her maid outfit, and Reina and Mavis were in fluttery dresses, which were a bit more chic than the average commoner's, and which they had purchased without any particular need for them.

The dresses really did suit the pair, though Mavis, who normally only dressed in boyish clothes and had been forced by Reina and Pauline to buy something a bit more feminine, looked a bit awkward.

"........."

The three of them acted as though they had not even heard Mile's question.

"You really like them, don't you?"

"........."

Silence persisted until Mile announced, "All right then, let's head into the next town like this!"

"What?" the other three asked.

"Well, it's a small town, so there probably won't be very many jobs, right? We will need to at least stop in and check the job board, but why don't we spend the day as a pair of rich sisters, their maid, and the rookie hunter hired to guard them? It'll be a bit of role-playing."

"Th-that does sound kind of fun..."

Every little girl dreamt of being a princess. Even Reina, technically an adult at the age of sixteen, was still a young maiden. Of course, she would still harbor these dreams as well.

"I guess I better change then," said Mavis. "There's no way a guard would ever go around wearing clothes like these."

Mile stopped her.

"No, stay as you are, Mavis. I'm going to be the guard this time, so you should play the role of the older sister."

"What?!" Mavis, certain that her role had already been cast, cried out in surprise.

"I mean, you did already bother to put on those cute clothes... and I got to be the noble maiden last time, so this time it's your and Reina's turns. As for Pauline..."

"I'm fine with this, actually," replied Pauline. "Rather than playing the young maiden, it's more fun to tease the maiden and stir up trouble around her. I'm more than happy to play the maid again."

"Pauline, I swear..." Reina sighed.

And so, the plan was now in order. When they arrived at the next town, the curtain would rise on the one-day run of Reina and Mavis's make-believe maiden show.

Wait, wasn't Mavis already a highborn maiden?

Technically, while she was the daughter of a count, she had been raised as a precious jewel, hidden away in the inner rooms of their estate with no one besides her own family, their staff, or her tutors to talk to. Beyond the various attendees at family parties, she had only ever had contact with the outside world as a rookie hunter, aspiring to be a knight. This was the very first time that she would ever be out in the world having interactions with townsfolk as a normal girl. Suddenly, the pressure on Mavis felt incredibly high.

The four girls then discussed the details of their charade.

"This time, we're just looking to have a bit of fun, so if anyone else happens to get involved, try not to let things get out of hand."

Nod nod.

"Lying about one's status is incredibly inappropriate, so we mustn't ever lie outright. We'll just explain things away in a way that doesn't require us to lie. And if it seems like that sleight of hand won't work, we give up the act and admit the truth."

Nod nod.

"No matter what, we all have to endeavor not to break our roles until we set out for the next town."

Nod nod.

No one found anything objectionable in Mile's instructions.

Then Mavis raised her hand. "Um... It'll feel weird not to have my sword on me."

Unlike Reina and Pauline, who could still use their magic even without their staves, Mavis's battle potential dropped exponentially without her sword. It was natural that she would feel uneasy, thinking of the small chance that something might occur.

"Umm, well then, how about just keeping your knife on you? We'll say that, even if you don't know about blades, you still like to have a weapon for self-defense. You only have the one guard, after all, and you worry for your maid and your little sister."

"Ah, yes. I would feel better like that. With this dagger, at least I have something I can stake my life on!"

As Mavis spoke, Mile felt as though she saw the dagger trembling, but Mavis did not appear to notice this at all.

Finally, they arrived in the next town, which was just barely big enough to have its own guild branch.

"All right, let's head in!" Mile said, pushing open the door of the guildhall, the other members of the Crimson Vow following behind her.

Ka-cling!

There was the familiar chime of the doorbell, and the familiar feeling of the hunters' gazes focusing on them. Some of those gazes lingered with interest, while... Actually, *none* of the gazes wandered back to where they originally were. Without exception, every eye that had turned toward them remained there, unwavering, as a look of dread spread across the hunters' faces. A single guild employee stood quickly from his seat and ran up the stairs.

The Crimson Vow was dreadfully perplexed, but there was no use in them just standing around staring. They moved over to check the information board, each of them leaning into their respective roles.

"Now then, miladies," said Mile, "I'm going to check the information board, so you two might look over the job boards or such to kill some time while you wait."

"All right then, thank you," Reina replied, heading over to the job board with Mavis and Pauline.

Meanwhile, the guild employees and other hunters continued to stare at them, silently.

Th-this is creepyyyyyyy!!!

Before Mile could finish looking the board over, a dignified gentleman who seemed to be the guild master descended from the second floor, shouting over to the Crimson Vow, "Just what the heck kind of job did you all come here on?! There are no bandit infiltrators in this Guild!!!"

The secret's out!!!

Indeed, there was no way that word of something that was such a huge incident for the Guild would *not* have already spread to the Guilds of neighboring towns...along with information about the girls who had played such a central role in it.

"Well, that was a huge failure..."

Even as the sun began to set and it grew dimmer outside, the Crimson Vow continued to move down the highway. Obviously, there was no way that they could remain in town after the huge embarrassment that was having their plans foiled immediately, so they decided to head back out right away.

"That was terrible!" The redness still had not fully faded from Reina's cheeks.

Meanwhile the nanomachines in the knife at Mavis's side, who had never got to make their debut, were sorely disappointed.

"Well, I guess we should have expected that," Pauline muttered. "It was a pretty big deal for the Guild, so of course they would have to get the information out to neighboring guildhalls to warn them and prevent something like that from happening again. Unless you tell the employees and the hunters as well, it's not much of a safeguard, so naturally, anyone affiliated with the Guild would know about what happened... As far as us being an all-girl party, well, I know that there aren't a lot of them, but it can't really be *that* rare. That said, a party of four girls dressed as nobles stopping by a guildhall is a little..."

She trailed off with a shrug.

"Y-y-y-y-you! If you already realized that, you should have said so from the start! Why didn't you say anything?!"

"Because it was more fun this way?"

"Why are you saying that like it's a question?!?!"

No matter what, Pauline was still Pauline...

And so, that night, the Crimson Vow made camp outdoors, far away from the town.

✧◈✧

A few days later, they arrived at a town of a more reasonable scale. They still had yet to cross the border, so word that, "the noble maiden's party is not to be messed with," had probably reached this place as well. Thus, everyone was dressed in their usual garb as normal hunters.

"I'm tired of dealing with all these petty little things. We are the up-and-coming C-rank party, the Crimson Vow! Nothing more and nothing less. We need to fight some honest, head-to-head battles and raise our ranks!"

"Yeah!!!"

As per usual, they entered the guildhall, waited as everyone looked them over, and then headed to the information board, when...

"What?"

They all froze.

B-Grade Special Bulletin: Forces from the Albarn Empire have invaded the Kingdom of Brandel. All travelers bound for the region should take caution.

"Whaaaaaaaaaaaaaaaat?!?!"

The Kingdom of Brandel! It was a country where they had stopped just a short while ago and then had left behind. As well as...

"Mile, that's where you're from, isn't it?"

"It is. And my family's lands are near the northern edge, which shares a border with the Albarn Empire..."

A land that had abandoned her, and which she had abandoned in turn. A country that she had left behind, never to return to again. A kingdom with which she no longer had any connection...

And yet, Mile began to look queasy.

"Come with me!" Reina shouted, dragging everyone to a reception window. "Please tell us everything that you know about the invasion!"

The clerk replied with a smile, "General information is free, but detailed information will cost one-half gold..."

"Give me all the details!"

"All right, please go right over there. Wellis, if you would!"

The clerk called over the young lady who appeared to be in charge of information and directed the party to follow her into another room...a natural course of action when sharing information that came with a fee, as you wouldn't want to go blabbing it to everyone around.

"Now then, I shall explain what we know about the situation."

After receiving the one half-gold payment, Wellis began to explain. According to her information, several days ago, the Albarn Empire had suddenly invaded the Kingdom of Brandel, its neighbor to the south, without declaration of war. At present, there were reports of fighting from the territories closest to the border. Currently, the Ascham fief was not involved in the fighting, but should those other territories fall, the Ascham lands would be next.

"As of yet, the Empire does not seem interested in engaging in an all-out war. Of course, this assumption is based on an expert analysis of the power of the troops they have deployed, the state of their supply lines, and various other statuses; however, it is not a guaranteed fact... What we can assume is that this is a tentative strike and that they hope to claim territories that are in geographically strategic locations, possibly for the purpose of afterwards engaging in a full-scale assault.

"While the Kingdom is of course enraged by this, the difference in military strength between them and the Empire is overwhelming. Furthermore, they lack any preparations for warfare, so it would be foolish to try and quickly scrape up some troops and toss them at the imperial forces until something sticks. They probably intend to forfeit the backwater territories close to the border to focus on their own preparations and launch a counter-assault later.

"Obviously, the Kingdom is in the right in this situation, but it seems that the Empire is insisting on some false claim about the successor of the house of Ascham, whose fief currently has no official ruler, and is launching a sortie on those grounds. Naturally, there's no other kingdom who would believe them, but that's the reasoning that they seem to be operating under, nevertheless."

"How do you have so much information?!" Reina exclaimed.

It was shocking. Considering what they had just received, one half-gold was cheap.

"Wh-where did you get all that information from...?" Mavis continued, equally surprised.

However, the guild employee known as Wellis merely gave an impish smile and said, "That...is a secret!"

As down in the dumps as she was feeling, Mile could not help but be reminded of something from her past life—and could only barely stop herself from offering a reply. Truly, she was a twisted girl...

After Wellis had finished her explanation and exited the room, the Crimson Vow remained inside. Given that they had paid the fee, it was agreed that they might have the room to themselves for a little longer.

"So it seems like the Empire has their sights set on the Ascham lands... What are you going to do?" Reina asked, facing Mile.

"I-I'm not going to do anything about it! I no longer have any connection with that country nor with those lands. I am Mile, a C-rank hunter of the Crimson Vow!" said Mile, feigning serenity, though her trembling body, pale face, and wrought expression betrayed her.

"So then, what of the land where you were born, the place where you were raised? Aren't there people there who you knew? People who looked after you?" asked Mavis.

"........."

"Officially speaking, those are your lands, Mile. Aren't the ones who live there your people?" chimed Pauline.

"........."

Mile, her head hung, could not reply.

"Well then, I'm going to place a request," Reina said abruptly.

"Huh?"

Mile was not certain what she meant.

"I'm assuming that you're thinking that you don't want to get the rest of us wrapped up in your personal affairs. So I'm going to place an independent request to the Crimson Vow—to get out there to the Ascham lands and do something about this!"

"What...?"

An independent request: i.e., a job requested directly of a hunter from a client, without going through the Guild. These were useful for those who did not wish to pay a handling fee to the Guild. It also meant that it was fine for the job to contain provisions that the Guild would disapprove of.

The flipside of this was that the hunters would receive no contribution points from the Guild. It also meant that neither the client nor the hunter received any protections in the case of either side lying or breaching contract—in other words,

withholding payment or falsifying job results. Furthermore, neither side had any guarantee that the other was who they said they were, and so forth.

In short, it was possible that the people you hired to be your escort could actually be the bandits themselves, lacking any qualifications as hunters, and you would have no way of knowing.

An independent request could be dangerous if the people with whom your formed the contract were not people with whom you were closely acquainted, in whom you had complete faith. However, as long as you knew the other side and could trust them, they were usually fine.

"I am requesting an independent contract with the C-rank party, the Crimson Vow. The stipulations are as follows: Travel to the lands of Viscount Ascham and rescue anyone associated with our good friend Mile. The payment for the job is one silver piece. Will you accept my request, Miss Party Leader?"

"I humbly accept your request, my beautiful lady..."

"Beau...?!"

Though she was the one who had begun this charade, upon seeing the sincere and serious expression with which Mavis replied, Reina went red in the face. She still had a long road ahead of her in the study of looking cool.

"Y-you guys..."

There were tears in Mile's eyes.

Pauline looked to her and said warmly, "You've saved us so many times, Mile. And several of those times involved the personal affairs of myself, my family, and Mavis's family, didn't they?

Still, even if that weren't the case, that wouldn't change the fact of us accepting this request now. And that's because..."

Pauline, Mavis, and Reina all cried, "As long as the blood flows red through our veins, our friendship is immortal!!!"

Mile clung to Reina, sobbing, while Mavis's shoulders slumped, wondering why she was never the one who got the hugs. Pauline looked on with a shrug.

Didn't I Say
to Make My Abilities
Average in the
Next Life?!

Good Luck, Mariette!

A LONG TIME AGO, Mile took on a home tutoring request, the goal of which was to prepare a young lady named Mariette, the daughter of the owner of a mid-sized mercantile company, for the scholarship entrance exam of August Academy. She crushed the entrance exam and made a glorious school debut, but what had become of her after that?

Dying to know, Mile slipped away to see for herself one rest day.

"Um, excuse me, are you all students of August Academy?"

The three uniformed girls were surprised to be asked such a question by someone they had never met before, but this stranger was a cute young girl, who seemed to be more or less around their age and had something of a dull look about her. Factoring this in, and seeing as they outnumbered her three-to-one, they did not feel the need to be especially on their guard.

Plus, one could tell fairly easily what school they attended at a glance, based on their uniforms, so there was no real need to conceal the truth.

"Yes, that is correct..."

Whether it was because they were raised well, or because Mile appeared to be older than them, the girls answered her politely.

"I actually wanted to ask you a few things about your school... Oh! I'm not anyone suspicious, though! I'm currently a hunter, but I used to attend an academy in another country, so I was feeling a bit nostalgic... If you don't mind talking with me for a bit, I'd be happy to treat you to whatever you'd like at that café over there!"

"Huh?"

The girls were a bit shaken. The café that she had pointed to served sweets and cakes that used a lot of sugar and juices made of expensive fruits, meaning that it was out of the budget of most young women. Though their school was one attended by the children of nobles, it was still the lesser of the two academies in the capital, which meant that the students were neither royals, the upper classes of nobles, nor the children of wealthy merchants, but rather, the lesser sons and daughters of lower nobles and the children of middle-class merchants. Thus, the students who attended their school were not the sort to receive ample allowances.

In truth, Mile had spent the day lurking about town observing the various students of the academy for a while, finally leaping upon the group who seemed like they were the most lacking in funds.

The three girls, who had been so suddenly assailed by this strange girl and offered a deal that was delicious in more than one way, startled to bristle, putting up their guards... *Not*.

The three were young ladies of a middle-class but comfortable nobility, after all.

Were they of a lower class—in other words, normal peasants—they might have been more cautious. And if they were of any higher class, such as wealthy merchants or high-ranking nobles, they would be likewise on their guard, having had a certain amount of self-defense ability and knowledge of their own status drilled into them. Those ranking in the middle had the least sense of the potential danger in such situations.

Plus, there was Mile's appearance to take into account. She was perhaps one or two years older than the three ten-year-olds and had a somewhat vapid, somehow comforting face that seemed to put you at ease. She did not appear to be a bad person.

The girls quickly winked at one another and replied, "Gladly!!!"

Except for the details of the security system, there wasn't really anything about the academy that they couldn't let other people know. There was nothing that the girls themselves needed to hide, and it was not as though there were nondisclosure agreements they had signed or any other privacy regulations they were obligated to comply with.

"...And that's how Crooktail, the 'Cat with Seven Names,' came to live in my dorm!"

"Ahahahaha!"

By now, the girls had already eaten five plates of sweets and downed three glasses of juice each. They listened and laughed as Mile told stories of her academy days. Until...

"Hang on! How come I'm the only one talking heeeeeeeeeere?!?!"

"Ah..."

Finally, Mile realized that there was something a bit off about the whole situation...

As it was the first time they had met, and it seemed a little weird to be drilling the girls for information right off the bat, Mile had begun to give a bit of a dramatized self-introduction in order to put the girls at ease and make the conversation a bit smoother. As the conversation went on, she began giving them advice on the subjects they had trouble with in school, and giving them tips on how to use magic, and before anyone realized it, the topic had shifted to Eckland Academy, with Mile doing all the talking.

"W-well then, I suppose it's our turn to tell you about our academy, then..."

Sweat began to pour down the backs of the girls' necks as they spied the mountain of plates and cups piled up on the table. The conversation shifted, and finally Mile got to hear some stories of August Academy. After listening to them talk about this and that for a while, she finally cut to the chase.

"So, I believe that there is a Miss Mariette at your school..."

"You know her, Miss Mile?!" the girls all chimed.

"Ah, y-yes! Only by name, though..." Mile was a bit taken aback at how readily the three replied.

"Ah, the defender of the academy, Lady Mariette..."

"The sacred maiden, Lady Mariette..."

"Lady Mariette, the goddess..."

The three then began to tell Mile the tale of a legend.

Of Lady Mariette, who rescued a freshman who became entangled with an upperclassman.

Of Lady Mariette, who always corrected the teachers' mistakes.

Of Lady Mariette, who brought someone back from the dead.

Wait! Waitwaitwaitwaitwaitwaitwait!!!

The first two tales were perfectly fine...but what the hell was with that third one?!

Mile was amazed. Yes indeed, it was as usual.

She was amaz-eggs and bacon!

✧◈✧

On a weekday the following week, Mile stood near the gates of August Academy, wearing her old Eckland Academy school uniform and using light magic to hide her form.

It sounded weird to say that she had any form while she was hiding it magically, but, nevertheless, she did.

She had donned the academy uniform as a contingency for the off chance that the light magic dissipated and her true form was revealed, figuring that, rather than a geared-out hunter suddenly appearing on the campus of an academy attended by the children of nobles, someone who was clearly a student undertaking a formal education in another country—even if they were not a student of this school—was far less likely to cause alarm. If she were a student of appropriate age from another country, there were plenty of reasons one could think of as to why she might be there, such as that she had been invited, or was someone's friend, or an exchange student. Either way, Mile presumed, she was far less likely to cause a stir in her uniform.

And so, Mile strolled boldly in, right through the front gate.

Now then... It's just a jump to the left and then a step to the right... No, wait, go in through the gate and turn to the right...

Even if she was only speaking to herself, Mile could not neglect the opportunity to make a joke.

Now, I think the first-years' classrooms are in this building?

She followed the instructions she had been given by the three girls she had spoken to the previous week, finally finding the classroom with a nameplate reading, *Year One – Blossom Class.* Mile stared at it silently.

Incidentally, the classroom just beside it read, *Year One – Kitten Class.*

These aren't consistent at all... It seems like they aren't broken up by academic levels the same way Eckland was. Still, class names normally go by letter or number, so I wonder if naming them like this was actually intentional... I mean, I guess I can understand picking a different method, but why are these names all so cute?

It was almost like a kindergarten.

As all the students were not yet assembled in the classrooms, the doors were still wide open, so Mile easily slipped inside.

Now, where is Mariette...? Oh, there she is!

There she sat, in a seat toward the front of the room.

It's been a while, but she's looking well. And as adorable as ever...

Mile's standard suspicious grin spread across her face.

Finally, the teacher arrived, and it was time for class to...

Huh?

For some reason, Mariette stood from her seat and walked up to the chalkboard. The teacher then sat down in the seat where Mariette had been sitting...

"Now then, let us begin our lesson!"

Whaaaaaaaaaaaaaaaaat?!?!

Mariette began giving the lesson, the teacher taking notes along with all the other students.

Wh-what the heck is going on heeeeeeeeere?!

On Earth, even in the distant past, the study of mathematics was fairly advanced. Thus, it was fair to assume that it would be decently advanced in this world as well. However, that only applied to knowledge shared between the most qualified individuals. Complex math was not something that was typically conveyed by the typical methods of information transfer and teaching methodology, so one would not expect the average layman to be able to solve complex equations. Likewise, one would not expect a teacher in charge of instructing ten to thirteen-year-olds to be a top scholar. Indeed, the sort of person who would

be hired as a teacher would likely be the sort of individual who was only slightly more advanced at mathematics than your average citizen, while also being in charge of teaching other subjects concurrently.

Were the math lessons that I drilled into her during those few days too much? Did I overdo it again?!

Sweat began to pour down Mile's forehead.

Now then, next up should be combat lessons...

Mile, still cloaked, observed the students as they moved outside of the building.

Hang on, they've already moved the first-years up from wooden swords to metal practice swords with real blades?!

Indeed, the students appeared to be having real contact matches, though blows to the head and other vital areas were still forbidden.

Still, they're gonna seriously hurt themse—

Just as Mile thought this, one student took a fast and fairly heavy blow to the side. They had almost certainly broken a rib. But then...

"Please take care of that," said the teacher, bowing his head... to Mariette.

"Of course! Broken bones, be as you were! Gather what you need from the body and repair yourself! Torn muscles and bruised organs, return to full form! Heal!"

The injured student, who had been crouching on the ground, stood up, good as new. None of the other students appeared surprised. In fact, they all seemed to be quite accustomed to this.

"You really are a savior, Lady Mariette. The fact that everyone can have sparring matches with real blows from the very start means that their rate of advancement is well beyond that of their other peers. At this rate, they might even be able to practice with *real* swords, soon."

Apparently, even the teachers had taken to calling her "Lady."

Even though the teacher seems like he's a noble, and Mariette is just a commoner...

Mariette's day continued, with her peers, the upperclassmen, and the teachers all looking to her in reverence. During their breaks, students from other classes and years came flocking around her.

It seemed like it should be quite the bother, but seeing how happy and full of energy Mariette was, Mile was able to breathe a sigh of relief.

Well, I suppose it's about time for me to get out of here, Mile thought, taking break time as an opportunity to begin her exit.

Still, I'd love to be able to see her face up close, just one last time. She's such a lovely girl, it's sort of puts my mind at ease to watch her...

Mile snuck up right beside Mariette and peered closely at her face, when...

"You creep!" Mariette shouted, thrusting her right hand out into a space where there was nothing.

"Gaaaaaaaaah!" Mile shouted.

"Waaaaaaaaaaaaaaaaaaaaaah!!!" the students screamed.

The space that should have been empty began to tremble, and in that spot, a human shape appeared. The students instantly began to panic. One girl swooned in shock.

"H-h-h-how..."

"Teacher?" asked Mariette.

"Teacher???" her classmates echoed.

The whole situation had gotten out of hand. Just as it always did...

"So you came to check in on me because you were worried about how I was doing?"

"Ahaha, well, something like that... Please, don't report me to the guards!"

"I mean, sure, that's fine..." Mariette said with a bit of a cringe, though she still appeared happy to see Mile.

"L-Lady Mariette," said one of her classmates from behind, "What did you mean earlier when you called her 'Teacher'?"

"Oh! This lady was the one who tutored me so that I could get into this academy. She really taught me a lot."

"What?! She t-taught *you?* That means that she must be even *more* amazing than..."

"........"

The classroom fell into silence.

A voice then piped up once more, this time directed to Mile.

"Oh, Miss Mile! Thank you for all the advice you gave us the other day! Thanks to you, I've started to get a handle on all the math I couldn't understand before, and I think I was able to get over a few hurdles with my magic, too! What are you doing here?"

Mile turned toward the voice, only to see the three girls she had spoken with the previous week standing there. They had apparently come over from their own classroom during break time, though it was unclear if this was because of Mariette or merely because they had some other friends they wished to speak to.

"Hm?"

Creeeeeeeeak...

Mariette's head, which had been directed toward the three girls, turned toward Mile with a certain unmistakable sound.

"Wh-why would you come here and watch me from the shadows when you're out there talking to other people and teaching *them* things?! What is the meaning of this?! Huh? What is the meaning of thiiiiiiiiiiiiiiiiiiiiis?!?!"

Mariette grabbed Mile by the collar and began to shake her.

"Huuuuuuuuuuuuuuuuuuuh?!?!"

It was the first time that the other students had seen such rage from Mariette, a girl who was always calm, collected, and beaming. They couldn't believe it. They looked on, stunned at Mariette's behavior. Moreover, they looked at the mysterious girl, who had apparently taught Mariette so much. If they could get that girl to teach them, then they too could...

Naturally, they all had the same thought at once.

"T-teacher! Won't you come be my private tutor, too?"

"No, tutor me! You have to come teach me! Just name your fee!"

"No, me! Focus just on me..."

"You fools! Obviously I will be the one to hire her!!!"

"Gaaaaaaaah! I knew this would happen! This is why I hid! Mariette, I thought I forbid you to speak of me! No one must speak of me! Farewell!!!"

With that, Mile ran straight to the window and leapt outside.

"Whaaaaaaaaaaaat?!?!"

The students crowded around the windows in a panic to see...

Nothing. There was nothing there but the blowing winds.

After that, no matter how much her classmates begged and pleaded, Mariette would not speak to them anymore of her mysterious teacher.

All that the other trio of girls knew of Mile was that she was a "graduate of a foreign academy," and, having heard the gag order that comprised her parting words, they refused to speak further on the subject as well.

Soon after that, Mariette, who was looked up to by everyone but had unfortunately no close friends with whom she was on equal footing, found a sisterhood in those same three girls...

Didn't I Say to Make My Abilities Average in the Next Life?!

Mile vs. Reina

"**M**ILE, I want you to go out with me."

"Hm? Oh, um, I'm not really looking for a *soeur* or anything..."

"'Soo-er'? What language is that? I was saying that I want you to go out and do some shopping with me."

"Oh. I see..."

Despite Mile's initial misinterpretation, going shopping was totally fine with her. Still, there was something that bothered her about the proposal. "Reina," she asked, "you seem to invite me out now and then but never Mavis or Pauline. Why is that?"

"That's because neither of them make me look good... Oh."

"What?"

Mavis and Pauline were silent, but both of their faces spoke volumes. *Now she's done it...*

Mile's head turned toward Reina, her neck creaking with a certain unmistakable sound. There was a stiff smile upon her face, but her eyes were not smiling at all.

"What did you just say?"

"Oh, um, I didn't actually say anything?"

Reina hurriedly tried to take back her words, as though she realized how bad they sounded. However, she'd said them far too loudly and clearly to pretend otherwise.

"*I. Said. What. Did. You. Just. Say?!*"

"Oh, j-just shut up! Look, when I'm with you, it's just that it makes me look a bit bigger! In height and bust!" Realizing that there was no way she could cover this up, Reina explained herself clearly. However, with Mile, that was a bad move.

"I-I can understand the height, but our busts are pretty much the same size! Plus, you're already sixteen, but I'm only thirteen! That's like being proud of yourself for having a bigger bust than a five-year-old! That's just sad!"

"Wh—?! Wh-wh-wh-wh-wh-wh-what?!?!"

"What is it?!"

"Y-you little!!!"

Th-this is bad!!! thought the other two.

Mile, who almost never got angry, was filled with rage. Reina had merely refused to back down after realizing that she was in the wrong, but Mile was well and truly angry. This was turning very quickly into a bad situation. The way things were going, the next step was inevitable.

"I challenge you to a battle!"

"I accept!"

With little other choice, Mavis allowed herself to be designated as the referee.

"Can we not just come to a compromise?"

And so, the battle began.

Naturally, this was not a battle of swords or spells. Were it to come to that, things would not end well for either of the combatants or for their surroundings. Thus, the method of battle was as follows:

"Now then, let the one-round, no-limits, no-holds-barred 'Roast Battle' begin!"

With Mavis's signal, the match was underway. Reina was the first to lob an attack.

"You flat-chested shrimp!"

"Guh... You growth-stunted runt!"

"Gah! You! Y-y-y-you stumpy little bean pole!"

"Gwuh! L-Look, it's Reina the hag, so ugly even an orc would pass her by!"

"Gwah! Well, there goes Mile the washboard, so flat that when she goes to a public bath, the people tell her, 'The men's baths are that way!'"

"Fwah!!"

"Um, it looks like you coughed up some blood... Mile, are you ready to forfeit?" Mavis asked worriedly.

However, Mile shook her head side to side.

"N-not yet! I'm still in this!"

Then she summoned up all her strength, and...

"My, if it isn't Reina, the woman of sixteen years, who, when she tries to smile and flirt with Ash at the weapons shop, gets scolded, 'Whoa, settle down there, kiddo!'..."

"Gyaaaaaaaaaaaaaaah!!!"

"Oh, she's fallen down twitching... Looks like we have a winner! The victory goes to Mile!!!"

Mavis grabbed Mile's hand and lifted it high in the air.

Pauline, wishing to compliment Mile on her victory, then said, "Congratulations on the win, Mile! Still, it must be nice to have such a small chest. I'm so jealous. I bet it doesn't even bounce around and get sore when you run. They don't get sweaty underneath, your shoulders don't get stiff, you can crawl faster, and you can even talk to guys without them ogling you! I really am jealous of you..."

"Gwaaaaaaaaaaaaaaaaaaaaah!!!"

"Oh, she vomited blood and passed out... The victory goes to Pauline!!!"

"Huh?"

Pauline stared on blankly as Mavis grabbed her hand and hoisted it into the air...

Afterword

LONG TIME NO SEE, everyone. FUNA here.
Welcome to Volume 7. It's been nearly two years since the release of Volume 1.

This time, Faleel was rescued from a mysterious organization!

Mile brought down the wrath of the heavens on the fiends who kidnapped her favorite little catgirl!

Reina proved she has a mind like a steel trap, and Mile has a mind like a swamp.

Mile was granted a small glimpse into the secrets of this world, courtesy of the kidnapping incident. Then there was the continuation of the Leatoria arc and the tale of the bandits. I hope you've enjoyed it.

Then, as I'm sure you may have heard... We're getting an anime! The production planning is underway! Of course, there are plenty of productions that have flopped before they even started. It's too soon to relax! We mustn't set our hopes too high!!!

Even so, an "anime," huh? That has such a nice ring to it, and I can't help but have high hopes...

Of the over 550,000 works published on *Shousetsuka ni Narou*, only a few hundred have made it to publication. Of those, only a few dozen have been made into manga. And of those, only the smallest proportion have been made into an anime.

Of course, I dreamed of something like this, but I never thought I would see the day when it would actually come true...

Even having my work published was a dream come true. Two years and four months ago, I published the very first chapter of my first serialized work, *Saving 80,000 Gold in an Another World for Retirement*, with that dream in my head.

I began publishing *Didn't I Say To Make My Abilities Average in the Next Life?!* on the same day that I concluded my second work, *I Shall Survive Using Potions!* About eight days later—which was two years and two months ago—I received an offer of publication.

One year and ten months ago, Volume 1 of my first-ever published work was released.

And then, I was contacted about the first stages of planning for an anime version.

These two years have really passed in the blink of an eye.

Well, of course, I spend most of my waking hours in front of a screen now, so even as the days roll by, there really isn't much about those two years that stands out in my memory...

Publication, manga version, anime version... As the beat marches on, I feel as though I've already surpassed the 'Narou Dream,' but please let me keep dreaming just a little while longer.

This wonderful dream of an exciting fantasy world, along with Mile and the others—and you, the readers...

Along with the release of Volume 7 of *Didn't I Say To Make My Abilities Average in the Next Life?!*, Volume 3 of the manga version is now available. Volume 3 of both *80,000 Gold* and *Potions*, along with Volume 2 of both their manga versions, will soon be available from Kodansha's K Light Novel Books imprint.

It's a jet stream attack!

Please enjoy both series from Kodansha alongside the *Average* books.

The manga version of *Abilities* can be read online at Comic Earth Star (http://comic-earthstar.jp/), and the manga versions of *80,000 Gold* and *Potions* can likewise be read online at Wednesday Sirius (http://seiga.nicovideo.jp/manga/official/w_sirius/).

Please enjoy these adaptations alongside the novels.

And finally, to the chief editor; to Itsuki Akata, the illustrator; to Yoichi Yamakami, the cover designer; and to everyone involved in the proofreading, editing, printing, binding, distribution, and selling of this book; to all the reviewers on *Shousetsuka ni Narou* who gave me their impressions, guidance, suggestions, and advice; and most of all, to everyone who's welcomed my stories into their homes, I thank you all from the bottom of my heart.

I hope we can meet again, in Volume 8, and that we can stay together just a little while longer, for the sake of my hopes and the Crimson Vow's dreams, and for the success of the anime...

Now then, everyone, let's say it all together, softly.

"Just one step closer to our dreams...!"

—FUNA